HOPE COMES WITH A STRANGE HEART

AND OTHER STORIES

**Phyllis Murphy,
Harold Raley, and Landy Raley**

TotalRecall Publications, Inc.
1103 Middlecreek
Friendswood, TX 77546
281-992-3131 TEL
www.totalrecallpress.com

Copyright © 2021 by: Harold Raley
Drawings by Trudie Murphy

ISBN: 978-1-64883-128-7
UPC: 6-43977-41287-4

FIRST EDITION
1   2   3   4   5   6   7   8   9   10

To Trudie

Table of Contents

Introduction

These are stories from the heart. Most have their genesis in events set in the Deep South with the accents, rhythms, and pathos of the unique Southern experience. Stories are not real until they have a past, which means that we cannot return to our yesteryears in fact but only in the wellspring of memory. But this turns out to be life's real fallback alternative. The only way we can understand our human and personal past and our prospects for the future is by telling our human tales, not by reciting facts and statistics. For more than biological creatures, we believe we are biographical creations, the stuff of our stories, the novelists of ourselves. And always behind and before us, we acknowledge the Creator with gratitude and humbleness and seek to conform our musings to his miracles. These convictions and the colorings they cast over our human condition have guided the authors in crafting these tales, which we offer with our good wishes to the reader.

HOPE COMES WITH A STRANGE HEART

by Phyllis Murphy

Part I

I started life like a Spartan warrior assessing the field of battle to be either prey or predator. Little wonder that I have always been cautious, and a beat removed from the spontaneity of others. As a child, I felt "set apart," contemplating the day's events as I lay in bed each night. I've tried to be in control of my destiny but am sometimes jostled like one of those silver pinballs, spiraling and bumbling into barriers before landing in a strange and foreign place not of my own choosing.

I was yoked with the name of Ebenezer Torplotnamun, in honor of my great-grandfather. Fortunately, I was nicknamed "Eb." My surname, Torplotnamun, I couldn't shorten; I just had to live with it—despite the fact that it was hard to pronounce and almost impossible to spell. Pa told me to represent the name well, and laughed when he said, "You can't do nothin' bad enough to shame that name, son! Just be thankful it ain't Beelzebub!"

I spent many hours researching the origin of my surname but could find nothing in genealogical records or by questioning old-timers to explain its genesis. I concluded that it must have been a misspelled signature on a document which my ancestors adapted. Pa wasn't as conciliatory. "Whoever signed that document must have been drunk out of his gourd. What man in his right mind would want that name!" I had no recourse but to accept it.

My mother's maiden name, "Nairn," was equally as odious. Sometimes, I think my ancestors spontaneously generated—like something primordial crawling out of the ocean. No one knew how to identify them, so they were given these strange appellations. Pa scoffed at the notion, not realizing I was joking. "Naw," he said scornfully. "No Torplotnamuns come from the sea. The way my grandpa told it, they come from Georgia about a hundred and fifty years ago when the Clarnell gang run them out of the state for horning in on their whiskey trade. Our kin kept on runnin' til they settled down in this area where didn't nobody know them."

Over the years, the uniqueness of the name became more appealing. Since the only Torplotnamuns on the planet live within a ten-radius of Aeolian County, it's a blessing that the people who share this name are conscientious kin, and not bank robbers, anarchists, or chicken thieves. I've learned to live in harmony with the name, just as I have learned to deal patiently with all the other challenges in the life. To paraphrase Paul the Apostle, "I have learned to be content in all things." As Pa reminds me, "Some things you can't do nothing about, so you might as well live with it."

As I narrate my life story in the Year of the Lord, 1966, I am 35 years old—a robust man in outward appearance—the prime of life as some would say—but there are major fissures below the surface that I try to conceal. I've been straining to hold up the walls of impenetrability too long—because I am sometimes so tired that I have verged on hopelessness. Faith has been my salvation: "A light to my path and a lamp to my feet." So, I pick up my sword and shield of faith and move on, praising God for being a survivor.

I was born in 1931 in Brattam Hollow, within five miles of easy walking distance to the town of Cyril Gouldingsburg, so-named for two Pennsylvanian geologists who traveled south in the mid-1800s to map out the richest coal seams in Central Alabama. Eventually Nehemiah Goulding and his partner, Edward Cyril, founded Goulding & Cyril Coke and Coal, abbreviated to GCC&C (which the townspeople laughingly and quietly referred to as "Didja See C&C? –although never in earshot of the company owners, who were too dour to see the humor).

Mssrs. Goulding and Cyril were hard-working Pennsylvania Dutch who disdained ostentation, relying instead on thrift and industry to advance in life. One of the main tenets of their faith was helping their fellowman attain dignity through hard work. To achieve this goal, they founded a community in the hopes that decent housing, fair play, and working conditions would incentivize workers to be good laborers.

Thoroughly pragmatic, the owners hired civil engineers to design the town, with bisecting streets at perfect right angles. Coal workers rented small, "shotgun" houses with yards big enough for gardens. Once a month, company inspectors examined the houses to make sure they met the standards of the GCC&C company. In the commercial part of town sat a general store, two churches, a rudimentary hospital where the doctor and his family lived, and a small jail supervised by two officers of the law.

The owners and executives built plain two-story homes near the center of town and planted oak trees to shade the sidewalks. Eventually the metropolis grew to a population of over two thousand people. As a result, in 1922 the state replaced the ramshackle wooden school with a brick building containing classrooms for first through twelfth grades.

To encourage financial prudence, the owners persuaded the president of the Southern Merit Bank in Tuscaloosa to build a branch in Gouldingsburg Cyril where workers regularly deposited their meager wages. The population thrived and appreciated a steady income and the amenities of smalltown life.

Since the dawn of civilization, society has been divided into various levels of status as exemplified by the town of Gouldingsburg Cyril. The founding fathers took a paternalistic role in the lives of workers by donating money to pension accounts and taking care of the indigent, Gentry started a "Lady's Mission" to encourage church attendance. Once a week they visited the school to teach etiquette, personal hygiene, and domestic skills to young coeds.

The men had a similar association called "Soldiers of God." Members taught weekly lessons in citizenship and woodworking skills to boys. As a highlight, the "Soldiers of God" leaders chaperoned eager cadets at an annual summer camp. For three days, boys camped out in tents mounted in the Talabithious State Park to hone their skills in fire safety, the identification of birds and trees, techniques of archery, and the location and identification of Indian artifacts. Lessons in knife safety had to be eliminated when bandaged boys returned home with deep cuts and abrasions.

When the town first formed, people struggled between the strictures of civilization and personal freedom. Most of the citizens descended from native Creek Indians intermingled with various ethnic groups whose progeny were self-sufficient:

keeping gardens, living frugally and respecting law and order. First generations revealed their Creek ancestry by their need to wander free as clouds and their reverence for the mystical arts. "Healing women" ventured into woods in search of medicinal herbs. Men escaped from the chafing harness of modern life to hunt, fish, and roam the wilderness before returning home. No one thought it blasphemous when oracles predicted futures through signs and omens.

However, after a few generations, only a few restless souls explored life outside town. Some woke up one morning, smelled the air, and followed a compulsion to walk unknown roads in search of answers. They might be gone years before returning, restless to return to the road within a few days. A few sojourners returned home for good.

The people who remained married, settled down, and had families. As their Creek genetic ancestry became diluted, they lost their wanderlust and tethered themselves to the town. If their lives became less adventurous, they were still fulfilling as people worked hard and enjoyed simple pleasures. Outliers were tolerated as long as they did not force their ideas on others, but rude nonconformists were viewed as barbarians invading the gates of Rome.

It was a tight-knit community with all the ramifications associated with people who know one another's business twenty-four hours a day. Neighbors were quick to lend a helping hand, and everyone banded together during times of crisis. However, minor disputes could divide neighbors into petty rivalries over who owned a dog or prodigal chicken. Usually, disputes were settled and forgotten until the next problem reared up and new alliances were formed.

There was a tavern of sorts on the far edge of town where adventurous souls gathered to drink amid boisterous storytelling, song, and fistfights. Police officers snuffed out any mischief with a stern warning that lawbreakers would be deported twenty miles south to the county seat of Elysium where the sheriff was rumored to enforce hard labor on miscreants who refused to comply with the rules. Although lawbreakers were slothful in practicing their faith, most were sensible enough to stop their deviant behavior before being consigned to a chain-gang.

In the valleys, pliable, maroon-colored soil enriched with iron and other minerals, produced an abundance of crops. The loamy soil was easy to till because it contained few rocks. When plowing time arrived each spring, fields emitted the earthy aroma of roots interlacing dirt and decomposing vegetation so identifiable that a blindfolded person could find their way home just by the smell. People returning to the hollow after a lengthy time away were known to scoop a handful of dirt to inhale "home."

Surrounding hills were pitted with slope mines cut deep into the earth like the diggings of giant moles into coal seams. Huge slags of coal were pumped out of shafts and down a long metal chute into steel wagons where they were baked into coke. Afterwards the coke was loaded into railroad cars and taken to foundries where blast furnaces melded it with molten iron to forge steel.

It was the coal trains that stoked my early desire to travel to unfamiliar places. My brother, sisters, and I went to the railroad tracks to watch the coal trains until the horizon swallowed them. I always got a sad, wistful feeling, watching the tail end of the train vanishing in the distance as the whistling of its steam engine faded away. Long after it was out of sight, I imagined it traveling northeast until it arrived in Birmingham—a place that seemed as exotic as the Far East to me.

Most of the men in my family rarely ventured beyond the county line, spending their lives instead working in the mines until they dropped dead from exhaustion or disease. Five days a week Pa rode to and from work with other men on the bed of a flatbed truck protected by a tarp in rainy weather. When he got home, he'd walk into the woods and bathe in a large tub of hot, soapy water to scrub off the soot. I'd bring fresh clothes in a duffel bag to him and take the soiled ones home for Ma to wash outside the house. Small specks of coal permeated our house, cluttering into corners like dusty spiders despite Ma's efforts to expunge it by mopping and sweeping.

No matter how hard Pa scrubbed, there were always traces of coal under his fingernails and the ashy smell of soot. To this day, when I smell smoke, I think of Pa, a gentle, contemplative man enjoyed venturing into nature to restore his soul.

In warm weather, he'd call the family after supper to sit with him on the porch and narrate our day. Ma rocked quietly back and forth in her chair while the rest of us sat on the porch edge. Our legs dangled in various lengths like the chambers of a pipe organ. Pa joked that if he attached our legs to a keyboard, we could play music, although he insisted the music of the woods was the most beautiful.

In cold weather, we stayed inside, nestling close to the fireplace and listening to the comforting hiss and roar of flames stretching in fluid yellow blazes. Eventually, everyone quietened as Pa lit a pipe to signal that it was time for Ma to read the Bible. We'd sit and listen under the amber light of a kerosene lantern.

In later years, when Central Alabama Power connected homes with electricity, lamps diffused gentle light into the room.

After Ma finished reading, Pa nodded and reminded everyone to "do right in God's eyes," which was as close to a formal prayer as he ever said. But it was a solemn admonition to us. Although Pa rarely administered whippings, when pressed he could deliver a painful wallop.

The pulsating murmur of insects and the far-off call of night birds in warm weather; the wind scuttling leaves and rustling limbs in the colder months reminded us that God is all encompassing—there to protect us in the darkest of nights. I took comfort in God's presence when I had to deal with discouragement and danger.

I was the oldest of two boys and two girls. Pa's paycheck was steady but stretched like a rubber band about to snap. Out of necessity we learned to work hard and be content with simple things. Ma was fanatic about personal hygiene and appearance. None of us ever left the house to attend school without brushing our teeth and hair, putting on clean clothing, and taking a final glance in the mirror before getting on the bus. I suspect Ma was aware that "country folk" at school were looked down upon by our more polished classmates, so she compensated by making sure we were presentable. Sundays were even worse. Ma carefully styled our hair and we suffered in scratchy clothing, stiffly starched and pressed.

Both Pa and Ma put great store in hard work. In winter the "men" hunted, mended fences, split logs into firewood, took care of the livestock, and fixed whatever else broke down. The men, as we jokingly referred to ourselves, got up around four o'clock in the morning to feed livestock, milk cows, and gather firewood.

In the early spring we plowed, planted, and slaughtered a few hogs—a task I dreaded. We'd salt portions to hang in the smokehouse for ham, sausage, and bacon. In the summer we chopped weeds in the fields, and in the fall, neighbors worked together to bring in the crops. Our years were rounded by hard labor, school and church attendance, with pockets of freedom as dear as a desert oasis.

It seemed like Ma and my sisters, Martha Leona and Deborah Noel, never quit working. They pulled weeds from the garden, processed food, sewed, quilted, cooked, cleaned, laundered, and helped out on the farm. In the winter, they sewed, quilted, and read in front of the fireside to stay warm. Although winters were fairly mild, the house had little insulation, so a fire had to coaxed continually to warm the house.

Occasionally we traveled to town in Pa's wagon to buy a few staples and squeezed fun into our Saturday afternoons by playing outside or relaxing inside the house. Sundays, everyone attended the Welsh Road Christian Church, a half mile from our house. Usually we walked the distance, but in bad weather we rode in Pa's wagon. Afterwards, we'd invite a few relatives over to eat a big Sunday dinner.

Once a month on a Saturday afternoon my brother, sisters, and I walked the five miles of red dirt road into Gouldingsburg-Cyril. Having made it through the worst of the Great Depression, the town prospered sufficiently to acquire a small diner, pharmacy, and movie theater, even managing by herculean effort to keep the bank in business. Daniel and I made extra money by hiring out as field hands to neighbors to pay for expenses.

We bought "Co-Colas" and peanuts at the movie theater Saturday afternoons, sipping it as we watched cartoons, newsreels, serial programs, and double features. To top it all off, we'd buy hamburgers and malts at the diner before walking home in the evenings. As we got older, Pa bought an International truck that I drove into town, stopping and picking up friends who rode in the truck bed with our sisters. I remember what fun we had on those golden afternoons when life glistened like sunshine.

My siblings were honest, hard-working people, content to live in the same area all their lives, but I was restless to see the world. One time when I accompanied Pa into the woods, he gently picked up a Box Turtle to show me its markings. Watching the turtle regressing into his shell, I listened as Pa explained that Box Turtles spend their entire lives within a small radius and would perish if placed outside their home range. "Maybe that's why they're call Box Turtles 'cause they're all 'boxed in,'" I said, Pa studied me as if he knew I would be the one, out of all his children, to leave home; and he was already missing me, even as I stood next to him—the way you miss someone intensely in that minute before they depart.

As I matured, I needed to go where treacherous landscapes matched the restlessness in my soul. After watching a Western, I'd be lost in thought for days, imagining windswept rocks carved into monolithic shapes; the craggy terrain of canyons; and otherworldly "Badlands" where outlaws hid. I wanted to walk on pebble-strewn beaches where savage waves crashed into rocks, feel the cold spray of the salty wind, and watch receding currents sweeping out to sea.

My need to do well academically paled in comparison to my quest for adventure. The only subject I excelled in was math where each problem had only one correct answer. I was uncomfortable with the ambiguity of literature with its subjective interpretations.

Always someone who enjoyed manual labor, I preferred wiring a house or working on a car engine to studying. My friends and I fixed cars rusting in barns and backyards, hunched over engines and learning the intricacies of automobile repair. We sanded, primed, and painted exteriors in a futile attempt to improve the appearance of these jalopies. Often the cars broke down on excursions, but we didn't mind; it just gave us something more to fix.

When it came time to graduate and decide on a calling, I never considered college because of my anemic grades. Mr. Philman, my math teacher, encouraged me to get a degree in math, but I didn't have the interest, finances, or transportation to attend the University located 26 miles northwest. I certainly was not a candidate for scholarships; nor could I work and attend college simultaneously, so I didn't pursue it.

"Son, you've got the brains to make something of your life, if you'd only apply yourself," Mr. Philman said in exasperation. "Just what do you intend to do with your life?"

I pondered that question many nights afterward, anxious that I had no real goals. For a few months, I worked at the lumberyard, planning plywood, all the while realizing this type of work held no appeal to me. It was hard work, as I sweated in the sun, wishing the day would end. One hot August afternoon while driving home, the transmission in my car failed, and I was stuck on the side of a weedy country road when a buddy stopped and gave me a ride. On the way, we talked about joining the army. It was 1949 and no wars were likely to occur since World War II had ended only four years earlier.

Enlisting seemed like a good idea. Like most country boys, I was a skilled marksman. I had seen enough war movies to be in awe of soldiers on the battlefield. I was tough enough to endure boot camp and was used to taking orders from my family. Enlisting would give me the opportunity to travel. Hopefully, with any luck, I could become a career military technician and retire after twenty years, which was a much more appealing prospect than working forty years in a lumberyard of coal mine.

Ma and Pa looked none too pleased when I shared my plans; but they agreed to talk it over before deciding. A week later, over breakfast, Pa said I could enlist. Within a few short weeks, I was saying goodbye to my family before boarding a train to report for basic training at an army base in Oklahoma.

On the long trip west, I stared at the landscape and wondered about the lives of people who lived in the houses we passed. What would life be like if I simply got off the train and walked into a community to start a new life, leaving my past, and forging ahead to marry and raise a family? It gave me a lonely, displaced feeling, as if I were moving to a distant planet like characters in a science-fiction movies.

I sloughed it off as foolish speculation—just idle thoughts to ward off the rising sense of homesickness I felt as each mile separated me from family. Halfway to Arkansas, I had such a burning lump in the throat that it was hard to swallow, but upon seeing the swirling currents and massive dimensions of the Mississippi River, I was overwhelmed. My spirits soared as I realized that I was traveling to places I'd only read about in books or seen in movies.

Further west I noticed changes in the landscape. Rice fields gave way to the rolling hills and flat plains of southern

Oklahoma. I saw vast spreads of cattle ranches surrounded by the sandstone ridges of the Ouachita Mountains. Narrow rivers wound through the rugged landscape in crooked furrows. Further west, oil derricks pumped rhythmically like giant dinosaurs bobbing their heads up and down.

We stopped to fuel, and I saw long-tailed Magpies hopping on the ground before taking flight. The autumn heat and arid climate make me so thirsty that I drank copious amounts of water. By the time we got to the rocky, sienna-colored soil of western Oklahoma, I was excited about my new phase of life. It was a consolation to remember that I had enlisted for a three-year stint to learn a trade. With the optimism of youth, I was buoyant with options and could make my own decisions. If I decided to return home, I might use the G.I. Bill for college, or re-enlist and become a career man. If I trained as a diesel mechanic, I could work at the county airport or open my own machine shop after retirement.

The first few days in boot camp were filled with activities. Upon registering at camp, we were processed, given a uniform, and immunization shots. Then we visited the army dentist who fixed any dental problems we had. (For many of us it was the first time we'd been to a "tooth doctor.") We met our commanding sergeants who took us to the barracks where we were allotted either a top or bottom bunk. I quickly got acquainted with my squad of ten men who shared the barracks with a platoon on the bottom floor and an equal number on the floor above.

After lunch we went through a battery of tests which everyone passed. Gus, from Gloryville, Alabama, and I became quick pals. He was apprehensive about qualifying since he was tall and scrawny. When he passed the exams, he laughed in unabashed delight. So infectious was his good humor that we all laughed until a stern sergeant told us to "shut up." Afterwards, we were given buzz cuts that exposed our scalps to sunburn on long marches.

I was used to long days on the farm, but by the end of that first week, I was sleep-deprived and more exhausted than I had ever been. We trained six days a week from five in the morning until ten at night with intermediate breaks for food. We looked forward to Sundays so we could rest up for the following week. In our free time we wrote letters to families back home and discussed topics of interest—namely women.

Each day was crammed with intensive training in military procedures. We learned to assemble and clean our rifles so instinctively that we could reassemble them in pitch dark. I did well enough in target practice to assist a few soldiers who needed extra help. Gus had such a hard time mastering basic marksmanship that eventually I hit the targets for him so he could pass the required course. He was thankful for my help and grinned good naturedly when I called him a "city boy." Gus kept practicing until he became a proficient marksman which really boosted his confidence.

My platoon went on long, brisk marches in all kinds of weather, hauling supplies in knapsacks strapped to our backs. Sargent Yakanovich was such a fanatic that if a twister had touched down, he would have ordered us to jump in a ditch until it passed. It stormed so violently on one five-mile march that we considered ourselves lucky not to have been struck by lightning. Toward the end of the trek—when we were covered in mud and limping back on blistered feet—we jokingly prayed to be electrocuted to end our misery. During those interminable months of training that summer and fall, we'd come back to the barracks enmeshed in dirt and sweat, shoulders aching from hauling supplies, and just tired enough to be ripe for fighting. I can vouch for the fact that fifty irritable, hungry soldiers have short fuses. More than once, fistfights broke out when men jostled to be first in line for food and showers.

Sometimes we camped in the woods to simulate battle conditions. While being eaten alive by mosquitoes, we dug foxholes—not an easy task in the blazing heat of summer—learned camouflage and night combat maneuvers. We used bayonets and participated in hand-to-hand combat—something we enjoyed as a way to let off pent-up hostility. Over the weeks, we grew lean by eating C-rations. At the end of a long day, we fell into exhausted sleep, oblivious to body odor, heat, and the intense pain of cramping muscles.

During our last weeks of training, we learned to fire machine guns, rappel up a cliff, run an obstacle course, orient ourselves using maps and compasses, throw a hand grenade, and gain a rudimentary knowledge of advanced weaponry. Also, we trained in marathon marching maneuvers and learned basic first aid. By the end of three months, each soldier had toughened up to pass a grueling physical fitness test. Gus bulked up and became as wiry and strong as a bantam weight boxer and as unrelenting as a bulldog if provoked. Most importantly, we learned discipline and how to work together as a unit.

At the end of four arduous months, we received our stars and bars in an official ceremony. Now we were full-fledged army soldiers prepared to engage in combat. My parents couldn't attend the event, so they sent a letter of congratulations along with a hundred-dollar check in the mail. I preserved the letter along with other mementos in an album and cashed the check the next day. Then I wrote a thank you letter home with the news that I was coming home for a month's furlough before being sent to Okinawa, Japan for training.

During the hiatus I enjoyed visiting with family and friends. It was nourishing to relax, rest, and catch up on all the latest news and gossip during the holiday season. Preacher Amherst took me aside one Sunday after service for a talk about "remaining chaste and spreading the Gospel" to others. I assured him that I was trying to set a good example. Clasping my hand, he said, "Good. We need young men and women to lead others to righteousness."

Pa gave me a Bible and told me to read a chapter or two every night. "Remember to always do right in the eyes of the Lord," he said quietly. Ma fussed over me, clucking that I was too thin and stuffing me with delicious food. My younger brother and sisters hid their newfound admiration by teasing and playing practical jokes on me. I spent time hunting in the woods with Pa, my brother Daniel, and the hounds. The dogs kept sniffing and nudging me with their noses. I petted them for a tactile memory while I was separated from them on another continent and knew that my family would take good care of them while I was away.

In church I noticed girls sneaking stares and giggling when I walked by. I joked that as a seasoned "Man of the world," I attracted women with my rugged looks. It was true that girls who had never given me the time of day before now vied for my attention. Some of my buddies had started settling down with girls they courted. It seemed like only yesterday these same guys had nothing more serious on their minds than fixing up cars, guffawing over jokes, and playing pranks. How could we possibly have turned into adults in such a short time?

I spent an afternoon visiting Mr. Philman, my math teacher who was especially interested in my boot camp experiences since he'd served in World War II. When I got ready to leave, he hugged me and brushed away tears that dribbled on his cheeks. Composing himself, he gruffly slapped me on the shoulders and said, "Be good. Come home safe and get that math degree, son. We might even teach together one day!"

I drove my brother, sisters, and friends into town on Saturdays for ice cream, to watch movies, and eat at the diner just like old times. Visiting the old haunts made me nostalgic like someone who returns home to realize that it will never quite be the same again. In only a few short months, I had attained a broader scope of life outside my community. Although I was restless to travel new paths, I was also sad to leave. I remembered a poem by Robert Frost with the line: *Home is the place where, when you have to go there, they have to take you in*. Only now did I understand the deeper meanings of those lines. Home is a place that's always in your heart regardless of distance and time.

On January 5th, 1950, I said a tearful goodbye to my family and got on a bus in Tuscaloosa, Alabama en route to Dallas, Texas, where we boarded a train for a week's journey to Seattle. Along the way, we saw majestic vistas. In the Midwest We saw wheat and corn fields covered in deep snowdrifts. Further west, in the Great Plains, we saw vast expanses of high desert with indigo-blue skies that seemed to stretch forever. Deep snow covered the Dakotas before we crossed the Rocky Mountains in Idaho and descended into the flat, stony fields of eastern Washington. After crossing west through conifer-covered mountains, we saw orchards and fields in rolling plains and a cold, drizzly mist persistently fell near the coast.

Part II

We disembarked at a military station in Seattle to be processed and get supplies for our assigned quarters. We had plenty of free time during our three-day stay to visit attractions. I ate seafood at a dockside restaurant on Puget Sound, took a ferry ride to an adjacent island, and visited a temperate rainforest. Every day we came back to our barracks drenched by a constant drizzle. It was beautiful, but the gray clouds and ubiquitous rain made me long for the clear skies of home.

When three days had passed, we boarded a ship and were ocean bound for two of the longest weeks of my life. I was seasick and unable to keep anything down before finally getting acclimated enough to walk around the ship and enjoy the view. I had thought the Mississippi River was vast, but it couldn't compare in size and grandeur to the ocean.

We arrived at the army base in Okinawa, Japan, in the latter days of January. It took a few weeks to get accustomed to the smells, sights, and sounds of a port city. Servicemen didn't attract much attention because the U.S. military had occupied the region since the end of World War II. Merchants in crowded marketplaces vied for our attention by screaming out their wares in broken English. Everywhere new construction signaled revitalization.

I learned a few basic Japanese phrases which came in handy when socializing with young Asian women whose graceful mannerisms and speech were as mysterious as those of mythical princesses. Bright silk dresses caressed their slender bodies and flowers accentuated black, shimmering hair. Their mesmerizing smiles haunted my restless dreams. Many years later, when I was back home in Aeolian County, I'd smell spring breezes and remember their perfume, as ephemeral and aromatic as blossoms. Looking up on a spring day, I'd feel closer to these women, as though the skies over both hemispheres connected us, and I'd wonder if they ever thought of me.

For several months we trained in advanced weaponry, learned the rules of war, practiced army combat maneuvers, and learned trades. I was well on my way to being ranked as a Private First Class Specialist qualified as a diesel mechanic to work on heavy tanks and machinery. As summer rolled around in 1950, I felt confident in my future as a mechanic now that I had been in training for almost a year. Even experiencing my first earthquake didn't shake my resolve, although I was terrified when the ground rolled in undulating motions, tumbling people and objects in its path.

In life as in war, unexpected attacks do the most harm when you're least prepared. On June 25th, 1950, the North Korean Army captured most of South Korea. U.S. intelligence agencies had greatly underestimated the aggressive determination of communist superpowers, so when South Korean officials asked repeatedly for training and military, their pleas had gone unanswered. Therefore, the South Korean army was ill-equipped when North Korean forces invaded their country. Terrified South Korean civilians fled to the Pusan Perimeter where freedom forces fought valiantly to ward off invading communist soldiers. As the fighting escalated, people in the "Free World" worried about the spread of communism.

I was deployed to South Korea in July 1950, as part of the 24th Infantry Division Task Force of the Eighth Army. Although scared sick, I was assured by Captain Dobbins that we'd whip the

"Reds" back to North Korea with tails tucked between their legs. The U.S. military, fortified by United Nations Forces of South Korean and Allied Forces, could easily defeat them in a short period.

At the time, I was inspired by patriotic optimism and respected our commanding officers who put their lives on the line every day. Looking back, if I find fault with anyone, it is with the people whose job was to collect intelligence to plan for the exigencies of war. To paraphrase a saying, "Old men plan wars; young men die in them." I was soon to learn that in war, as in life, one should never underestimate the opponent.

Although I was a soldier in the Korean War for almost a year, I am not going to elaborate too much on my experiences. First of all, I suffer from Post-Traumatic Stress Disorder (PTSD) and don't want to burden anyone with terrifying flashbacks. Secondly, it's too painful a subject to discuss casually. Unless you have been in combat, you'll never understand the true nature of war, and I don't want to glorify my role in it. All I can say is combat duty is a combination of long stretches of boring regimentation followed by unpredictable episodes of sheer terror.

I'll summarize the fundamentals of my war experience. We landed at the port of Pusan in July, 1950. By this time, North Koreans occupied all of Korea except the Pusan Perimeter, a one-hundred-mile rectangle in the southeastern corner of the Korean peninsula. Despite the fact that we were outnumbered by the North Korean army almost two to one, we fought hard in the steaming heat and rain of August and September in a frenzied effort to hold the last free remnant of South Korea. By the end of August, we were exhausted, depleted of food and equipment, and had sustained heavy casualties. We rejoiced when shiploads of fresh soldiers and American tanks rolled to reinforce Allied strongholds as we continued to fight for our lives.

In September, Navy ships brought 75,000 Marines and Army infantry to the Port of Inchon on the west coast in a surprise amphibious assault. North Korean casualties mounted under heavy naval bombardments. Marines, Army infantry, and the ROK (Republic of Korea—South Korean forces) captured the city to deploy troops, supplies, and tanks to the front lines. In a few days, Marines and U.N. forces marched twenty-five miles to recapture Seoul, the capital of South Korea. Allied victories turned the tide of the war. North Korea's army, suffering from heavy casualties, hastily retreated.

We pursued the North Korean army aggressively past the 38th parallel into North Korea. By the middle of October, the remnants of the North Korean army were on the run. General McArthur, the brilliant strategist and Supreme Commander of Allied Forces, demanded that North Korea officially surrender to unify all of Korea as part of the "Free World." Instead, wanting more leverage, North Korean forces retaliated by slaughtering South Koreans in several cities. To further complicate matters, Chinese communist forces loomed as an ominous threat.

Although we heard rumors of Chinese forces massing to aid the North Koreans, we discounted their strength. How true the expression: "When you *assume*, you make an *ass* out of *u* and *me*. Intelligence agencies assumed the Chinese army was as poorly trained and supplied as they had been during World War II. How could they know that the invigorated Chinese army had become automatons indoctrinated to spread communism? They say that every trial teaches a lesson. On a personal level, I learned not to take the status quo for truth and to conduct reconnaissance to defeat enemies.

Tanks led the way as we rode northeast in jeeps, ascending and descending mountains. The plan was to connect the Army with Marines and X Forces along the northern boundary of North Korea. During marches, we became as surefooted as mountain goats. Along the way, we cleared out pockets of guerilla resistance. Towards the end of October, the weather turned cooler as we traveled north into hilly terrain. Sometimes the only sounds we heard were howling winds and the rumbling of tanks and jeeps over snow. Thousands of trees leveled by artillery fire lay on the ground like matchsticks. Strangely, we heard no wildlife which fled in terror when they heard the sounds of jeeps or gunfire.

When November rolled around, fierce Siberian winds chilled the temperatures to subzero levels at night. Our feet got soaked and blistered from marching in boots. At night, sweat-soaked socks turned frosty. We'd dry them by holding them over a fire with sticks. Little wonder that most soldiers, including me, developed cases of frostbite. I adapted by running and walking on the balls of my feet. The rest of gear was just as inadequate. Uniforms were not thick enough to keep out the chill. At night, we slept in large, warming tents heated by kerosene; each soldier wrapped in thin blankets on the ground, barely warm enough to keep from freezing to death.

It was so cold that batteries froze, and artillery wouldn't fire. We kept jeeps running overnight to charge other vehicles the next morning. Men huddled tightly around exhaust pipes to keep warm, rifles close to our stomachs. It became a nightly routine to douse bunches of weeds and lumber with gasoline to start a small inferno in a large barrel. An anthropologist would say we reverted to the primitive survival skills of our ancestors. We looked like ice-age hunters as we sat on haunches before bonfires eating thawed food from a can, grizzled and lean from long months of battle, staring out in constant alert. The hard, frozen edge of the Cold War pierced our bodies. Little wonder we took so much comfort from fires which defied the cold.

We had Thanksgiving on top of a snowy mountain that November. I remember how good the turkey and dressing tasted after weeks of eating K-rations. We sat in huddled groups savoring hot food and swilling cold coffee in metal mugs. I'd think back to that meal during the grueling days ahead and remember how delicious the food tasted. Sometimes at night around a campfire, I'd describe succulent turkey and dressing until I drove everyone crazy with hunger. They'd tell me, "Shut up or you're gonna get roasted on a stick!" I knew they were only kidding, although a few of them did have a hungry look in their eye.

We soon received insulated uniforms, coats, socks, gloves, and ponchos parachuted down from cargo planes like manna from heaven. Everyone who fought in Korea will vouch that military pilots were heroes. They landed and took off on makeshift, frozen runways dug out of fields, endangering their lives to deliver fresh supplies and troops. Under heavy fire, they dropped bombs to decimate communist forces and help clear the way for allied troops to continue fighting. They also transported thousands of wounded soldiers to hospitals in Japan without losing a single man. Helicopters were first used in the Korean War, landing where planes couldn't and helping to transport wounded soldiers and MASH units.

We started traveling continuously northward, only taking breaks to eat and rest. Marines and X Corps battalions were the first to arrive in the remote region of Chosin Reservoir high in the mountains bordering North Korea and Manchuria, China. The Chinese were very protective of the Chosin Reservoir because dams supplied energy to Manchuria and North Korea. Allied troops were on high alert to the presence of the encroaching Chinese Army. One night, lookouts in tanks spied Chinese encampments signaled by glowing campfires. Deer bolted frantically out of the woods to escape the rumblings of Russian tanks used by the Chinese military. Radio operators detected Chinese communications in close range. Like a phantom army, the Chinese assembled for war.

To the sound of bugles, cymbals, and beating drums, thousands of Chinese soldiers, camouflaged in white uniforms to match the snow, came to the rescue of the North Korean army at "Frozen Chosin." For two weeks, Allied forces battled the Chinese to prevent a siege. Suffering heavy casualties and greatly outnumbered, Marines and X Forces regrouped and fought valiantly to open an evacuation route from Hagaru-ri to the port of Hungnam. Our battalion joined them to maneuver south through a seventeen-mile, narrow valley opening called "The Gauntlet" to allow access to an evacuation route called "The Long March." Through grueling conditions, we marched seventy-five miles in the longest military retreat in U.S. history.

Allied forces desperately bolted between ridges heavily occupied by Chinese forces with Marines clearing the way forward. Like rats in the bottom of a barrel, we were easy targets for the Chinese whose positions on the hills gave them a vantage point to attack fleeing Allies. U.S. tanks and artillery were destroyed and jeeps carrying soldiers overturned as the narrow passage became a graveyard of soldiers and vehicles.

Men jumped out of overturned jeeps in a terrifying maneuver known as "Bugging Out," which meant every man for himself in a hellish dash to stay alive. Fueled by adrenaline, I was running as fast as I could, knowing I could be blown to bits. Death seemed imminent when I heard heavy explosions bombarding the mountains. Like avenging angels, American Air Force pilots came to the rescue, bombing Chinese encampments. Through the haze and noise, we escaped over the high, frozen Taebaek Mountains bordering the east coast. Refugees poured after us in a desperate attempt to outrun the encroaching Chinese army who despite heavy losses, continued pursuing us with maniacal determination.

We continually moved night and day, escaping the pursuing Chinese. It was hard to keep going when I was so overwhelmed by exhaustion and terror that I just wanted to lie down and sleep. I'd heard that in the last few seconds of life, a freezing man felt warm as if bundled in a snowy blanket. I had to force myself to keep going until something happened that inspired hope. A naked infant, covered in blood and mucus and abandoned on the side of the road, sobbed for his dead mother lying beside him. He was too young even to crawl to safety. Suddenly, a terrified woman, fleeing for her life, stopped and cradled him in her arms. He looked back at his mother one last time before curling into the arms of his savior who ran for shelter. The infant inspired me to continue living. Surely, God would rescue me if I trusted in him. I prayed for protection and the strength to push forward with renewed hope. I have continued praying every day since then.

The Funchilia Pass was a sixteen-foot gap that separated sides of a mountain over a gorge thousands of feet deep. In order to reach the other side, engineers had to devise plans to build a portable bridge. They quickly telegraphed a list of materials and a blueprint to headquarters. Shortly afterwards, Air Force pilots dropped sections of the bridge by parachute. Soldiers worked quickly to assemble a treadway bridge in time for jeeps, tanks, soldiers, and hundreds of refugees to cross safely. The last jeep teetered close to the edge before miraculously crossing safely. Afterwards, U.S. forces burned the bridge to prevent the passage of Chinese. As we continued, morale dropped to rock bottom as tired and humiliated soldiers and civilians trudged to the western shore. Ranks were depleted from combat exhaustion, and starvation.

One night Chinese troops fired heavily at our battalion from their encampment on an adjacent mountain peak. We were in danger of being besieged and captured. Lieutenant Davis ordered fifty men to run up the hill where the Chinese were encamped to distract them and force them to use more ammunition. You've heard the Aesop Fable about "Belling the Cat" where the wisest, elderly mouse comes up with the idea of putting the bell around the cat's neck. Well, naturally, none of the younger mice volunteered because they had more sense than to run straight into the jaws of a deadly feline. None of us volunteered to the be "mice" either because we had no desire to run headfirst into the jaws of death. Better to be a live soldier than a dead hero.

With infinite bad luck, Gus and I, along with forty-eight doomed soldiers were selected as decoys. Scared out of our wits, we charged up the hill in the dark under heavy fire. Blinding flashes of artillery lit up the night like lightning. Grenades rocked and bullets whizzed as men screamed savagely in aggression and fear. I saw soldiers running in all directions like lost souls in hell.

Air Force pilots dropped bombs with the force of an earthquake, and I bolted downhill, running as fast as possible. When shrapnel exploded in my shoulder, the sinewy tissue that attached my bones ripped apart. Spasms of pain shot out with each stride as I ran blindly, stumbling and sliding over snowbanks, cowering in dark crevices from pursuing Chinese. Eventually, I made it down the hill and tumbled headlong over a moaning soldier. For a split second, I continued running until his pleas make me turn back. I half carried, half dragged him, as I stumbled back to camp as fast as possible. Have you ever run through thick mud in agonizing pain, carrying a sack of rocks while trying to outrun a hungry lion? That's what it felt like as I heaved ragged breaths, feeling as if I were running through a thousand miles of jagged glass before seeing the camp lights of my battalion.

I collapsed once I made it up the hill to my battalion, disengaging myself from the soldier I had carried, before falling to the ground. Luckily, It was so cold that I didn't bleed out as I was laid on a stretcher and taken into a medical tent where medics assessed me. I saw that Gus was lying on the stretcher beside me. The medics put a vial of frozen morphine into our mouths and covered our wounds with bandages. My last thought was a feeling of gratefulness that I had rescued Gus and could escape into peaceful death.

I left my body and hovered over the scene in the medical tent. Everything was calm and remote as if I were watching a movie. I saw medics working frantically on me, compressing my heart with the flat of their palms. Gus pleaded for me to "come back."

Instead of being frightened, I felt a wonderful sense of peace like the endorphins that elevate one's spirit after running an arduous race. I evaluated life as it revealed itself in episodic spools.

Have you ever looked into a clear pool of deep water and your eyes misjudged the dimensions? As I reviewed my life, it was as if I were looking into the depths of my life deepened with meaning and purpose.

In a panoply, I saw people on earth. Why was Gus so troubled? Didn't he know that joy was being manifested? I drifted upward gaining momentum as I sped through a bright tunnel, encountering people I had loved in life who welcomed me to glory. Reaching Heaven's gates, I was met by my Savior who hugged me. With infinite love, he told me I had to go back to Earth. My story wasn't finished. So I fought my way back to life on Earth, like Lazarus rising from the dead. As soon as I was back in my physical body, I turned to Gus who stared at me as if I were trailing glimmers of light. It was impossible to tell others that I hadn't died at all; I had been elevated to ultimate life. I knew they wouldn't understand, so I remained quiet.

Part III

Later that night, Gus and I were transported by helicopter to a hospital in Japan where we spent several grueling months: I, recuperating from burns, abdominal wounds, and a fractured shoulder; and Gus, having the shattered bones in his legs replaced with steel rods. We gritted through months of punishing physical therapy before being discharged in July, 1952. Although we had the option of serving two more years as clerical staff in the Army, we both decided to take a medical discharge and continue to serve as reservists.

I wrote a letter to my family informing them I was going to spend a few days at Gus's house to reacclimate to civilian life before he drove me home. We arrived in the military airport on a sultry July day in stifling humidity and heat and stayed a few days, filling out paperwork. Since I had grown accustomed to the regimentation of military life, it was difficult adjusting to so much personal freedom. I felt guilt-ridden that I was not in active service.

I was astonished when Mr. Ozem Jackson, the livered chauffeur greeted us at the waiting area, picked up our meager belongings, and led the way to a gleaming cream-colored Cadillac in the parking lot. He opened up the back doors for Gus and me to sink into plush beige seats and loaded our duffel bags into the trunk. During the two-hour trip southeast to Gloryville, we chatted amiably as hot air circulated from open windows. The ride was so smooth and quiet that I might as well have been carted around in a Sultan's palanquin. Gawking in astonishment, I looked at Gus to ask what this was all about; but he just smiled and explained that he was the fourth and youngest child of Elwin

Leavenson, descendant of carpetbaggers who came to the South during Reconstruction to make a fortune in the cotton industry. Four generations later, his family continued to prosper as owners of Leavenson and Sons Textiles, a mill factory that employed two hundred people to produce socks and undergarments.

Gus's house was located in a quiet section of town where expensive lawns showcased mansions. We drove through ornate gates opening to a long, circular driveway through acres of immaculate grounds before stopping in front of an Antebellum mansion. Massive windows bisected vast sections of painted white brick. The entire second story was fronted by a semicircular balcony supported by Corinthian columns standing on a wide portico. A heavy curtain parted inside the house before Gus's parents opened double-paneled entry doors to greet us effusively with hugs and handshakes.

"Wonderful to have you back, son!" exclaimed Mr. Elwin Leavenson, a corpulent, ruddy-faced man in his sixties whose sparse graying hair framed a smooth, good-natured face. Gus's mother, Mrs. Taulia Plainfield Leavenson was a tall, distinguished woman with graying strands of dark hair swept up in an elaborate coil. She insisted on being called "Tutu," which was about as incongruous as addressing her as "Big Mama" or "Tootsie." Behind her welcoming demeanor, she evaluated me coolly with light blue eyes, honing in on my gauche uneasiness and ill-fitting clothes. "Gus, I'm so glad you're home from that awful war. All these months, I've prayed that you'd return safely," she said, hugging him tightly to her. She looked at me appraisingly and said, "And, of course, we are honored to meet the man who saved your life. Ebenezer, we than you immensely," she said, extending a slender hand to mine. Then she commented,

"Come inside. Phillipi will show you to your rooms. Get freshened up and meet the rest of the family for lunch at one."

Although I'd only known "Tutu" for five minutes, I surmised that she ruled the house. Gus informed me later that everyone abided by her dictates just to keep the peace. She took charge of her family with as much planning and attention to detail as a Prussian general. Gus had been shipped off to boarding schools since he was twelve with the goal of continuing his education in a prestigious Ivy League College and marrying a respectable young woman of impeccable pedigree. He joked that his mother was obsessed with improving the bloodlines of her horses, dogs, and family members in equal measure. One of the reasons he'd enrolled in the service was to get away from her domineering control and constant criticism. As he put it, "Serving in the military is easier than living with her."

As we walked up the stairs, Gus muttered, "I'd rather fight the armies of Genghis Khan than deal with her every day. I'm sick of having her find fault in everything I do. I'm the only one who has enough gumption to tell her to back off."

I followed Phillippi through a spacious hallway to my bedroom where she deposited my bag on the bed. "The bathroom is through this door and here's the closet," she said, opening two interior doors. If you need anything, just press this button on the wall." I thanked her and she left with a wry expression like a guard releasing a Christian to hungry lions in the Colosseum.

Open windows overlooked a spacious, meticulously groomed lawn shaded by strategically placed trees. I looked down to see water descending in steady trickles from a three-tiered fountain. A German Shepherd lapped clear water from the bottom well where goldfish swam languidly. Throughout the house, the craftsmanship of nineteenth-century builders was evident in opulent details such as carved balustrades, windows and doors framed in oaken wood, and hand-carved furniture. Thick insulated walls blocked all noise in the house except for the sleepy droning of the ceiling fan spinning over the bed. Polished floors gleamed under ornate crown moldings edging high, tin-plated ceilings. The house emitted the mellow scent of history that I associated with museums and stately courthouses.

I took a shower and dressed in a clean pair of pants and a worn plaid shirt before walking down the wide curving staircase to the living room where Gus and his family sat on sofas and chairs. Spouses huddled with their children as if posing for a photographer. The adults stood up and introduced themselves to me when I walked into the room. They were cordial, but I felt about as out of place as a pauper in a palace.

The women were attractive, similarly dressed in muted summer dresses with perfect posture like actors in a stylish movie. They emanated affluence with their soft, lilting voices, expensively coiffed hair, and elegant clothing. I detected the aroma of expensive perfume like hyacinth flowers in early spring.

The men, dressed in pastel polo shirts and pressed pants, smiled and chatted easily with me. Gus, in plaid shorts and tee shirt, sprawled out in a chair with a cryptic smile on his face, looking like a sociology professor observing a field study on some remote island.

We took seats at the dining room table and got quiet, so Mr. Elwin could lead prayer before the meal. The place settings were so elaborate that I had to watch Gus to see which fork to use as Vashti delivered and took away courses with clockwork regularity. I complimented her on the delicious meal, but Tutu smiled sourly as if she disagreed. Then she held a goblet up the sunlight and observed, "I must talk to Vashti about polishing the crystal, so she gets rid of all the water stains."

After dessert, we retired once again to the living room for another hour of polite conversation while Tutu served coffee and dessert like a queen dispensing afternoon tea. Finally, the interminable visit ended, and Gus and I gleefully escaped to the backyard pool with his young nieces and nephews.

That evening after the grandchildren left, we dressed for supper with Tutu and Mr. Elwin. As we ate, the conversation turned to Gus's plans. He announced that he had decided to enroll at the University of Alabama where he was going to share an apartment with me and requested that Mr. Elwin pay my tuition in appreciation for saving his life.

I was mortally embarrassed and interjected, "No, I really don't want you to do that. I can use the G.I. Bill and work my way through college."

However, I knew it was useless to protest when Tutu raised her palm like a teacher shushing a class and announced with firm deliberation, "We will do this. The matter has been settled."

Mr. Elwin said, "Ebe, I think Gus's request is perfectly reasonable and I'll make the necessary arrangements. However, the caveat is that you study hard, make good grades, and represent yourself and our family well." Then glancing from one of us to the other, he asked, "What do you intend to study?"

Gus replied, "I'm focusing on pre-med. I talked with the doctors in MASH units in Korea and learned quite a lot about the medical field during my time at the hospital." I looked at Mr. Elwin and said, "I plan on being a math teacher." He smiled at us fondly while Tutu vigorously nodded her head in approval. "Those are good fields of study," she said. Then looking pointedly at me, Tutu surmised, "As an educator, you will not make a large salary, but you'll be compensated by helping others succeed in more lucrative fields."

Then she addressed Gus, "Augustus Plainfield Leavenson, as you well know, my grandfather and your namesake was a highly respected surgeon at Johns Hopkins. I'm sure that after you finish your bachelor's degree, you will take this into consideration when continuing your education in medical school."

Tutu sighed and my stomach contracted because I knew she was preparing for an onslaught of criticisms. Looking pointedly at me, she said, "My family are staunch New Englanders; and yet, I've married into Southern society, with all their whims and fancies. For the life of me, I don't understand why my son doesn't apply to Yale or Princeton for his undergraduate degree. They have fine facilities with students of long lineages. But instead, he associates with southerners whom I simply don't understand. I mean no offense to you. Thankfully, you understand your place as a member of the working class; but really, those of a higher caste in this town are so insufferable."

As a member of the Boston Brahmins, evidently Tutu held rigid ideas about social milieu. She elaborated, "How I wish Gus would find a sensible young woman to marry, instead of one of these regional aristocrats." Then, huffing with injured pride, she added: "All my children married southerners who despise me because I'm an outsider. For forty years, I've tried to make friends and break into society in this small town, and I'm still not accepted. What I wouldn't do to have a sensible woman of good Yankee stock marry into the family, someone with whom I could converse and who could bear grandchildren!"

After Tutu quit talking, I had to squelch a joke about breeding good livestock on the farm since I figured levity would not be appropriate.

"Mother," said Gus, setting down his fork resolutely before he stabbed his mother with it. "Have you forgotten that you married a southerner? Even though my father's ancestors emigrated here from Massachusetts after the War, they've made their home in Gloryville for almost a hundred years. Besides that, I don't really care if your ancestors were senators from Boston or Quakers who lived in commune. The fact is that I'm not going to college for the sole purpose of marrying and siring offspring. Believe me, I'm as ready as any other red-blooded male to find a mate, but it won't hinge on some girl having ancestors straight off the Mayflower.

Mr. Elwin, evidently resigned to such outbursts, absented himself from the entire conversation while Tutu and Gus fired off a verbal blitzkrieg before staring in an icy standoff. I squirmed in my seat like a neanderthal at the Court of Versailles, wishing I could go back to my room and sleep. It made me thankful for my uncomplicated family who accepted situations with grace and humor.

In an attempt at breaking the tension, I began relating Nairn and Torplotnamun family lore as Gus and Mr. Elwin listened in rapt fascination, laughing at some of the outrageous adventures while Tutu wavered between disgust and shock, looking at me as if my family had woven moccasins out of her forebears' skin before cannibalizing them.

"Well, I must say you certainly have colorful people in your family!" she said primly.

Throughout the rest of the week, Tutu listed her grievances with as much fervor as Martin Luther nailing his theses to the church door. At dinner, she fumed aloud about her garden and church committees, incredulous that her proposals were met with sullen silence or dismissive smiles. Tutu lamented: "I go to these meetings and the women waste their time voicing all their concerns. When I give logical solutions, they simply smile and say 'thank you', then go back to the usual routines. They don't want progress; they just want to fuss."

She changed topics and said: "By the way, I simply must talk to Vashti about her cooking. All this foot is too rich for my palate. And is it too much for her to quit making all these fattening desserts? I realize we have company, but she's baked enough sweets to feed an entire village. Elwin, you won't fit into your pants if you continue to gorge yourself with her pies."

"My dear, I'm afraid I'm the culprit," said Mr. Elwin. "You know how I love rich food. Please don't say anything to her. She takes such pride in her delicious recipes and it will hurt her feelings."

"Oh Elwin, really!" snarled Tutu. "We pay her enough that she should be thankful to comply. A good manager is not dependent upon the approval of employees. That's why I wrote down the protocol and procedures that each servant is to follow. You'd think the staff would remember after I've gone over them so often."

"I am speaking to her tonight about preparing simple, nutritious meals or I'll be applying as the 'fat lady' in the circus. Also, I need to talk to Mr. Jackson about his incessant need to talk when he drives me to meetings. How I long to sit in silence instead of having to reply to all his questions and observations.

That's the problem with southerners, they're always prattling in long-winded narratives. And if I ask a question, every answer is so rambling that I might as well be a Byzantium ruler to unravel all the plots and twists.

"Yes, we all appreciate your attention to detail. However, you are becoming vexed with too much responsibility. Perhaps, dear, you should think about spending some time with your sister in Boston," said Mr. Elwin. "I think it would do you good to get away for a short vacation."

Yes, I believe I'll do that. I need a two-week respite before returning with ideas of improvement," she squawked. "I'll give my itinerary to you tomorrow at dinner. As you well know, I cannot stay too long, or things fall to pieces. Why just yesterday, for instance, I told the Iris Club about how business is conducted in Boston by using *Robert's Rules of Order* at meetings. Yet, they just stared at me as if I were a Martian explaining how to grow an herb garden. Mrs. Evelyn Caulders even had the temerity to say, "Honey, we're just talking about garden bedding, not amending the U.S. Constitution."

Gus and Mr. Elwin covered their mouths with napkins to stifle laughter. For all her intelligence, Tutu had no insight into the most basic concepts of social interaction. Throughout the week, I observed her issuing admonitions to servants and family as if she were a Russian empress. When she phoned colleagues, she dominated one-sided conversations with advice.

I joked that she needed to use *Roberts Rules of Order* at family get-togethers so everyone could express their views. Gus replied, "No, that would mean people get to vote on things, and she wouldn't allow that."

After I became less intimidated by Tutu, I realized that she had many good traits. She took her duties seriously by giving money to the needy and improved health and education in the area by serving on hospital, school, and college boards. Although she imperiously ruled the house, she treated family and servants equally, dispensing advice to the gardener and family with the same fervor. In her eyes, a person who worked hard and achieved goals should be rewarded with respect. Ironically, she balanced autocracy with diplomacy in equal measure and was ahead of her time in appreciating diversity.

She took frequent sojourns to visit her sister because she was lonely. Mr. Elwin spent most of his time conducting business and her family studiously avoided her. Servants kept out of her way because of her constant meddling. Her friends and colleagues distanced themselves to avoid her admonitions. Everyone breathed a sigh of relief when she was away.

One afternoon, I said to Phillipi, "I bet it's hard working for Tutu," assuring her that our conversation was going to be kept confidential. Evidently, Phillipi trusted me because she said, "Miss Tutu ain't really so bad. She's bossy but fair. Ain't many bosses will pay the help a good salary and come to family events. Miss Tutu got a lot of respect for people. Even though she get on my nerves, she means well. She's a Christian woman, which is a lot more that I can say for some other people around town. And she don't think she's too good to come visit my church when I invite her for sermons. That show she's a good lady."

On my final day, Tutu summoned me to her office where she sat behind a desk like the chairman of a corporation. Broad shafts of sunlight filtered through window blinds to illuminate oak-paneled walls containing family portraits. She motioned for me to sit in a comfortable wingback chair in front of her desk.

"Well," she said, "I don't mind confiding in you since you have no ulterior designs and can look at things objectively. I suppose you've noticed that I have strained relations with everyone in Gloryville. It's not pleasant to be *persona non grata*, as you probably observed."

"Well, Tutu," I responded, "I can empathize with you since most people have experienced rejection or felt the sting of being ostracized at one time or another."

Tutu nodded, exhaling quietly before speaking. "Gus has relayed that you had an out-of body experience, so perhaps you have spiritual insight. Frankly, although I'm a sensible woman, I do put certain stock in the clairvoyant. Perhaps your ascent into the afterlife has given you powers of discernment. Do you have any suggestions to improve my situation so that I can relate better with people?"

"Tutu, I'm just a simple person with absolutely no clue how to get along in high society, so you probably want to consult someone who is in your social stratum."

"Go ahead and speak your mind," commanded Tutu. "I'm an astute observer of human nature and can plainly see that have common sense and discretion."

"Tutu, I am deeply appreciative of your offer to pay my tuition. I admire you and your husband. It cannot be easy to run an estate this size. The only advice I can give you is to let down your guard and quit trying to act like the warden of an asylum. People don't like being bossed around, even if you have great ideas. It makes them feel unappreciated and worthless. Your family obviously loves and respects you, but you make them uncomfortable because you smother them will well-meaning advice instead of listening to them. They want to lead their own lives, make their own choices, and deal with the consequences. Deep down, you're afraid that if you lose control, somehow everything will fall to pieces. When you keep an iron fist over people, it shows you don't trust them—and that you are infantilizing them because you don't have confidence in their abilities to do the right thing." I paused to soak in her reaction.

"They know you love them, and they love you also. Even Gus loves you very strongly and he wants your approval. But he's not going to base his decisions on whether or not you agree with him. Just remember that no matter what happens, people know you have done your best. Now trust them to do their best in life."

She stared at me for a long period before taking a long breath and exhaling slowly. For the first time, I could see vulnerability the person behind her armored persona.

"Well, what do you suppose I should do? I'm bored with my clubs, have no friends, and my family avoids me as if I carried the plague."

"What did you do before you married?" I asked.

"I studied art and ballet at Wellesley and acted in drama productions." She smiled and I could see a warmth come into her eyes and the edges of her lips in memory of herself as a young woman. "I do miss performing. I was quite a good ballet dancer and had I not gotten married, I wanted to pursue a career on stage. However, in 1912 ladies of a certain class simply were not performers, so my father forbade it. He was adamant that no Plainfield was going onto the stage. I might as well have expressed interest in becoming a sword-swallower or circus acrobat. So, at the age of twenty-one I married Mr. Elwin and moved to Gloryville, Alabama, where I've been an outcast for over forty long years.

"Tutu, tell me something, how did it make you feel when your father forbade you to perform?"

She looked out the window for a long while as if seeing long-ago memories before answering. "I . . . hated him to be perfectly honest. I mean, I did love him and understood his reasoning, but it made me feel thwarted and it struck a divide between us that never really healed. I felt sad that I never got the opportunity to follow my dream." Then she laughed and added: "That's why I demand that everyone call me by the silly name of 'Tutu'. It was my father's nickname for me."

"Tutu, you are a good person and good leader if you'll allow others to express their ideas. It's not too late to follow your dream. You have the money and clout to spearhead an arts council at the local college. Think about all the wonderful things you could do by being part of a group to promote the arts. You could foster programs in local schools and hire teachers to direct plays, teach music, and instruct dancers."

Tutu sat in silence for such a long interval while staring at me that I began to squirm uncomfortably before she began to speak.

"Well, you know, you may be onto something, Tutu said thoughtfully. "We do have some very talented local artists and I'm sure that with the right instructors we could channel energies into dance, theater, art, and music. I've always wanted to head the committee to renovate the college auditorium. Once that's completed, we could use it for community productions."

"Tutu, you could leave a legacy as a great patron of the arts. You could denote money and help write grants to improve the local college art department, direct plays and dance productions, and even hire teachers to instruct students in schools here in Gloryville."

Tutu's eyes began to sparkle. "I think I'll do that. While in Boston, I'll make preparations. Thank you for your input," she said. Then she winked and added, "You see, I can appreciate the ideas of others, and I'm not as stubborn as people think."

I was surprised when she walked over to me and clasped my hand in hers. "Ebenezer Torplotnamun, I have enjoyed your company. Please come back anytime." She turned away as tears filled her eyes. Clearing her throat, she regained composure before looking straight into my eyes. "Thank you for saving the life of my son."

I'm very proud to say that Miss Tutu lived up to her word. For the rest of her life, she funneled considerable energy to form art instruction in local schools. She coordinated money to build several humanities buildings at the local college whose state-of-the-art facilities attracted professors and students from many regions. Through her philanthropy, scholarship programs enabled students to major in the humanities. Eventually, she was honored when the new Humanities Buildings were name for her.

She accomplished all this through indefatigable hard work and by forming close friendships with people in the community. She became what she never expected to be: a beloved friend to many who inspired others to fulfill their dreams.

I like to think that maybe I had something to do with that.

Part IV

Gus drove me home to Brattam Hollow in late August where he spent an enjoyable week getting to know my family and friends. It was quite a cultural shock for him to go swimming in a creek, fishing in a rowboat, and working on a corroded car engine. His face turned while as a ghost when he stumbled over a log and dislodged a copperhead which I picked up on a stick and threw into a ravine. "Shh," I whispered. "Don't tell anyone I saved the life of a copperhead. The way I see it, he wasn't attacking us, and we need him to eat vermin."

I knew that most people in these parts had a natural repulsion toward snakes which they viewed as the offspring of the Serpent in the Garden. Danny and Gus looked at me as though I had lost my mind when I explained that "Snakes are a part of the natural order."

Ma and Pa thought Gus was a handsome, down to earth young man. My sisters and the girls at church clustered around him like planets orbiting the sun. Despite the fact that I still moved gingerly due to war wounds, I also captured my fair share of female attention.

Friends and kin visited the house to pay respects, bringing heaping platters of food. One night the community gathered for a barbecue at our house. Men sat in clusters singing, playing guitars and telling stories while the women prepared the meal and the children played. After everyone had eaten, the men gathered in a fraternal bond to talk about their war experiences.

Danny, who was in his last year of high school, asked my advice about what he should do with his life. Gus and I told him about training in the army before showing him our rather gruesome scars. We warned him that if he enlisted, he might be deployed to fight in Korea. By the end of the week, he had narrowed down his options to either attending college or joining the army. Fortunately, his grades were better than mine so he could apply for scholarships.

In late August, my family drove me to the apartment that I was sharing with Gus. We started college one shiny day when the sky bathed everything in a clear shade of indigo blue. When I looked at the eager, innocent faces of the students, I felt so much older than they because of my experiences.

I managed a full load of freshman classes while working as a clerk in the Geology department. I was such an adept typist and file clerk that I finished my work and still had plenty of time to study on the job. Before long, I worked my way into the administrator's offices to file applications and other paperwork. Between attending classes, working on campus, and my part time job at the airport as a mechanic, I was very busy. Each week I went to the V.A. hospital where I had physical therapy sessions with a beautiful young nurse named Cheryl Lake.

Pa developed a persistent cough which forced him to retire in his mid-forties. For the rest of his long life, he parceled his time between resting and helping out on the farm. My family managed to survive on his small pension and by raising livestock and crops. Eventually Pa had to sell some of the acreage after Danny enlisted in the army, and the farm became too much of a burden.

Once a month I borrowed Gus's car to visit my family, attend church, and share Sunday dinner. Before leaving, I gave them money to help out with expenses. Over the years, Ma saved money by canning vegetables and fruit. She and my sisters were resourceful in foraging for poke salad, watercress, and herbs to supplement their diet. They also created a profitable business of selling fruit and pecans to local merchants. They exemplified the woman in Psalms 31:18: "She perceives that her merchandise is profitable. Her lamp does not go out at night."

When I could spare the time, I accompanied Gus to a popular hotspot close to campus where G.I.s gathered to talk and relax in the evenings. Some of the younger men exaggerated their success with women, and we laughed when they couldn't generate any sparks of interest from the females they encountered.

I was a sturdy, introspective man who was a willing accomplice to men with more confidence. I had to smother laughter when my buddies approached women with lines so sappy that they couldn't lure a fly, much less an intelligent female. My knowledge of women at the time was limited to few casual friendships with girls and furtive conversations with friends which ended in explosions of laughter. The rest of my biological education I gained from living on a farm, interpreting "interesting" biblical passages, and reading lurid articles in "Poignant Confessions" magazines that Ma tried to keep hidden in the house. Everything else I gleaned from the local gossip mill.

Years earlier, Pa took my younger brother, Daniel, and me aside when we were, respectively, eight and eleven, to explain the "facts of life." He advised that we not "know" a woman in the biblical sense prior to marriage lest we get trapped into "a shotgun wedding." Although many of the marriages he knew had started off with "one in the oven," it was better to remain chaste until the wedding night. "That way, you ain't gon' be disappointed like someone who's been around too much," he surmised. Pa elaborated "that carnal desires are fine, but not to let them take over your life. The happiest people are satisfied with what they have. Better love the one you got than pine for the one you can't have."

Now that Pa had our attention, he sermonized like a preacher at a camp revival. "Chasing fun like a dog with his tongue hangin' out will lead to destruction. It's like a fat man who can't think of nothin' but food. He spends all his time eatin' and when he's finished, he still ain't never satisfied. And he just gets fatter and fatter thinkin' about food and lookin' for something different to eat. Anyhow, food's just food, no matter how good it tastes or how different it looks on the outside. You can only eat so much without feeling sick. And before you know it, you're digging your grave with your teeth. Boys, now don't you grow up and dig your grave with your teeth or any other part of your body, you hear! 'Take heed, lest you fall.' Like Paul says in the Bible, 'Buffet yourselves'!

After this exhortation, Pa looked sternly at us as though he had just given the Sermon on the Mount. We stared at him with faces furrowed in puzzlement. What did knowing a woman have to do with digging our grave? Seeing our perplexed expressions, Pa said, "Well, you'll figure it out one day. Don't worry about it for now. You'll find out soon enough." Then he stared a long time in the distance, slumping his shoulders while simultaneously shaking his head and sighing deeply. Turning away, he walked to the barn to check on a newborn calf. Over his shoulder, he admonished us: "Boys, now don't you tell Ma what I said. Women don't understand our take on these things."

Alone, we stood for a long while, thinking about all the worrisome burdens of adult life. "How we gon' marry a woman if we don't know her?" I asked. We finally concluded that Pa and

Ma would most likely pick a bride for us like they did in the old days.

"Well," Daniel sighed, "I sure hope they pick out somebody nice who can throw a ball and hunt or she ain't gon' be no fun at all. Besides, what else can you do with a grown woman?" he exclaimed, drawing pictures in the dirt with his toe. It was little wonder that most men look like "sad sacks" after they'd been married a few years. How dreary domestic life seemed. Nothing compared to being a hero like Daniel Boone in the wilderness chasing Indians and building forts.

"You reckon that's what happened to old man Selser?" I asked. Hezekiah Selser had recently died at age ninety-nine years and had been buried in Welsh Road Cemetery. His visage was so grim throughout life that no one ever remembered him smiling. Maybe his grim countenance was a result of eating dirt for a considerable long period of time. "Did ole Lady Selser just get a new oven?" I asked. "Pa said when a man marries, it's best not to get your wife an oven or she'll get uppity and you chew dirt."

"Naw, said Daniel, "I seen them undertakers 'a diggin' up the grave the day before he was buried, so I know he didn't gnaw none of that out."

After brooding in silence, I brightened and said, "Well, if Pa and Ma bring home some awful girls, we'll just stay single. That's a heap better than lying in a hole we dug out with our teeth. Reckon why women make their men eat dirt?" We grimaced at the disloyalty of womenfolk. Surely Ma wasn't like that. The prospect of turning into a dirt-eating, avaricious semi-marmot gave us the shivers. What a truly ironic and sad ending to life, we thought, and vowed to keep Pa's words in mind.

Many times over the years, I wished I had heeded Pa's advice.

If only I had listened to what Pa was trying to tell me, then everything would have been a lot simpler. Only now with the wisdom of age do I realize that sometimes even mistakes can turn out to be blessings.

When you are young, life holds so many prospects. Even when you encounter difficulties, hope and strength make you resilient, so that if one path doesn't work, you can easily take another. I was carefree, with no pressure to be encumbered by a serious relationship. At the age of eighteen, I had all the time in the world, or so I thought. However, the old adage, "Life happens when you least expect it," became the Damocles Sword hanging over my life.

I was a naturally cautious young man who thought about consequences before leaping into action. As a cadet, I listened to lectures and saw graphic movies about the effects of "communicable diseases." We took those lectures to heart and either abstained or took precautions. None of us wanted to take penicillin shots to ward off ancient diseases. We knew we could not depend on fickle fate which could spin lives around like a weathervane in a windstorm.

It's strange how a simple event can alter the course of one's life; it's as though you are driving on an ordinary street and suddenly an oncoming car swerves into your lane. You're never quite prepared for calamitous events in such a mundane setting. It's as if the course of one's life sometimes hinges upon a random encounter or event. But it happens more often than we realize. I should know because it happened to me.

One Thursday night in the middle of October, 1952, Gus and I happened to be at the nightspot when Cheryl walked in and my life changed at that moment. I knew her because she was my physical therapist at the V.A. hospital. She was a tall, statuesque beauty with curly, auburn hair cascading to her shoulders. Unlike the coeds with their unpretentious, down-to-earth innocence, Cheryl possessed a sensual presence as she assessed her surroundings to capture the attention of everyone.

Then she recognized me and with graceful, cat-like strides glided over to the table, sat, and introduced herself to my friends. Sometimes a girl disappoints up close when you notice slight imperfections, but she was more beautiful than any woman I'd ever seen. Her skin was flawless, with a faint peachy blush on high cheekbones, hazel, almond-shaped eyes tipped upward, fanned with long eyelashes like a model in a fashion magazine. Her only flaw was a nose a little bulbous at the point where it dipped down. I decided this made her look more interesting. Besides, who was I to criticize since I was hardly anyone's idea of an Adonis?

She had controlled energy like a beautiful feline. She lasered her attention on me and ignored the other guys who competed for her attention. I was thankful that her focused attention raised my status. When it was time to leave, I figured my night of glory would end in a whiff of smoke. I'd joke with Gus and the guys about my tantalizing charms, and they'd get a kick out of bringing me down to size.

I was shocked when she asked me on a date for the coming weekend. "Wow," I thought, "I must have done something right!"

Cheryl said, "Come to my apartment at 7:00 in the evening." Then she gave me her address on a slip of paper. "I'll cook supper," she said. "I bet you haven't had a home-cooked meal in a long while." Too shocked to talk, I just nodded my head up and down enthusiastically, trying not to choke on my Adam's Apple.

When we got back to the apartment, Gus slapped me on the back. I laughed when he joked "How did a country boy like you attract Rita Hayworth?"

I figured she just wanted a platonic relationship for laughs. Maybe a beautiful woman got tired of fighting off admirers. I didn't expect she was infatuated with me. We'd have a good time before she moved on to someone more suitable.

The next weekend, as planned, I went to her apartment where we talked over dinner about our lives. She was twenty-six, and I was twenty-one at the time. Her first husband, a veteran of World War II, had died in an accident a few years earlier, leaving her with a daughter named Eve to raise. She'd used money from his life insurance to attend nursing school and had worked at the veteran's hospital for the past two years while Eve lived with her grandparents in Western Mississippi. When she settled down, she planned on bringing Eve to live with her.

We sat on the couch after clearing up and putting away dishes and listening to music on her record player. She asked me to dance, and I awkwardly did the best I could. I was five feet nine, but she was taller in her high heels than I by a good two inches. After dancing. We sat down to drink some wine. To this day, I don't know what happened. I had drunk only a few ounces before feeling faint and weak as if I were going to pass out. I lay down in a daze and was immediately asleep. When I came to my senses the next morning, I was shocked and disoriented. It took me a few minutes to remember where I was and was embarrassed at overstaying my welcome. Walking over to the mirror, I examined my face, brushed my hair and prepared to leave when she walked in the living area, wearing a luxurious emerald satin robe over her diaphanous gown, looking like a movie heroine.

Swallowing hard, I offered my profuse apologies, stumbling around in an effort not to stare at her. I had never been alone with a woman before, much less one dressed in such intimate apparel. It was like being in a movie with an alluring woman whose husband would come bursting through the door any minute, grabbing me by the collar and asking who I was in a belligerent voice before beating the stew out of me. I averted my eyes even though she was covered by a robe whose lapels and cuffs bore fluffy white feathers. My face reddened in embarrassment as I kept flitting my eyes to her outfit. I'd never seen anyone wearing such attire, except for the time I'd sneaked a peek at the negligee section of the Sears catalog.

"Oh, don't worry about it. You have nothing to apologize about!" she said brightly. "Sit down, and I'll make breakfast." Luckily, she was a great cook, and I gulped down pancakes, milk, eggs, and bacon, becoming more interested in food than anything else. I relaxed and began talking to her as if she were one of my sisters.

Luckily, it was a Sunday, so I still had a few hours before returning to the apartment. Still, I had an uneasy feeling. As a creature of habit, I attended church every Sunday where I enjoyed studying the Bible with friends, I felt guilty at missing services. Then I thought, "How in the world can I explain this to the preacher?" Having grown up a community where one had little privacy, it took time for me to realize that I didn't have to telegraph everything that happened to me. I'd keep this innocent escapade a secret, to chuckle about when I was older; but for right now, I had no intention of ruining the reputation of either of us.

Besides, we hadn't done anything illicit.

Still, I had an uneasy feeling about the events of the previous night. I wasn't a heavy drinker and had never been intoxicated. One or two beers was my limit for the entire week. "How could a sturdy man like me get woozy off only a glass of wine?" I asked. "Maybe I'm more exhausted than I realized."

Before leaving her apartment, I offered to meet her the upcoming weekend as a friendly gesture. After all, I thought, I can't very well sleep overnight on somebody's couch, and leave without asking if they want to meet again. For a split second, I had an irritating feeling that I was obliged to be at her beck and call just to make amends. "The old ball and chain!" I thought. But looking at her innocent face, I felt ashamed for having those suspicious feelings.

"Oh, yes," she said in a breathy voice as mellifluous as a cat's purr. "Let's have another dinner at my apartment and then we'll chat and listen to music. I really enjoyed talking to you and telling you about my life. You know, I have been so lonely ever since Billy died. And when I go out with other men, they expect certain things from a widow like me," she said, waving her hands over her body.

"Well, I can understand that. Nature's been bounteous to you," I gently interjected. "I enjoyed the conversation and dinner and I'm sorry I passed out like a doofus last night. You're a gorgeous woman and as out of my league as Rita Hayworth to Groucho Marx. I mean you're like a leading lady and I'm a supporting player," I said, trying to salvage my dignity. "Neither of us is interested in anything more than friendship, so let's meet at Joe's Bar. We'll buddy around with our pals. I'm sure you've got friends you could bring."

For a moment, she looked disappointed, but then nodded her agreement. "O.K.," she said, "but I still want you to come over and listen to my new Sinatra album." I nodded in agreement, wondering why she was so attracted to me. I was reasonably good looking in a nondescript kind of way, with sandy brown hair, of average height with a sturdy build, but certainly nothing special.

"I guess you're comfortable with me," I laughed. "It must be my exceptional intelligence and striking good looks." I left, red-faced when she'd kissed me on the cheek.

I walked back to the apartment, where Gus kidded me about spending the night with such a goddess. I assured him that nothing happened. "I could write home to my preacher and not feel ashamed about anything I did last night," I said, intentionally leaving out the part about passing out. He guffawed and laughed at me for being such a "square!" "Eb, you beat all, throwing opportunity away!"

Soon I forgot about the strange experience at her place. Had I been a little more mature, I would have paid more attention to that nagging feeling that something wasn't "kosher." Try as I might though, I could recall nothing "untoward" happening, so I relaxed and quit worrying. At twenty-one, I didn't brood on things for long periods of time. Everything reverted back to the usual routine, and I quit worrying and fretting about it.

When I saw Cheryl at physical therapy, she was friendly and reminded me about the meeting for drinks at the club. That weekend, everything seemed normal. We drank a few beers, laughed with friends, and had our usual fluid conversation. I went to her apartment afterwards, ignoring the guys who were winking at me as we left together. We sat on the couch and listened to the dulcet singing of Sinatra. I declined any offers of drink, although my throat was parched for water. Even though I was powerfully attracted to her, I wasn't under any illusions that she felt the same about me. Any bumbling advances I made would only make her laugh in derision. She had better looking fish to fry than me.

Much to my surprise and delight, Cheryl and I started dating regularly. Within the space of few months, I introduced her to my family, and we began to contemplate marriage. I was looking forward to getting to know Eve and having a ready-made family. Although my parents liked Cheryl, she was something of a mystery to them, as if I had brought home an exotic princess to marry. Pa voiced his reservations when he said, "She's awful pretty. But son, are you sure she is ready to marry someone as down-to-earth as you?"

With some trepidation, I replied, "Well, we love each other, and we can work out our differences." I was so blinded by infatuation that I didn't realize that people often marry an idealized version and then have to live with the real person.

I graduated from college in 1956 and was hired as a math teacher at a high school in town. Cheryl and I agreed to marry now that I had secured employment. She took a two-week vacation for the wedding to be held at her home church in Mississippi and a weekend honeymoon to Memphis.

Part V

I bought a used Oldsmobile from Uncle Lewis to drive to Cheryl's in late July, 1956, accompanied by Gus and my brother Danny who was on a two week furlough from the army. We took turns at the wheel on two-lane highways to Desoto's Landing, a small town in Mississippi about twenty-five miles east of the Mississippi River. As we neared the delta, a misty patina of humidity coated everything. Our clothing was so drenched in sweat that it clung to our skins, with rivulets of moisture rolling down our backs. We hooked elbows on windowsills to ventilate the car and cool ourselves. Heavy rain clouds darkened the sky, making the humidity and heat as oppressive as a sodden blanket. All living things seemed to be paralyzed. We rode in silence, unable to expend the energy needed to talk.

Extensive fields stretched in all directions, dotted here and there by small clusters of houses which stood as mute testimony to the occupants. I made up stories about the tidy, peaceful lives of those living in well-maintained farmhouses as appealing as decorated cakes atop a table. I thought about the lives of the sharecroppers and working class who lived in small, weathered houses with patchy areas of dirt in the yard. Deserted homes riddled me with wonder about why they had been abandoned.

We arrived in Desoto's Landing around nine at night, saturated in exhaustion and sweat. Each of us booked separate rooms at the local motel after being cooped together on the hot drive. It felt as if I had been working in the fields all day when I lathered off sticky residue of perspiration and grime in the shower. Feeling clean and relaxed, I crawled into bed and read before drifting off to sleep. The next morning, we rose around nine, got dressed, and ate breakfast at the "Sit A Spell" café. Afterwards, we walked around the town square for an hour before getting in the car and driving the eight miles to Cheryl's house.

A person remembers the most mundane details with vivid clarity when their life is about to change. For instance, I recall the sunlight accentuating sparkling dew clinging to ever grass blade, leaf, and flower. Everything glistened with the overnight rain and life stretched in hope and promise like a rich field when I knocked on Cheryl's front door.

Cheryl's mother, Mrs. Devotia Brooks, opened the door with a wide smile on her face, inviting us inside in a heavily accented delta drawl. Waving her arms outward in a wide arc, she clasped each of us in a bear hug. She gave the appearance of someone desperately clinging to youth and beauty. Her face powder accentuated a lined complexion, and her features were highlighted with eyeliner, mascara, and vivid scarlet lipstick. Heavy penciled brows effectuated an expression of perpetual surprise. A shirtwaist dress in bright floral print was stretched over her ample frame.

"Oh, I'm so happy to meet each of you! Cheryl has told me so much about y'all that it's just like meeting kinfolk. Sam, Cheryl, Eve, company's here!" she sang out.

Presently, Sam, Cheryl's father, walked inside the room to pump each of our hands enthusiastically. He was a tall, corpulent man with a fleshy, ruddy face. Wide eyes, a pronounced nose, a thick head of trimmed red hair spiked with gray, and generous mouth made his outsized features look as if he were a cartoon character. I was thankful that Cheryl had inherited the best of her mother and father's genes.

"So glad to meet you!" he bellowed. "Please come into the living room and have a seat. You'll have to excuse Cheryl. She's still asleep from her long trip. I don't know where little Eve is, but she's lurking around somewhere!" Sam chortled conspiratorially.

We walked into the living room where I settled into a chair while Gus and Daniel sank into a cushiony couch in front of a large window. At attic fan cooled the house, pulling drafts from the open windows, which made the lace curtains billow like fluttering ghosts. Looking around, I noticed the roomy house was cluttered but well maintained with buffed wooden floors and polished furniture. Every available surface was covered with paraphernalia. Magazine racks and bookshelves were overflowing. Floor to ceiling shelves were stacked with decorative plates, cups, saucers, and glass and ceramic figurines.

The fireplace mantle was covered with framed photographs of Cheryl in formal and casual poses. Mrs. Devotia noticed my interest and said, "Oh, I see you're admiring Cheryl's pictures. Isn't she a beauty? When she was growing up, I drove to Jackson every Saturday for her to attend Stella Tyrone's Professional Charm School. And do you know that she compiled an impressive portfolio which was sent to modeling agencies in New York City!" Devotia said while raising clasped hands in rapturous jubilation.

"Well, what happened? I mean, did any of the agencies offer her a contract?" asked Daniel.

"No!" thundered Sam, startling everyone by banging his hands down on the small table beside him, scattering several small figurines to the floor. "Can you imagine! We spent hundreds of dollars paying professionals to instruct her in grooming and deportment, but no agency was interested. It made no sense! She outshone all the competition like a thoroughbred among mules."

"Now, Sam, whatever their reason, it wasn't a complete loss," Devotia said soothingly patting her husband's plump hands. Then sighing in satisfaction, Mrs. Devotia looked at us and said, "With all that training, and Cheryl's spectacular looks, she entered the Miss Delta contest and won first place. You can just imagine how envious the other girls were. But she did let jealousy dampen her outlook. Why, she went on to compete in the Miss Mississippi Contest and won a thousand dollars as third runner up! She met her husband, Bill, when she was chosen to represent his family's business as Miss Pecan Queen with her portrait on the label of Flynn's Pecans."

During this exchange, I listened incredulously while taking in the jumbled room as if watching an especially absurd play. The central character were Cheryl's mother and father and the rest of us were startled audience members pulled onstage as impromptu players.

Sam said "We're so blessed with Cheryl. From the minute she was born, she was special. I'm afraid we've spoiled her. She was such a beauty with those red curls and green eyes. You see, we'd tried for years to have a child; and finally, Cheryl was born as our little miracle. All she had to do was flash those eyes at us and we ran to do her bidding."

"Yes, Cheryl's one flaw is that she's spoiled and headstrong. Gently guide her, but don't ever make the mistake of telling her 'no', or she'll throw a fit. Unfortunately, Bill, her first husband, never quite understood this and it caused problems in their marriage," said Devotia.

"Yes, Cheryl, mentioned her first husband. She's never spoken much about his accident. I don't want to pry or be insensitive, but what happened?" I asked.

"Well," replied Sam, lowering his voice to a near-whisper, "we never discuss it because it causes Cheryl such pain. But it happened like this: late that night, Bill left the house to drive twenty miles to work on some accounting business at the orchard. Normally, he would have left early in the day, but Cheryl had been sick, so he'd stayed home to tend to her. By the time he left around midnight, he must have fallen asleep at the wheel and run off Hollis Ward Bridge into the creek where he drowned in the car. Because of heavy rains, rescuers had a hard time pulling the car out of the swollen current. Such a tragedy. If only he had waited until the next day. I don't know why he left in such a terrible storm."

"Oh yes. Every waking hour, we are reminded of his death. Cheryl was so overcome with grief that she had to move away. That's why she left Eve with us while she went to nursing school and then got that job at the Tuscaloosa hospital. She had to get away or she would have lost her mind," Devotia explained.

As if summoned, Eve walked into the room with all the poise of an actress playing the part of a stoic eight-year-old child. She was a quiet, reticent girl whose solemn, light green eyes took in everything around her. Stout and tall for her age, she resembled her grandfather with her robust physique, coarse red hair, and oversized features. While no beauty, she had a calm dignity that was appealing.

She looked steadily at me when her grandparents introduced us. I was cordial but not overly friendly. I've always thought children are intimidated by overly affectionate adults and I hoped that gradually over time, we'd get to trust and like each other.

Daniel, Gus, and I gaped in utter shock when Cheryl walked into the room clad in a satin robe barely concealing an elaborate gown in a peacock pattern of green and blue plumage. Had she taken flight and soared out the window, we could not have been more aghast. Who in their right mind wore such intimate apparel in mixed company?

Devotia and Sam hardly seemed to notice. "Why look, everyone. It's our dear Cheryl," effused Devotia. Cheryl welcomed each of us with a warm hug, much to the embarrassment of Daniel and the amusement of Gus who was nonplussed. Apparently in his circle of friends, eccentric elites were renowned for such outlandish stunts. Certainly, I didn't want my wife to parade around in intimate apparel and made a mental note to talk to her about being modest in polite company.

Thankfully, Cheryl went upstairs and put on a more acceptable outfit. When she walked into the dining room where we had gathered to eat lunch, she looked sophisticated wearing chic yellow capri pants and a bright pink top. I had no clue about all the hours she spent shopping in upscale stores to compile a wardrobe that fit her every mood.

Later that Friday evening we had a simple wedding rehearsal, then ate a meal at a local restaurant attended by half the town. That night as I lay in bed, I said a prayer for a happy marriage, realizing that this was my last night as a bachelor. Early in the morning, I awoke from a dream in which I was floating down into a forest that was covered by deep, dark water. It was so disturbing that I had a hard time going back to sleep and spent hours staring at the full moon as night breezes billowed thin curtains through the open window.

Part VI

Family and friends gathered inside Desoto's Landing Baptist Church the next afternoon for the wedding. Cheryl was decked out in an elaborate wedding dress festooned with lace flounces puffed out by so many layers of tulle that the bottom edges stuck out in a wide circle. Guests sat on pews decorated with bouquets of pink roses, gladiolus, and peonies which emitted such a cloying fragrance in the hot church that people fanned themselves to disperse the smell. Eve, her only bridesmaid, wore a simple yellow grown that hung below her knees. She was overshadowed by a pair of cherubic twins: a five-year old flower carrier and her brother, the ring bearer.

During the afternoon ceremony, I nervously sweated in a black suit while my two groomsmen, Daniel and Gus, stood beside me for moral support. Afterwards, Cheryl and I stood in a reception line greeting each guest. We went to separate dressing rooms to change into more comfortable clothing during the reception. I wore a simple dress shirt and slacks while Cheryl was outfitted in a pink lace dress more appropriate for a coronation.

Apparently, all the guests felt compelled to bring gifts, so we spent the entire reception opening them. I smiled so enthusiastically at household appliances, cookware, towels, oven mitts, and aprons, that my face began to hurt. After a five-hour reception, and a lengthy goodbye to all the guests, we piled gifts into the beds of two pickup trucks and drove them back to her parents' house, spending another two hours unpacking and storing the gifts in the hot, crowded attic. Then we ate supper with a houseful of relatives before finally going to bed. I was so tired that I was distracted, and matters were not helped knowing that our kin were sleeping in close proximity to the wedding chamber. But nevertheless we quietly persevered.

The next morning, we said lengthy goodbyes before packing our suitcases into Cheryl's maroon Chevrolet and driving to Memphis for a three-day honeymoon.

On the way back, we stopped at Cheryl's parents, packed up the gifts, and drove to Tuscaloosa in separate vehicles. Gus and Daniel had ridden back home with my parents after the wedding, so I would have access to my car. I led the way in my Oldsmobile with Cheryl and Eve following in their car. Cheryl's mother and father completed the caravan by driving a truck hitched to a trailer loaded with presents, suitcases, and supplies. Each vehicle contained so many possessions there was barely room for the occupants to sit. Had any of us stopped suddenly, we would have smothered under an avalanche of household what-nots.

We rented an apartment in the military housing unit which had enough room for most of the supplies that Cheryl had brought with her. After setting up housekeeping, Cheryl started back to work at the hospital. I held down two jobs that summer, working as a diesel mechanic at the airport and at a local neighborhood grocery store.

I didn't think it was a good idea to leave Eve, an eight-year-old girl, alone in the apartment all day by herself. So, on Sunday evenings, I drove her to my parents' farm to spend the week. Each Friday afternoon, I drove her back to our city apartment for the weekend. After a few weeks, Eve began smiling and talking more as she blossomed under my family's attentive care. She enjoyed being around my teenage sisters and didn't complain when she worked alongside them on the farm.

My sisters, Martha Leona and Deborah Noel, taught Eve to sew, quilt, crochet, and cook. Eve especially enjoyed sewing and spent hours creating new dresses for her dolls out of cloth scraps. A black and white cat named Slider accompanied Eve and Pa when they fed the cows. She enjoyed the soft muzzle of the mule nibbling sugar out of her hands and laughed when Pa squirted milk from the cows' udders into the cat's mouth. On evening strolls, Eve enjoyed walking with Pa and my sisters as the dogs trotted ahead.

By the end of the summer, Eve had toughened up and slimmed down. Like a butterfly, she crawled out of a chrysalis of silence, gaining confidence in work and companionship. For the first time, she had a family who cared for her, rather than pushing her aside.

As the summer wore on, Cheryl became too exhausted to accompany me when I picked up Eve on Friday and returned her on Sunday. Although I was sad that Cheryl remained home, at least it gave me some time to get to know Eve who began telling me about her life.

Eve didn't remember her father since he had died when she was an infant. As she matured, she overheard unsettling conversations between her mother and grandparents about why she had no contact with her father's side of the family. She found out that they suspected Cheryl of staging their son's accident for profit and had disowned both of them. Her mother had squandered most of the inheritance within a few years and had been forced to get a job as a result.

Cheryl's parents had lavished so much attention and love on Cheryl that they had little left to give to Eve. She felt like an unwanted nuisance for so long that she learned to stay out of the way. Living in a dysfunctional family had taught Eve to isolate herself and distrust her mother. She had never felt accepted or valued until my family supported her with unconditional love.

By the end of the summer, Eve and I developed such a good relationship that she and I conversed freely. I'd ask questions about her week and listen as she told me about sewing, doing chores, and playing with cats and dogs. She was awestruck by my pretty teenage sisters who taught her how to fix her hair and apply nail polish. One day she sighed, "I wish I was pretty like your sisters. I'm so plain and ugly with my freckles and kinky orange hair. Why couldn't I be beautiful like my mother?"

"Listen here," I said, "You are very pretty. Beauty comes in all shapes and sizes. I think your hair is beautiful. Besides, Doris Day has freckles, so what are you complaining about!" Then I looked at her and said, "You are perfect exactly like you are. Don't ever compare yourself to others. Just be you and that's good enough."

Eve looked at me, blinked her light green eyes, and turned away. I could see that she was ruminating over what I'd said. After a few minutes, she said, "You know something, you're right. I can be my own kind of person and make my own kind of songs!" Then she started singing in a high falsetto voice like an opera singer. We both started laughing and I felt my heart opening up to her. "She's my daughter. I always get the giggles when I try to be serious," I thought with pride. She must have gotten that from being around me. On the rest of the ride home, we laughed over jokes. "This is love at its purest," I thought. And I was right.

I had gotten to know some people in the apartment complex that summer during cookouts. On Saturdays when Eve was home, she became friends with a girl her age named Carol Lee and was overjoyed to know they would be in the same grade at school. It was such a relief to know she would have a ready-made friend once she started third grade in late August.

Cheryl and I fell into a routine that summer. She'd come home from work so exhausted that she'd lay on the couch reading romance novels instead of cooking and cleaning. Eventually, I grew so tired of eating cold sandwiches and living in a messy house that I started making supper and straightening up. I tried not to compare Cheryl to my hardworking sisters and mother since she held down a fulltime job. Occasionally, irritation caused me to nag Cheryl to do her share of the work, but she shrugged off my complaints and went back to reading.

On Sundays, we dressed up to attend a local church which Cheryl liked because of the affluent members. There were times when I wondered if she went to services just to show off her latest outfit and make friends with the well connected. She spent so many hours getting ready for church that she was like a queen at court, cinching herself into expensive dresses. I could never understand why she insisted on dressing so formally on sweltering summer days.

Although she had natural beauty, Cheryl sat in front of the vanity table applying makeup, fixing her hair, and dousing herself with perfume. To this day, when I smell hairspray, I am reminded of the days when I sat beside her in the hot church as she waved an accordion fan back and forth during the sermon.

Her church friends cooed like doves over her clothing, jewelry, and coordinated accessories while I received little notice at all. It was like she was a preening peacock followed by guinea hens, but I didn't mind. I only wished she would put as much effort into keeping house as she did on her trousseau. Her closet was packed full of shoes, purses, belts, and clothing. I thought it was a colossal waste of money since she wore a uniform to work and could only display her wardrobe at church or when we occasionally went out to eat or attend a movie. When I advised her to sell or give some of her clothing away, she scoffed, "Don't tell me what to do."

One Friday afternoon Eve walked in to show off her new hairstyle and dress to Cheryl. "Look at my dress, Mama. I made it myself. Do you like it?" Eve asked.

Cheryl made Eve twirl around. "It's pretty good," she said. "What kind of material did you use? It looks like you made it out of an old flour sack!"

Eve replied, "Yes, it was all I had, and I thought it was pretty." She was so crestfallen that my heart ached as she walked quietly off to her bedroom.

"Cheryl," I said indignantly, "Eve spent hours making that dress. The least you could do is compliment her on it. What kind of mother are you? How many eight-year-olds do you know who can make a pattern and sew a dress?"

"Well, so what? she muttered. Then she picked up the novel she was reading and dismissed me with a wave of her hand.

I was so incensed that I went to Eve's room to comfort her. "Eve, I'm sorry about your mother. Your dress and hair are really pretty." Then I hugged her. "Don't feel too bad. Your mother works hard and comes home in a bad mood. Don't let her get to you. Honestly, I don't know why she acts the way she does, but I know she loves you." After a few minutes, Eve began to smile and tell me how she cut out the pattern and maneuvered the sewing machine.

When I walked back into the living room, I talked softly so Eve couldn't eavesdrop on us. "Cheryl, your daughter needs you to teach her things and pay attention to her. She's going through a lot of changes right now—moving to a new city, making new friends, getting to know me and my family. Why don't you spend the day with her tomorrow? Take her shopping. Buy her some new things for school."

Cheryl put down her book and looked at me. "You just don't get it, do you? Saturday, I'm going shopping with friends from church, and we don't need a kid tagging along and complaining."

I had to control my temper when I spoke. "All right then. Next weekend I'll take Eve and my sisters shopping, and they can spend the weekend. My sisters hardly ever get to go anywhere."

"Oh Eb," Cheryl sighed. "Why must you always involve your family in our plans? You know how I detest company. Honestly, you have absolutely no consideration for my feelings!"

"Look Cheryl, when you married me, you married into my family, and I married into yours. I never complain when your parents visit, so don't complain when my family does. I'm taking the girls shopping whether you like it or not; and believe me, shopping is not my idea of fun. Afterwards, my sisters are spending the weekend with us. It's the least I can do for all they have done to help us out and I wish you'd show them some respect."

"Whatever, Eb," huffed Cheryl. "Just don't expect me to cook and clean up after them."

Then she picked up the book, gave me a long withering look, and went back to reading a novel whose cover featured a bronzed pirate swinging on a rope with his arm around a sultry woman whose ample bosom was close to bursting out of her dress.

Most Saturdays, Carol Lee's mother and I took turns watching as Eve and Carol Lee went to the playground and each other's apartment. Afterwards, Eve and I went grocery shopping and came home to put everything away, tidy up, and get ready for supper. Late in the afternoon Cheryl would come home laden with bags of clothing and more music albums and books from her shopping.

That fall I started teaching math to high school students. Eve rode the bus with Carol Lee to the local elementary school. She was a quiet and respectful student who dutifully turned in homework assignments and studied hard for good grades. She and Carol Lee often visited each other to do homework before playing outside or watching cartoons.

After a few years, we saved up enough money to put a down payment on a small house with an unfinished attic that I planned to remodel into an extra bedroom, office, and bathroom. My marriage continued to hum along, although Cheryl's excessive spending caused resentment. It wasn't the harmonious union I had envisioned, but at least we managed to keep the peace. We became one of those couples who rarely communicate from the heart.

After five years of marriage, it was to my great surprise and delight when Cheryl announced that she was pregnant. She quit her job when her doctor forced her to take bed rest because of her turbulent pregnancy. On April 3rd, 1961, Cheryl gave birth to an eight-pound baby boy with a dusting of light red hair whom she insisted on naming Antonio after one of her fictional heroes. As Tony matured, he began to favor me, although he had the same shade of hair and eyes as his mother.

Eve was a loving sister to her brother, tending him when

Cheryl was tired or distracted. Since Cheryl had gotten in the habit of staying up past midnight, she napped during the day. Often, I'd come home to find Cheryl reclined on the couch asleep while Tony entertained himself in a playpen strewn with toys. I worried that he was being neglected so I'd look for cast-off diapers and empty baby bottles just to make sure Cheryl had changed and fed him during the day.

Eventually, Carol Lee moved to a neighborhood close by, so she and Eve frequently visited each other after school. Sometimes I helped them with math problems at the kitchen table before supper. Eve and I played with Tony and tended to him after Carol Lee left, then bustled to cook supper and clean up. After Tony took his bath and fell asleep in his crib, the house was still. Eve went upstairs to bed, and Cheryl and I read or watched a few television shows. With very little variation, our routines remained the same throughout the years.

In comparison to our humdrum lives, the new decade of the 1960s sparked seismic shifts in music, art, and technology. NASA was sending people into orbit as the space race heated up. Heightened anxiety about the Cold War caused fear as we learned about communist invasions and governmental upheavals. In Alabama, civil unrest energized a need for equality. President Kennedy and his glamorous wife initiated new ways of dressing and entertaining. The world was changing, and I wanted to be a part of the revitalization. But when I tried to involve Cheryl, she was apathetic. "I have no interest in any of that stuff," she said when I talked to her at night. At night, she motioned for me to go to bed. "I need some time alone. Goodnight." Then she would read until the early morning hours. I felt lonelier than ever when she came to bed as the rift between us grew.

Although my marriage was faltering, I treasured my children. Tony was a sweet-natured little boy who loved exploring nature and being with his family, I gauged the passing years using my kids as a measuring stick. Too soon it seemed, Tony turned five and Eve was a seventh grader in junior high school. Over the years, I'd tried to adopt Eve, but Cheryl refused. All I could figure out was that Cheryl was still trying to inveigle her way back into the good graces of her first husband's family. She probably still clung to the hope that if Eve kept the Lake name, she might be included in a share of Lake's Pecan business. I had no such delusions; but Cheryl adamantly refused to believe that the Lake family was done with them.

Cheryl got crankier and more restless until one night she announced that she and Betsy, her church friend, were going to start attending Bingo Night at the Lady Kingfisher's Lodge on Tuesday and Friday evenings. I was relieved when Betsy started driving Cheryl to these events just to have some peace in the house. In a few weeks, Cheryl was happier than I had seen her in a long time; although it was odd that she never brought back any prizes.

Some six months later, I got an urgent call at work from the bank. The teller told me that my checking account was in the red and several of my checks had bounced. After work, I hurriedly drove to the bank to talk to the manager. Surely there had been some accounting mistake. I'd always balanced my checkbook. Had someone been forging checks in my name?

Mr. Helms, the bank manager, ducked his head and looked at me over the rim of his glasses as we sat in his office. "I'm sorry, Mr. Torplotnamun," he said. Then he started clearing his throat before lifting his head, sighing, calmly taking off his glasses, and gazing at me with an expression of concern.

"You've always been a highly respected patron of our bank and we certainly appreciate your business," said Mr. Helms. "However, your wife has been making large withdrawals from both checking and savings. Fortunately, you still have five thousand fifty dollars and twenty-eight cents in savings, but your checking account has a balance of minus twenty-eight dollars." He hesitated, then added: "I'm sorry, Mr. Torplotnamun, but I'm going to have to ask you to please make restitution. You'll need to transfer some money into your checking account."

My face blanched in shock. Had I held up the bank in my underwear, I couldn't have been more embarrassed. I had always methodically balanced the checkbook each month, making sure to cover Cheryl's expenditures. She thought nothing about throwing hundreds of dollars away on trifles. She was like the farmer who threw seeds on hard ground and the wind and water carried them away so they didn't take root. There was nothing to show for all her expenditures except vanity.

"Of course. I'll do just that." I hesitated before saying, "Transfer five hundred please to my checking. And could I make a separate savings account in my name only?" Then dropping my voice, I said, "It would be better for my family if only I have access to it. Cheryl doesn't understand financial prudence."

"I understand completely," said Mr. Helms. "And yes, that is a great idea. Many people do this—more than you realize. How shall I say it? We in the banking business do quite a few confidential transactions. We'll do just that today. And Mr. Torplotnamun, you're a good man. Please don't worry about this. I know you'll do the right thing."

I set up a savings account in my name with the bulk of the

remaining cash, leaving just enough in our joint savings account for Cheryl. I didn't like being secretive, but I had to keep my family financially solvent.

That's when I began to get suspicious of Cheryl. While she was gone, I'd look through her receipts, adding them up to see her expenditures. Even though she spent extravagantly, the amount still didn't add up to the hundreds she was spending each month.

I had a nagging fear that Cheryl wasn't telling me everything. Was she involved in some nebulous dealings down at the Lodge? Cheryl had long been a member of the Kingfisher Ladies Club, attending meetings and participating in events that raised money for disadvantaged children. My goodness, had the pillars of society started playing high-stakes poker?

When Cheryl was sleeping one night, I looked at her. In her middle thirties, she was more beautiful than ever. It was unsettling to realize that I hardly knew her; after eight years of marriage, she was still an enigma. I felt a shiver of fright as if I were looking at a foreboding statue encased in a crypt. "It's just a possum running over my grave," I thought, trying to explain my shuddering; but I knew that something far more ominous overshadowed me and I went to sleep, with dreams of drowning in dark water.

Part VII

Howdy 'Pardners', this is Pretty Boy Floyd, and I'm going to be your narrator in this chapter of the story. Ha! I gotcha with that introduction. Actually, my name is Floyd Yarkus of the Yarkus gang, but women say I am good looking, so I don't mind the nickname. You may not have heard of us if you don't live in Aeolian County; but around these parts, the Yarkus gang don't exactly rate high on anyone's list of upstanding citizens.

When we come around, none of your belongings is safe. We'll pilfer anything you got lying around or locked up, except we don't hurt nobody in the process. For instance, we don't bust into houses if people are in them. We ain't armed robbers who'd just as soon beat you up as look at you. We might be sorry and no-count, but we got a conscience. That's where we draw the line, 'cause we don't hurt innocent people; although we have been known to harm people who try to take any of our business. We ain't too keen on competition, I guess you could say.

I come from a long line of grifters, thieves, drunks, and ne'er-do-wells. My dad was too lazy to work so he sired eight kids and make them do the work for him. He was mean as a junkyard dog whether he was drunk or sober and slapped his wives around when they tried to get him to do better. I was the youngest boy from his first wife who died giving birth to me—her eighth child.

A year later, Pa married a woman of some means but little sense. My stepmom was as mean as Pa. She'd spit and hiss at his first wife's kids but treat her own two kids like they were angels from heaven. By the time she married Pa, she was in her 50s, and too old to have any more babies, which was a blessing. I'd hate to think what the offspring of a bobcat and a drunk would be like.

Pa taught us to thieve and grift our way through life with charm, sleight of hand, and keen planning. I teamed up with my brother Verndall who was a few years older than me when we in our late teens. Believe it or not, I was actually the first in my family to graduate from high school. I did fairly well, and if you notice, I can use proper English when I want to appear educated. Most of the time, I just speak some kind of hick jargon to blend in. I'm a chameleon, you might say.

We did fairly well thieving and selling stuff until the law caught us driving Preacher Amherst's tractor and bush hog through town on a drunken spree one night. That's how we got locked up for criminal mischief and driving under the influence for a six-month sentence in the local jail.

I ain't never lacked for women, being as how I'm a good looking, charming kind of guy. I got a smooth way of talking and a hot way of eyeing a woman that keeps me pretty well supplied with female companionship. I did o.k. in jail, except for one encounter where a guy tried to start some weird business. I was doing laundry at the time and broke his jaw because nobody takes advantage of me. After that, no one tried to coerce me into stuff that I had no interest in doing. And believe me, I got zero interest in that kind of activity.

The ambulance took the guy to the hospital. Sheriff Dubbs wrote up an incident report and apologized when I told him what happened. It was worth it just to gain a little respect. I told him, "You better start running a tighter ship."

It won't happen again," he said. And it didn't. The offender got his jaw fixed and had to work outside for a while with a pickaxe. I learned that good looking people have advantages. We can do bad stuff, and get forgiven; but then again, our looks attract people we don't want to have around. It's a double-edged sword, I guess you could say.

A few months later, I got into trouble again and was facing the possibility of serious prison time before the charges were dropped after I paid restitution. I started thinking about straightening up and living on the right side of the law after Judge Brent gave me a chewing out and said that if he saw either me or Verndall again, he was throwing the book at us. I guess you could say, I got "scared straight" before I regressed to bad habits again.

I admit I've done some stupid stuff in my time. My biggest problem started when I hightailed it out of Aeolian County to Tuscaloosa after my witchy stepmother snitched on us to the sheriff. It wasn't so bad because we had greater opportunities for stealing. Things would have been fine and dandy if we hadn't got so greedy and careless.

We made a lot of money pilfering auto parts, tools, and machinery in a lucrative black market. It was easy making a good profit since our only expenditures were the efforts we put into not getting caught. Our problem was greed which was hazardous to our well-being since neither of us had much sense. You've heard the scripture: "An idle mind is a devil's workshop." Well, let me tell you, it's true that when degenerates ain't engaged in nebulous activities, we're thinking of other opportunities for a quick buck. Verndall and I spent too much time swilling down booze and planning illicit business ventures instead of making an honest living.

One night, we broke into an auto ship and got caught by the owner who started cussin' and chasing us with a shotgun. I outran him, but Verndall got shot in the left buttock. He fell into a ditch and nearly broke one of his legs before I grabbed him, and we escaped. After that, I had to pick out the pellets once we got back to the house. We avoided going to the emergency room 'cause neither of us could come up with a plausible explanation of how he acquired the wound. He just about died in agony when it festered up into a smelly abscess. Thankfully, he went to a doctor who didn't ask too many questions and got some medicine for it to heal.

Verndall had so much free time just lying on his side in bed that he started thinking about all the bad things he'd done. One night, he picked up a Bible and started reading aloud the passage where Moses goes up the mountain to receive God's commandments, and nearly loses his mind when he comes down to find his people rioting in front of the golden calf. "You know," Verndall said, "you and I are just like those sinful people. If we don't get away from the devil, we're going to be swallowed up in the pit of hell too."

That night Verndall "saw the light" and proceeded to straighten out his life. Mired up to his eyeballs in sin, he cried out in repentance, started going to church, found a good woman to marry, and got a job at the local paper mill. His wife, Darlene, kept him on the straight and narrow. Every few years, she'd drop another kid, and if he ever slipped up, she'd scream at him to set a good example to his kids. Verndall became a righteous man, in part because he wanted to follow Jesus, but also because he was afraid of his feisty wife.

I was on my own after that. Without Verndall to be a guiding light of common sense, I became as unmoored as a leaking boat in dangerous waters. I was headed for destruction like some idiot in a barrel going over Niagara Falls.

Figuring I'd take a sabbatical from breaking and entering, I decided to lay low and make money playing poker at Fuzz Swarther's place. Fuzz was the kingpin of gambling in the region. He lived in an expansive compound in Natathala County, bordering Tuscaloosa to the northwest. His real estate holdings consisted of an expansive private dwelling where he lived in isolation, surrounded by smaller houses for his employees, and a gambling shack nestled in thick desolate woods. Fuzz's Place was a private retreat for fun-loving reprobates. Complicit county officials were paid under the table to look the other way.

To be a member of Fuzz's "Private Club," you had to pay large yearly dues and take a pledge of secrecy about transactions. If someone blabbed, they'd pay for it. Over the years, so many loose-lipped people went missing that the county became renowned as a place to hide bodies in deserted coal seams and untrammeled woods.

Anybody with sense was respectful of Fuzz and his bodyguards, known as enforcers. They made sure everything was square and all accounts were paid on time. Although they meant business, they were fair. If you got in a bind, you could pay on an installment plan. People got in trouble when they started borrowing from Fuzz to cover their debts because he charged a lot of interest. If they didn't pay up in time, they got a baseball bat to their head or a bullet to their heart. I knew that if I lost big time and borrowed from Fuzz, I'd better pony up in a few months or be "taken out" and dumped somewhere.

The problem with gambling is that people get too greedy and then blind chance starts turning south. It doesn't take a financial genius to know that your chances of winning start to dwindle the more you play the odds. For a while, I was a savvy poker player who played just for the fun of it. It was a way to pass the time and make a little money every week just for kicks. I'd saved up a good share of money from the thieving business and was even thinking about becoming a reputable citizen like Verndall.

At the age of twenty-seven, I'd done so much lawbreaking that I began to worry that my name wasn't written in the Book of Life. When Pa was dying of liver disease, he'd called his children to his bedside and made us vow to straighten up our lives so we wouldn't end up like him. Once he knew death was looming, he converted to Jesus after Verndall preached the gospel to everybody in the family. My family converted right then. Even my mean old stepmom caught the fervor and started going to the Primitive Baptist Church with my sisters and brothers. She invited them over for Sunday meals and occasionally took care of her step-grandchildren, although she was quick to point out the faults of their parents. My siblings overlooked her faults because they felt sorry for her. Her natural children rarely kept in contact because they were ashamed of her.

I vowed to end my youthful transgressions before settling down. I have never been one to do something halfway; so I justified gambling as my last blaze of glory before turning respectable.

Everything was going pretty well until I met Cheryl who refused to tell me her last name. At Fuzz's Place, we only did things on a first name basis—if you know what I mean. She was a beautiful redhead with a gorgeous figure who turned heads when she came waltzing into the joint with her dowdy friend Betsy. "Betts" as she jokingly called herself in what she thought was a witty double entendre, was plain as dishrag.

I'd had a lot of women before and if they got too serious, I'd make up some excuse and leave. I'm ashamed to admit that I left two of them in real trouble and they had to get married real quick to make their child legitimate. I've fathered two sandy-haired little boys who I met when they were just toddlers. It's kind of sad that I can't have anything to do with my own progeny, but some things are better left alone. Their adopted fathers assumed the boys were their own. I don't think it would be good if I demanded my parental rights and got some husbands hot on my tail.

I was fixated on Cheryl who was beautiful, smart, and kept a cool head. Sometimes she'd win and sometimes she'd lose, but she paid up and didn't sweat things, even when she had to borrow from the house. I liked how she acted under pressure—like a piece of carbon buried under layers of dirt to form a diamond. She was older than most women I was interested in, but that didn't matter, because she had them beat in looks and class, and I wasn't interested in a long-term relationship. Younger women seemed dull in comparison to her, like she was a prancing high-spirited horse and they were a bunch of nags.

Cheryl and I started meeting after games to drink and talk in a quiet corner of the room while Betts gambled. Fortunately, nobody paid much attention to our little illicit rendezvous. I'd ask Cheryl for dates, but she always refused, explaining that she had a husband. I told her that didn't matter to me; I wasn't looking for a long-term relationship and didn't demand exclusive rights, but she refused any further intimacy.

Then one night she told me how mean her husband was and said he smacked her around if she didn't clean the house right. Well, let me tell you, this struck me as hard as if she'd picked up a baseball bat and walloped me right in the chest. I'd seen my own pa beatin' on my stepma when she didn't cook his meals right or didn't work hard enough to please him. I may be a no-count, thieving low-life, but I have never advocated violence, especially toward the helpless. I have never touched a woman—except with her enthusiastic consent. Kids and animals are innocent, and I will beat anyone who abuses them. The Yarkus gang takes pride in the fact that we may steal you blind, but we ain't violent and have even gained the reputation of helping the needy.

By March, bad debts started piling up like magma buried underground until pressure prompts everything to explode to the surface. At first, I waged big bets just to impress Cheryl, hoping that if I made enough money, I could convince her to take our relationship to a new realm. Then I got addicted to the rush of winning. Like a drug addict wanting a fix. I had to continually up the ante for the ultimate buzz. I got so reckless that my luck turned sour. I tried to recoup my losses by waging even higher bets and ended up losing thousands of dollars. As my debt increased, I started being hounded by the loan sharks to pay back what I owed.

I went to see Verndall to see if I could borrow some money, but his wife controlled the purse strings and refused to help me out. She met me on the porch and shouted at me to hightail it out of town. "You best hitch a quick ride far out of town before your body is thrown in a ditch to rot somewhere in the next county. Ain't nobody gon' look for you there. That's what happens to people who try to swindle Fuzz Swarther. We can't help you 'cause we got two kids under the age of three and another on the way. You should have looked before you lept."

I tried to borrow money from Cheryl and Betts, but they were both in the same dilemma. We were like three idiots in a sinking boat smack dab in the middle of the ocean with hungry sharks smelling blood.

Betts was a tall, thin woman in her forties with a face better suited to a horse. Worry lines like dried-p gully washes furrowed her face. She was so spinsterish looking that no one would have guessed she liked to gamble. After our lives settled down, she corresponded with me in letters, so I'll fill you in on what happened to her after she paid off her debts and left Fuzz for good.

As a widow, Betts barely escaped bankruptcy by dipping into her savings to pay off gambling debts. Then she returned to a life of boredom, sharing her small home with her mother. Rather than flagellating herself as a sinner, she appreciated the guts it took for her to crawl out of pit of sin. "I've done the devil's work. Now I intend to do the right thing," she resolved.

With the fervor of a reformed sinner, she rededicated her life to good works by joining the church choir, teaching Sunday school to young children, and practicing charity. Her only indulgence was participating in weekly Bingo games on Thursday Lady's Night at the Kingfisher Lodge in which she became adept at winning prizes, culminating in the grand prize of an electric skillet to fry bologna sandwiches late at night. It was an illicit thrill to snack while her disapproving mother snored loudly in bed at such close range. "I'm such a daredevil," she giggled as she munched furtively.

Deep in her heart, Betts loved the Lord, but got a rush from skirting so close to danger. In prayer, she asked God for forgiveness and praised Him for taking her out of the valley of sin and far away from Fuzz's gambling joint. "Whew, I learned my lesson and I'm never doing that again!" she whispered.

As for me, I was as scared as a possum with a shotgun aimed at my head when I couldn't repay Fuzz. What was I going to do? Cheryl had lost her cool and was equally scared. Having drained most of the money in her family checking and savings account, there was no telling what her husband would do once he found out about it.

"Why, he'll throw me out of the house, and I'll really be destitute. I can't borrow from my parents either. They've already taken out two mortgages to get me out of binds!"

Fear and desperation make people come up with crazy ideas because Cheryl hatched one of the most imbecilic schemes ever conceived. The expression "Any port in a storm will do" applied to us even if we landed in the gallows with a noose around our necks. However, after a few weeks of desperate fear, we stepped off the ledge of rationality and into the surreal.

We had two months to pay our debt or both of us were going to wind up in the bottom of a mine shaft. Neither of us was making much progress on the installment plan; it had to be one lump sum for the both of us or we were dead. We talked Betts into picking up Cheryl as usual so no one got suspicious. Instead of going to Fuzz's joint we started going to Betts' house to connive and scheme. Betts said she didn't want anything to do with our situation and excused herself to watch television in another room, turning up the volume so her eighty-eight-year-old mother could enjoy the shows. For an entire week, we sat in Betts kitchen, talking over ways to get the money.

I convinced Cheryl that we should write down everything to make a list of good ideas. At the top of the paper, I wrote down the amounts each of us owed. My total came to two thousand and fifty-eight; Cheryl's was three thousand and twenty-two dollars. While bleakly discussing our prospects, Cheryl relayed the most harebrained scheme I've ever heard. If she hadn't been so intent, I'd have laughed in her face; but I was so scared, nothing was funny. A man drowning at the bottom of a well doesn't jeer when someone throws him a tattered rope.

Scribbling notes, I realized that Cheryl had been planning her escapade for some time. She explained: "Eve and Antonio are going to spend spring break with their grandparents in Mississippi. Eb and I will drive them there, spend a few days, and be back next Thursday. I'll act all lovey-dovey like we're on a second honeymoon with the kids gone. Every Thursday night, Eb works at the airport. He's the only one working in Building One. There's a few workers about a football field away in another hangar."

"I'll convince him to let me go with him to the airport to watch him work. Before I leave, I'll pack a thermos of tea and a sack lunch for him. Only, I'll douse the tea with sleeping pills that I saved up when I worked at the hospital. I've tested it before on him and it completely knocked him out, so I know it'll work. To get to the airport, you have to drive on Stokely Bridge over Titus Hapland Lake—you know that lake that got dug out about ten years ago over those woods. Anyway, it's a narrow, high bridge with a steep turnoff before you get to it in either direction. People drive down the dirt incline to dock boats, so I know it's pretty deep on the banks. You park on the side road that is closest to the airport and wait on me. It'll be safe. Nobody is going fishing late on a Thursday night in this cold weather.

"Eb told me that the security guard doesn't really check when people enter or leave the airport. I know this is true because a few weeks ago I drove there to deliver a meal to Eb. After he drinks the tea, he'll be knocked out. I'll put Eb in the seat beside me and drive out. Right before we get to the main bridge, I'll stop and get out of the car. You join me and we'll put Eb in the driver's seat and push him in the car down the ditch and into the lake. The water is deep enough close to the banks, so it'll cover the car, but it can be seen from the road the next day.

"After the car submerges, we'll drive off in your car so you can drop me off at the church behind our house. I'll creep back across the vacant lot to the house. No one will see me because it'll be late at night. I'll throw a biscuit if any neighborhood dog barks to keep it quiet. The next day, I'll file a missing person report and act hysterical that Eb didn't come home from the airport. The police will retrace his route and find him dead in the car when they cross over the bridge. They'll assume he fell asleep at the wheel on his way home late at night.

"I'll have a nice funeral service and play the part of the distraught widow to win people's sympathy. Nobody is going to suspect anything; and in a few weeks, I'll put in a claim for the insurance money. We'll pay off our debts to Fuzz and leave town. We can go to Reno or Las Vegas, get married, and start up our own casino where gambling is legal.

I just starred, open-mouthed while Cheryl talked. After she finished, I said, "How do you know this'll work?"

"Well," said Cheryl, flexing her long manicured fingers and smiling sensuously with a gleam in her eyes. "I've had experience with this sort of thing. I got ten thousand from my first husband's life insurance and it worked fine. Better than I expected—because he drank my tea right before we went on a midnight ride. It was a stormy night when I pushed his car into the water. I had to walk through the woods to get back home and creep into the house undetected. Believe me, it's the perfect crime. The police conducted an investigation and filed it as a tragic accident. The insurance company did a cursory evaluation and came up with the same findings. Neither wanted to prolong the agony of a bereaved widow, especially one with such a sterling reputation as a church-going beauty queen who represented her community so well. I got my money in a month. It's a cinch that if it worked before, it'll work again!" she said.

"How much does your husband have in insurance?" I asked warily.

"Well, I've gone through his records discreetly you know. He keeps them locked in a steel file, but I found the key. He's got fifty thousand in life insurance with double indemnity in case of an accident! Just think. That's plenty to pay off Fuzz, with a fortune left over for you and me. We'll move to Nevada and start our own casino where gambling is legal. And just to make sure that neither of us turns on the other, we'll marry. Think of all the money we'll make!"

Cheryl lit up like a neon sign at the thought of serious money. I knew it was up to me to discuss the fine details. My note taking was too slow for Cheryl, so by the end of the night, she had written detailed instructions on a sheet of paper and handed them to me to show her trust, saying, "We're in this together."

I gulped and nodded. Cheryl noticed that I was sweating and told me not to look so nervous. "Honestly, quit acting like an amateur. Desperate times call for desperate measures. Remember how I told you that he beat me. He deserves what he gets. Everything will be fine. In a few weeks, we'll get the money and can pay our debts and leave. Then we'll marry and get serious about making real money."

I looked at her and asked, "Cheryl, what about your kids? What's going to happen to them?"

She replied with a look of annoyance clouding her face. "I'll be spending all my time getting the casino up and running so I won't have any time for the kids. It wouldn't be fair to uproot them. I'll let them live with Eb's parents since they like it on the farm. Or they can live with my parents, and we'll visit them in Mississippi. Either way, they'll be just fine!"

"Well, whatever," I sighed, pocketing the paper. "Cheryl, we need to practice this plan for the next few days to we don't mess up. And another thing, if we do this, and you run off without paying me, I'll track you down and get the money one way or another! Don't try to double cross me."

Cheryl leaned over and kissed me playfully. Then she told me not to worry, assuring me again that everything would be fine. We'd practice the procedures in a few nights to avoid any mistakes. She picked up her purse and went to the living room to ask Betts to drive her home. Betts sighed and I could tell by her expression that she was more than ready to end their friendship. Cheryl was one of those people who nibbled you down to the nub.

I'd gotten in the habit of visiting Fuzz's place each week to render some earnest money just to show that I was serious about paying off my debts. The day after Cheryl told me her plans, I visited Fuzz's joint around midday, giving a twenty-dollar bill to the office manager. Then I ordered some tea, trying to figure out how I was going to come up with the rest of the money since I was as financially barren as dust.

All I had for the rest of the week was a dollar and eighty-two cents in change—not enough to buy a decent meal. I sat at a table, waiting on receipt of payment, deep in thought. One of the enforcers walked over, leaned down, gave me the receipt and said gruffly: "Hey, I'm the official accountant in this joint. Let me give you some advice, son. I've been in this racket now for over twenty years. Fuzz's cuttin' you a deal and shaving off five hundred 'cause you're young and stupid. I know you've taken up with that redheaded woman. If I was you, I'd tell her to take a hike. I've seen her type before and she's no good. She'd as soon slice your throat as look at you." Then peering at me with a glint of compassion, he added, "Buddy, take my advice, pay up and don't ever come back here again. This place is a one-way trip to hell."

"You'll get your money, but thanks for the advice," I said. Then I paid a quarter for the tea, trying to ignore the rumbling in my hungry stomach and went to the rental house where I spent the rest of the day figuring out what to do. "Floyd, you stupid idiot, you really messed up this time," I thought. I came with about fifty solutions and none of them worked. This fact is that I had dug myself into such a deep hole that there was no way out. I was facing the gloomy reality that I either had to leave town quick or end up dead, without even a marker on my grave.

I never even considered taking Cheryl's plan seriously. No way was I killing an innocent man and taking the rap for capital murder. Then I worried. "What if Betts or her mother overheard our discussion, and they told the police! I could be tried for attempted murder!" The sudden bleak realization that I was stuck in a septic tank of troubles caused me to wail. I put my head in my hands as destitute as Job when he covered himself with sackcloth and ashes as his boils festered. Let me tell you, I ain't ashamed to say that sometimes you just have to admit despair like a half-dead rat surrounded by vultures on a dead-end road. It's never a good feeling to be hungry, and scared witless with no way out. "I'm a dead man walking to the electric chair," I thought, but was somewhat comforted by the idea. "At least, that'd be better than Fuzz's gang taking me out on a one-way trip to a mine shaft."

I dried my eyes and lit a cigarette to calm down. Recently I'd read detective magazines to gain insights into the criminal mind. I was proof that most criminals are dumb and lazy; but, at least, I wasn't crazy and shameless, too. "At least, I've got a conscience because I'm sorry for stealing," I thought. I reviewed my life and asked God for mercy, hoping He'd find some goodness in me and give me a second chance.

When in despair, there's a tendency to compare your life with another. I measured my life against Cheryl's and came out ahead on the moral high road. Even though I was a common crook, at least I was sorry for what I'd done. On the other hand, Cheryl fit the profile of a sociopath. "This Cheryl lady is one crazy nut! The sooner I cut my ties with her, the better! Why, even if I was evil enough to be her accomplice to murder, I'd be killed once she collected the insurance money and got out of town. I mumbled: "She just wants to lure me out into the desert so she can keep me quiet and dump my body."

I finally resolved to drive out to my brothers and sisters in Aeolian County to beg for money, hoping they'd take pity on me once I explained my predicament. I'd write each of them a promissory note to pay them back with interest. Once I got some money, I'd drive to Betts house and get Cheryl's phone number so I could inform her husband over the telephone about his wife's murderous plans. At least, I could warn him; and if he didn't believe me, that would be his fault. My conscience would be clear that I'd done the right thing.

Afterwards, I'd buy a bus ticket to Detroit and live with Fletcher, a cousin, who'd given me an open-ended invitation to stay with him until I got on my feet. It sounded like a sensible idea. But when you think about things, you find kinks in the best-laid details. What if Fuzz found out where my family lived and started knocking some of them off as a warning to me that I better pay up!

I'd not slept all night. My eyes felt as grainy as sandpaper; my head throbbed, and all the black coffee I'd drunk made my stomach feel like I'd eaten a tar brisket. I was just about to get a glass of water and some antacid when I heard banging on the door around eight o'clock in the morning. Suddenly my heart pounded like a gong being beaten by a claw hammer. I walked to the window and peered out in dismay at a man dressed in a dark suit surrounded by two burly guys. "I'm fried," I thought. "It's the police."

Conclusion

It's Eb again and I'm going to narrate the conclusion of this odyssey. As I write this, I am looking back with a half century of wisdom since the unfolding of these events. Currently, I am seventy years old. If I can attain the age of one hundred and five, I will have lived three trimesters of life in thirty-five-year increments. As a mathematician, it would be fitting for my life to end on such a perfect linear scale. After I reach that milestone, I will be happy to join the Lord.

Writing keeps my mind active and allows me to help others

who are going through tribulations. I will relate the following events as told to me. So back to the story.

The gentleman banging on Floyd's door was Sol Goldberg, savvy and street smart as a good private investigator should be. Bodyguards came in handy in his line of work as he explained to Floyd when he introduced himself. Having grown up in an especially dangerous section of the Bronx, Mr. Goldberg was adept in assessing people's character. He had been hired by Gus to tail Cheryl and find out why she was going through my savings like water through a sieve.

After intense interrogation, Floyd was only too eager to explain the entire sordid situation in great detail. As evidence of Cheryl's masterplan, he handed Sol the yellow legal paper bearing her distinctive handwriting. When Floyd found out that Cheryl's intended victim was none other than me, he was flabbergasted. He buckled at the knees and would have fallen to the ground had Sol not grabbed him and thrown him to the sofa. When he came to his senses, Floyd said, "I can't believe it! I know the entire Torplotnamun family. They're nice folks who always treated me fair when I stole some of their ham hocks. There ain't no way that I'd ever kill Ebe. I've known him nearly all my life and he's a good guy!"

Sol examined the packed bag of clothing to corroborate Floyd's plans on hightailing it out of town, and finally surmised that he was telling the truth and had no malicious intentions. He called Gus who wired the money for Floyd to pay off his gambling debt. Floyd was so grateful that he wrote down Gus's address with a shaky hand and promised to repay the money with interest. Then he wrote a bill of sale and gave the title of his Dodge to Gus as partial payment, although it was not worth more than two hundred dollars because of a recent wreck. Floyd loaded his suitcase in the trunk of Sol's car, and they drove to the post office to pick up the money, and then to Fuzz's Gambling Hall. Sol and his men stood guard as Floyd gave the money to the accountant and received the receipt showing that he had paid in full, holding it as though he had received his walking papers out of prison.

As Floyd was leaving Fuzz's Place, the accountant blocked him from leaving with a hand to his chest, and for one long, heart-stopping moment stared at him in silence. Then he shook Floyd's hand and said, "Son, try and make good on your second chance in life. And remember, I never want to see you again. You're lucky. Usually, I say that to people right before I kill them."

Floyd swallowed hard and took a long breath to regain his composure before promising that he would comply. Sol and his posse drove to Betts' house to speak to her. She handed them a tape that she'd recorded about the conversation Cheryl and I had the previous night. "I won the tape recorder at the Bingo game and thought it might come in handy if I recorded Cheryl. You can have the tape, Mr. Goldberg. Maybe if she ever threatens to show her face in this town again, it'll come in handy."

Sol thanked her and took the recording. Then he drove Floyd to the Greyhound bus station on the outskirts of town. As Floyd was about to board, he was surprised when Sol reached into his pocket and pulled out a fifty-dollar bill. "Floyd, here's fifty dollars to get you to Detroit. Stay out of trouble when you get there," said Sol gruffly.

Floyd thanked him profusely and then surveyed the area he had called home for so many years. Breathing deeply, he could almost smell the newly turned soil back in Aeolian County. Teary-eyed, he boarded the bus, waving goodbye to Sol and the two guards.

Floyd eventually paid back his debts to Gus, and he always remembered to write thank you notes in his Christmas cards to Gus, Sol, and me for helping save his life and getting him on the right track. In his letters to me over the years, Floy wrote that he had gotten a job in one of the major automobile plants in Detroit, married a fine woman, and had children whom he encouraged to do good. After retiring, he enjoyed gardening and puttering around the house.

Floyd and his wife took trips back home to Alabama to visit relatives in Aeolian County, stopping by my house to talk. On one solitary visit, Floyd asked me to locate his two illegitimate sons. Sol investigated and sent photos to Floyd with the message that both still lived in Tuscaloosa and were maturing into good young men who enjoyed playing football as high school rivals, never realizing that they were brothers.

Floyd wrote back to Sol, stating his thanks and saying, "It's enough for me to know they turned out to be good boys. Maybe the Yarkus blood wasn't so bad after all." Eventually, as fortune would have it, both boys received scholarships as football players at the University of Alabama, never knowing that their biological father was in the stands watching both of them with pride. "Those are my boys," he'd say to his wife after they made an especially good play.

"I know, Floyd," she'd say. "You did good." Even after his sons graduated, Floyd and his wife never missed an Alabama football game on television.

As for Cheryl, she admitted to plotting my murder and

forfeited all parental rights. I didn't take the matter to the police because she could just explain that it had been an elaborate joke. Besides, I didn't want to drag my family's business into the public arena. I dipped into my meager savings to pay off Cheryl's gambling debt in exchange for her leaving town permanently. When things settled down, I got a job teaching in the same school from which I had graduated and it was an honor to teach math alongside my mentor, Mr. Philman. I sold the house in Tuscaloosa, and my children and I went to live with my parents in Brattam Hollow, which was a blessing to everyone since my father's health was declining and my parents needed help keeping up the house and farm.

I officially adopted Eve and she and Tony thrived in their new home. They made new friends at school. Eve and Carol Ann remained friends and made plans to room together at college once they graduated high school.

Ma and Pa especially enjoyed having Tony and Eve around since my two sisters had married and moved out of the house, and Danny was overseas. It was peaceful to worship at Welsh Chapel with my family and extended relatives. I'll always treasure sitting beside Pa on the pew. He'd put his worn fedora on his pant leg in a gesture that was soothing as we listened to the sermon. When a few people voiced concern about my marital situation, Pa silenced them by saying, "My son's an honorable man." His words had the same effect upon them as a judge slamming down a gavel. Justice had been served. He was always going to be there to protect his family.

Cheryl ended up divorcing me and marrying Fuzz. Her dream of riches and fame came true when she and Fuzz closed up shop in Natathala County, moved to Las Vegas and gained prominence in society as the esteemed owners of "Luck Be A Lady Casino" where they made a fortune. Her parents sold their orchard and moved out to live with Cheryl, basking in their good fortune like two cats sunning themselves in a fancy solarium.

All my life, I'd had a recurring dream like a premonition, warning me to stay away from deep, dark water. I thought about all those trees covered by water when the lake was dug out and flooded. How horrible to sink down into those subterranean depths and to look up with my last dying breath at trees whose branches continued to stretch upward, never reaching the surface. One night I dreamed that I was sinking to the bottom and grabbed one of those limbs, hurling myself to the safety of dry land. When I woke up, I thanked God for giving me dear friends and family who saved my life, and I never had that dream again.

THE PLUM CREEK ESCROW

By Harold Raley

On a Saturday afternoon in late November of 1934, Marlow Hardin, 27, took his 12-gauge shotgun from the gunrack, stuffed a couple of shells in his back pocket, and yelled to wife Betty, 25, that he would "be back directly." Then calling his dog Blue, the two of them headed down to Plum Creek. Blue went along strictly to keep Marlow company, and the shotgun was a prop in case he ran across people on the way. The truth was neither of them had any interest in hunting. Blue was too old and fat to jump rabbits anymore, and Marlow, too obsessed with another matter to bother shooting them. His main thought was brothers Dewitt and Howard Evans' sixty-acre fenced tract of prime land running along the east side of the creek.

As they reached the fence line, Blue barked half-heartedly at a startled rabbit bounding away in the tall grass, then hiked his leg and pissed on a fencepost to renew his marking before curling up to doze while Marlow did his usual thing. Blue did not understand some of the odd things Marlow did, but they were old friends and respected each other's space and ways. Marlow leaned the empty shotgun against the next post and for the umpteenth time began to rack his brain for some way to gain ownership of the rich Evans land that was central to his ambitions. And for the umpteenth time he could think of nothing even remotely possible. For one thing, as a business principle the Evans brothers did not sell their land, and for another, Marlow had no money and nowhere to get any even if they did. After half an hour his small stock of optimism was exhausted. He gave a dispirited sigh, picked up the shotgun, roused Blue, and they started back home.

"I need to quit coming down here," he said aloud, shaking his head. "No way I'll ever get my hands on that acreage and just thinking about it has turned into a blue misery I don't need."

At the mention of his name, Blue looked up sympathetically at his friend and wagged his tail but respectfully kept his silence.

Marlow knew that Dewitt and Howard had no practical use for the land. It had lain fallow for so long that the old cotton shed, the only structure on the property, had collapsed into a pile of rotting timbers, and sassafras bushes and pine saplings were beginning to take over. The brothers had not farmed land of any kind since the Evans family got rich. But instead of selling some of their foreclosed properties, they preferred to rent them to tenant farmers like Marlow and keep all the land. That way they got a share of what the renters produced and made money on loans. Their widowed father Amos had drilled it into their heads that land was the foundation of wealth and the thing to do was to get as much of it as you could and hang on to it for as long as you could. He died in 1930, leaving his three sons a respectable fortune and several hundred acres of farmland just as the Depression was starting to squeeze the economic life out of Hackworth County. When the only Hackworth bank failed, Dewitt and Howard began lending money at usury rates of interest to dozens of desperate cotton farmers; many of whom, unable to pay off their mortgages as the Depression deepened, eventually lost their farms to the brothers. By the mid-thirties, Evans Enterprises, the corporate name of their several ventures, was the largest agricultural conglomerate in their part of the state and the brothers the richest men in Hackworth County. But time and money did not satisfy or soften them. They were as deaf as statues to pleas for extensions of mortgages and liens, and the more they got the more they wanted.

Unlike his older bachelor brothers, younger sibling Gene did not share the Evans philosophy. Instead, he drank and gambled away his inheritance in two years, wrecked his marriage, and disappeared. Rumor had it that he ended up a panhandler in New Orleans. Remember the name; we haven't heard the last of him.

Variations of a joke circulated that Dewitt, the bigger and brighter of the remaining brothers, once died and, naturally, went to Hell. He talked the Devil into a scheme to modernize his outdated operation. It sounded too promising to turn down but turned out too good to be true. Before long Dewitt had a deed to half of Hell and a mortgage on the rest. Satan stormed and screamed, turned up the heat, and made all kinds of threats, but as usual Dewitt turned a deaf ear. Desperate to save what was left of his crumbling kingdom, Satan made humiliating concessions to the Higher Powers to get them to restore Dewitt to earthly life before he foreclosed on the rest and all hell broke loose.

Marlow's blue funk lifted, and he was grinning as he thought of the joke, when suddenly Dewitt Evans himself came stomping through the knee-high grass. Marlow had been so fixated on the land that he did not see his Buick behind the sassafras bushes.

"Hey, fellow, I've caught you trespassing on Evans land, and hunting to boot! Now dammit, that posted sign down there by the fence row tells any fool that both things are prohibited on Evans land. Who are you, anyway?"

Marlow and Blue were both startled. Blue whined and Marlow hurried to explain.

"I'm Marlow Hardin, Mr. Evans. I didn't see you and didn't notice the sign. I do ask your pardon. I meant no harm and didn't come here to hunt."

"Then why the shotgun and the dog?"

"Oh, Blue here's too old and fat to hunt, and I'm just not a hunter. I carry the gun around sometimes but never shoot anything."

"Well, Hardin, maybe what you say is true, but I've seen you over here before, though you didn't see me. So tell me, why do you trespass on posted land if not to hunt? Tell me that. You could get yourself shot, you know."

Marlow glimpsed a shoulder-holstered pistol under Dewitt's coat.

"I was just admiring the good land down by the creek, Mr. Evans. No other reason to come down here."

Dewitt laughed. "Just admiring the land, you say. Now that's a fool thing to do. Besides, what do you know about land?"

"Well, sir, I'm a farmer. A man gets to know land if he works it all the time."

"Hardin. The name is familiar. We have, or did have, a renter by that name. You him? If I remember right, he was farming what used to be called the Ferguson place just over the rise."

"Yessir, that's me. I've farmed it for three years now, ever since you all took it over. Good land, but this is a lot better."

"You up to snuff with everything you owe us, money, crop shares and such?"

"Yessir, with everything."

"So you say. I'll check to make sure when I get back to the

office. Meanwhile, you stay off this property if you know what's good for you. And I don't believe that bullshit about 'admiring the land'. A good farmer doesn't have time to waste on such foolishness. Now what were you really up to?"

"Nothing, Mr. Evans. I just like this place and . . ."

"And what?"

"Well, sir, since you ask, I wish I could buy it."

"Buy it!" Dewitt hooted. "With what? I doubt you have two pennies to rub together in your pocket."

"I have a little more than that, Mr. Evans," Marlow retorted with a shade of wounded pride in his voice.

"Well, good for you, Hardin, if it's so," Dewitt said, toning down his voice a bit. "But not nearly enough to buy this property outright, I'd bet, even if we were selling, which we're not. As a rule, we Evanses don't sell our land. It's the real foundation of wealth. But just out of curiosity, tell me how you would propose to pay for it?"

"Well sir, Marlow answered, his heart ticking up a notch, I thought I might pay for it by the year, the way we do with crop shares."

"I said we don't generally sell land, but for reasons that are none of your business, this sixty-acre tract—actually surveys out closer to sixty-two—could be an exception for the right man. All I'll say for now is that we're getting a little top heavy in land here lately. Got more farms than tenants, and I don't like to see land lying fallow and not making us any money. Tell you what, Hardin, I'll check to see if you really are in good standing with us. You come by the office next week, let's say Tuesday morning, and if your account is in good order, we'll see if there's anything we can do. But for now, you and that dog get off this property and stay off till we see what comes of all this. You understand me, Hardin?"

"Yessir, and I'll be there!"

Blue and Marlow ran nearly all the way home, and both were winded when they got there. Blue's tongue was hanging out and he was panting in clueless exhaustion. Marlow's heart was also pounding and his lungs heaving, but big ideas were dancing in his head.

Betty was not thrilled.

"Marlow, you've dealt with that Evans bunch long enough to know you can't trust them as far as you can throw a bull by the tail. Whatever Dewitt Evans tells you next Tuesday, if you're bound and determined to go see him, don't believe a word of it. I wish we could put a county or two between us and them and never have any more dealings with that pair of swindlers."

Leaning on his father's knee, four-year old son Johnny's looked up at Marlow with big blue eyes.

"Daddy, can you really throw a bull by its tail?"

Marlow laughed and tousled Johnny's hair.

"Well, I ain't tried lately, son, but I can sure pick you up!"

With that he tossed and caught Johnny who squealed with delight.

"Marlow, please don't do that!" Betty pleaded. "He's growing a lot and you might drop him. Johnny, of course your daddy can't throw a bull by the tail. Nobody can. It's just a saying."

"You mean it ain't so, mommy? But you told me to always tell the truth. How come you said something that ain't so?"

"Looks like he's got you cornered on that one, Betty."

She hugged Johnny and tried to tell him what she meant by explaining what she didn't mean. Then sending Johnny out to play, she reminded Marlow of old wrongs the Evans had done her family.

"Marlow, I told you how old Amos Evans beat my Grandpa Jenkins out of our family farm. He promised Grandpa he would hold off a year on the note he had on the place, and Grandpa believed him. But then slimy old Amos broke his word and foreclosed anyway and hung Grandpa and the Jenkins family out to dry. And you know as well as I do that his sons are just like their daddy. I don't like speaking ill of the dead, but it's the truth. Anyway, instead of trying to get that land you have your heart set on, you ought to be thinking about cutting loose from the Evans leeches and moving us out of Hackworth County. They poison everything they touch."

"Now, Betty, don't you fret. All I'm gonna do is to listen to the man. Probably won't amount to hill of beans. And even if there is something to it, I'm not gonna do anything till you and me talk about it and agree on things."

"You promise me that, Marlow?" she asked in a softer tone.

"Cross my heart and hope to die, little lady."

Marlow didn't die when he broke his promise the following Tuesday, but Betty almost did when she found out. And she was so incensed with him that for a moment he was afraid she might take him with her into the next life.

"Marlow Hardin, you made me a solemn promise and forgot it the minute you walked out that door!"

"But Betty, I had to say yea or nay right then and there. Dewitt Evans said if I didn't agree to the deal, he had another man waiting that would."

"And you believed him?"

"I had to or lose my chance at the land. Dewitt had all the high cards. I had to do it to get the land."

"You're my husband so I won't call you a fool. But you talk like he just handed the land over to you. But I know Dewitt Evans wouldn't give a sip of water to somebody dying of thirst. And all the money you had was that fifty dollars left over from the crop, money we have to live on this winter. You didn't give that to him, did you? You couldn't have been that dumb, could you? Oh, Lord, I see by the look on your face that's exactly what you did. Dear God in Heaven, what am I going to do with this husband you gave me? Tell me the truth of it, Marlow, or I'll sic Johnny on you, and he'll get it out of you."

"Whoa, woman, just slow down and I'll tell you, and it aint a mess but a real opportunity."

"Marlow, on top of everything else that's gone wrong, I've told you I don't know how many times that I don't like to be called 'woman'. My name's Betty and you better remember it, even if you can't seem to remember anything else."

"Betty, honey, I am truly sorry. But I did what I had to do. I had to put down some money to set up the escrow."

"All right, Marlow, tell me what kind of mess you've got us into this time. What do you mean by setting up an 'escrow'?"

"Honey, an escrow is where the owner of a property puts a deed into a bank or money handling kind of place like that and they hold it until the buyer pays for it. That way they don't deal directly with each other, but the owner gets his money, and the buyer gets his title when he makes the last payment."

"I know what an escrow is, Marlow. What I want to know is what you promised to pay Dewitt Evans for that land and what kind of safeguards are in place so that he won't beat us out of the money and the land."

"Man, you are one suspicious woman."

"I have a right to be. I know the Evanses."

"Well, just to put your mind at ease, look at this," he said, tossing a receipt on the kitchen table.

"So, Marlow, just what I was afraid of. You did put down the whole fifty dollars, which means we're facing the next few months without a penny to live on. And I don't see a signature on this paper."

"I asked about that, and Dewitt had his money man right there to answer my questions. He said that the beauty of the escrow is that nobody has to sign the deposits or deal face-to-face. You pay into the escrow account—there's the number, 505—and it's all recorded by the bookkeeper. And when the deed is paid off, it's right there waiting for the buyer to pick up. We'll have all the receipts. So you hang on to them. And as for money for our necessaries, I'll sell our two calves down there in the cattle pen. That and cutting some dyewood and timber for Tom Hannigan this winter will tide us over till I can make a spring loan."

"Well, maybe, maybe not. But about the deed, did you actually see it? Did they put it in the box with the papers with you watching?"

"I sure enough did, and they sure enough did."

"You didn't tell me how much you agreed to pay for the land and over how much time."

"Now, Betty, you have to understand that the sixty acres, really closer to sixty-two by survey, is not just ordinary sandy upland like most around here but rich bottom land with plenty of water. Maybe the best land in Hackworth County. It'll grow anything."

"You're hedging, Marlow. How much?"

"About eighteen hundred dollars, I reckon it was, well, maybe close to two thousand all told when the handling expenses are figured in."

"My Lord," she moaned, rolling her eyes, "I can't believe what I'm hearing. And how much time is the escrow set up for?"

"Four years from the first of this month and due the first of December."

"That's five hundred dollars a year, and to make bad matters worse this month's nearly over to start with. That leaves a little over forty-seven months to come up with two thousand dollars."

"Nineteen hundred and fifty now by my arithmetic."

"Marlow, what you've done is done, and it's an impossible mess you've got us into. I don't see how we can come up with an extra five hundred dollars a year, especially not in these hard times."

"But we can, Betty, we can. Like I said, I'll work extra hard at farming, plant more cotton, and after the crops are in, I'll find other work in the winter. You'll see. It'll work out. I promise you."

"Don't make me promises you can't keep, Marlow. And I just thought of one more thing to worry about."

"What's that?" Marlow asked apprehensively.

"What happens if we miss a payment, or come up short on one?"

"I guess I didn't think to ask, honey. So I reckon we'll just have to make sure we make the payments on time. But we'll manage. Don't worry, Betty, we'll manage. And that's a promise," he added, forgetting her plea.

Despite efforts not to think about it, at moments like this Betty's doubts about Marlow popped up again. Her parents,

Harmon and Sally Jenkins, were certain that it was a huge mistake for her to marry Marlow. They could not change her mind, but Harmon told them not to come crawling to him for help when they were down and out. Betty was deeply hurt by his attitude, but Marlow took it in stride.

"You know, Betty, Mr. Jenkins is right. It's not his place to support you now that we're married, and I wouldn't expect him to. That's my job."

Betty hoped that in time their attitude, especially her father's, would soften. As for her mother Sally, she was too subdued by her overbearing husband to question his decisions on anything. Time passed, and Mr. Jenkins did not relent. Instead, the separation widened over time and not even Johnny's arrival two years later made a difference. Betty sent them a card and a picture, but there was no response. They lived only fifteen miles away but never bothered to see their grandson. It was a shock to Betty to realize the kind of people her parents really were and how little she really knew them. Now that the battle for the Plum Creek acreage was joined and the outcome much in doubt, Betty was more afraid than ever that she someday soon she might have to beg her family for help.

But Marlow tried his best. In the spring of 1935, he rented an extra ten acres from Evans Enterprises to go with the twenty-five he usually farmed. It meant working seven days a week in summer with no time left for church or socializing. And things were not much easier after fall harvest. As soon as the crops were in, Marlow cut dyewood and railroad crossties the first winter, and hoped to get an easier WPA job the next. He and Betty cut expenses to the bone. Luckily, Betty was an excellent seamstress whose expert repairs extended the life of socks, underwear, and outer garments well beyond their normal usage. It was different with Johnny who was in a growth spirt, but with Betty's modifications, hand-me-downs from her Aunt Sadie's youngest son served nicely.

Because of the extra fertilizer, seed, and replacement equipment needed for the extra acreage, Marlow asked to borrow five hundred dollars instead of the usual four hundred. Howard Evans, who now busied himself mainly with liens and mortgages, approved the loan but told Marlow that he would have to pay an extra half percent more interest. Marlow complained about the increase, but Howard laughed and blew cigar smoke across the desk toward him.

"Tough shit, Hardin, but that's the way it is. And if you don't like it today, it'll cost you more tomorrow. And if you keep bitching about it, we might decide not to loan you anything."

They scrounged up the first installment with a little to spare, but in December of 1935 Betty discovered she was pregnant. She dreaded telling Marlow, who was thinner than ever from weeks of chopping and sawing dyewood and crossties from daylight till dark. But he had to know and soon would see the obvious for himself if she waited. She told him the next day at breakfast.

"Well glory be, Honey!" he said, rushing around the table to hug and kiss her. "We thought old Santa Claus wasn't gonna stop at our house this year, and here we are with the best gift of all on the way! Johnny, John boy, come in here! We've got something to tell you!"

"Then you're not upset?" Betty asked after baffled little Johnny went back to his playing. "I know this comes at a bad time with us trying to pay for the land and all."

"No, honey. News like this never comes at a bad time

regardless of the circumstances. No way I'm not going to thank the Good Lord with a happy heart. The land is one thing, and I'm doing everything I can to pay for it, but the family is something else and it comes first."

His delight with the news brought tears of relief and gratitude to Betty's eyes. Marlow's immaturity often frustrated her, but she reminded herself again that he never had a real boyhood, only endless toil as the oldest boy with four younger siblings in his widowed mother's impoverished family. If the suppressed boy in him was a worry for her, the good man he proved to be in moments like this was a reassurance. Dear Lord, she prayed that morning after Marlow left for work, help me to appreciate Marlow's good points and work more on my own shortcomings.

Molly Claire was born in late August of 1936, a healthy miniature of her pretty mother. The cotton was good that year, but with Betty unable to work in the field, it took longer than usual—into November—to harvest the crop. Johnny, now nearly six and a half and eager to prove himself, labored alongside his father like a little man. With both working every day until it was too dark to see, by the middle of November Marlow had enough money from his share of the cotton to make the second payment. Two down and two to go, he announced that night to Betty.

Now even she was beginning to think that Marlow's Quixotic quest for the Plum Creek land might be possible after all. She pluralized her concern, though, for the long hours her "menfolk" had to work, an inclusion that caused Johnny to swell with pride.

Life for the Hardin's changed little in 1937: thirty-five acres of cotton and another five in corn for meal and animal feed. Now that Molly was big enough to sit on a blanket under a peach tree, Betty duplicated her flourishing spring garden of earlier years:

tomatoes, okra, onions, and beans that helped, even though meat was scarce. On rare occasions when he could spare the time, Marlow would overcome his indifference to hunting and shoot one of the rabbits that hopped out from the woods into the fields at twilight.

Blue was now too old and tired to accompany his friend, though he would still rouse up briefly to wag his tail when Marlow and Johnny and would go down to the barn to check on him.

"Daddy, what's wrong with Blue?" Johnny asked. "How come he doesn't follow us around like he used to? Is he sick or something?"

"No, son, he's not sick, just old. He's sixteen, old for a dog. Dogs don't live as long as people."

"Why not?"

"I reckon God just made them that way."

A July drought reduced the cotton yield, and Betty's garden suffered, even though she carried water from the well to keep it alive. The extra ten acres of cotton, planted a few days before the main field, saved the day, and by the end of November Marlow had enough for the third payment.

"Three down; one to go," Marlow reminded Betty.

But she was thinking of another a problem: Johnny's schooling.

"Marlow, Johnny's going on eight and needs to be in school with children his age. He's already behind."

"Honey, can we hold him out till next year? I really need him to help me with the crop so we can make the last payment. Before he didn't make that much of a difference, to tell you the truth, but now he's big and stout for his age. Maybe you can give him some lessons yourself. You've got a good education, a lot better than mine. If we can pay off the escrow then he can start, can't he?"

"I guess so, Marlow, if we have to. You know the state has truancy laws, even though since the Depression set in, they don't enforce them very much, and maybe not at all in country schools. I guess I can start giving him some lessons in the meantime. But I tell you this, Marlow: the day we pay off that land, if we ever do, I'm going to shout hallelujah so loud and long that everybody in Hackworth County will hear me."

"And I'll be there too, shouting right along with you, honey!"

They had a major scare in February. Molly, now a talking toddler, was feverish for three days. All throughout the "escrow" years they had enjoyed good health, which made her illness all the more unnerving. Betty hovered over her, applying cool, wet towel compresses to her hot little forehead and body, and Marlow and Johnny came to her bed as often as they could to pray for the Lord to heal her and the angels to watch over her. The third night was especially disturbing. Molly's temperature had risen again, and she was verbally unresponsive. In chairs by her bedside Marlow and Betty drooped and dozed off from exhaustion. "If she ain't better come morning, we're taking her to the hospital," Marlow had vowed the evening before.

But the next morning Betty was awakened by a tiny hand rubbing her face and calling for "Mommie" to wake up. It was Molly. Her fever had broken in the night; she was up and alert, and to her parents' tearful delight, hungry as a bear cub.

Finally, in November the four-year ordeal was over, and the big day arrived. As soon the Howard's office opened, Marlow walked with the last payment in his pocket and asked for his deed.

"What deed are you talking about, Hardin? We don't have a deed for you."

"Yes, you do, Mr. Evans. It's been here in escrow, number 505, for four years while I paid it off. So, I've come to pick up the deed, you know, to the Plum Creek acreage you sold me."

Howard lit up a cigar, then went over and called in accountant Andy Johnson.

"Andy, come in here and answer me a question. Hardin here claims we have a deed of his that we've been holding in escrow. You know anything about that?"

"Let me go check my records. It won't take me long."

"Number 505," Marlow said hopefully.

Johnson returned in a few minutes, shaking his head. "Mr. Evans, there's no record of any transaction like that in my books. And I checked Troy Blankenship's books for when he was the company accountant before me."

"And—?" Howard asked.

"And nothing, Mr. Evans. There's no record of any such deed or escrow going back ten years."

"But there damn well is!" Marlow said angrily, rising from his chair, "I paid two thousand dollars for that land, and I'm here to pick up my deed!"

"Well, Hardin, I don't know where you got that idea. Everybody knows we Evanses don't sell land. It's the foundation of wealth. So, I tell you what, Hardin, you can hire yourself a lawyer and sue us, but without any evidence you'd be wasting your money, if you have any. My advice to you is instead of picking up a deed that nobody ever heard of, you pick your ass up and get out of my office before I call the security guard to throw you out."

"It's not right to cheat a man like this!"

"Well, I don't have any more time to waste arguing with a

fool. And by the way, by December 31ˢᵗ, and not a day later, I want you off our property. We won't be renting you that place next year. And you better leave the place and everything else in good shape, otherwise we'll be coming after you, and you won't like the consequences. Now, Johnson, get me the papers I need for my New Orleans meeting. I'm running late as it is. Always some damn fool around to waste my time."

Marlow started to say something but changed his mind and left in a trembling rage. When he got home an hour later, he brushed by Betty and went straight to the gun rack and took down his shotgun, loaded it, and stuffed shells in his back pocket.

"Marlow, what are you doing? What's wrong with you? What happened with the escrow? Marlow, Marlow, talk to me! Tell me what's going on. I've never seen you like this. You look like you're ready to kill somebody."

"I am. Stand aside, woman."

"Marlow, you must tell me what happened," Betty insisted as she tried to block the door. "Where are you going with that shotgun?"

"Huntin'," he said as he pushed her aside.

"But you're not a hunter."

"I am now."

Johnny stared at his father and kept his distance. Like his mother, he had never seen him livid with rage. Molly stood behind them and sucked her thumb.

"Marlow, wait!" Betty called after him. "There's something you need to know."

"Not now," he replied without looking back. "It can wait."

"No, it can't! Blue's dead!"

"What?"

"I said Blue's dead. Now Marlow, you put down the gun and bury that poor animal before you do anything else. He comes first. You hear me?"

Marlow came back, unloaded the shotgun and leaned it against the porch steps, then went down to Blue's bed to see for himself. Blue's body was cold and stiff.

"Everything's falling apart on me," he said to himself. "I tried my best with the escrow, the Lord knows I did. But it wasn't good enough. The Evanses were too slick for me. Now the land's gone, Blue's gone, and as soon as I'm finished with Howard Evans, I'll be gone too. But Betty's right; Blue comes first. He deserves a proper burial. The rest can wait."

Betty and the children came down to watch as he took a shovel and started digging by the edge of woods.

"Daddy, is this for Blue?" Johnny asked.

"Yeah, son. Blue's finished his life, and it was a good one."

"You told me dogs don't live as long as people."

"Yeah, I guess I did," he said.

"Yessir, will he go to heaven? Do dogs go to heaven?"

"I don't know, son, but if any of them do, Blue will."

After placing Blue's body in the three-foot-deep grave and covering it with the loose dirt, he tamped it down with the back of the shovel. Johnny brought rocks to shield against scavengers.

"Marlow," Betty said as calmly as she could after it was done, "dinner's ready. Come on back to the house and eat. You need to eat something after the morning you've had. You'll feel better. Everything else can wait."

He hesitated.

"Come on, Marlow, come on back to the house," she insisted. The food's ready, and I made tea."

"Daddy, carry me," Molly said, reaching up for him to take her in his arms. Marlow stood looking for a moment at the road to Hackworth, then down at his daughter. Molly won; he lifted her and followed Betty and Johnny to the house, picking up his shotgun on the way. During the meal he was silent. Then suddenly he slapped his forehead and laughed.

"Would you look at this! I plumb forgot about it."

"Forgot what?" Betty asked, bewildered but gladdened by his sudden switch of attitude.

"This," he said, pulling the envelope with the last payment from his pocket. "I was in such a hurry to get the deed I forgot to give Howard Evans the last payment. He swindled us out of three payments with that lie about the escrow, but we get to keep the last one. Just think, Betty, five hundred dollars free and clear! I know it's not all that much money to some folks, but after what we've been through these last few years it feels like we're rich."

"Oh, my goodness, Marlow. Thank the Good Lord you forgot at the right time. Now I feel like doing some of that shouting I mentioned a few months ago," she said with a big smile.

"Well, cut loose with it any time you please, honey, and I'll be right there with you!"

Johnny and Molly laughed at the sight of their parents dancing an awkward jig and shouting with glee. Later that night after Johnny and Molly were asleep, they sat and talked about their future.

"Honey, I guess I didn't tell you, but Howard Evans ordered us off this place by the end of the year. I wouldn't have stayed anyway, not after that crooked trick he played on us. Now you can have that wish of yours, Betty, what you said two or three years ago about putting a county or two between us and them.

We've both lived here all our life, but that's no reason to spend the rest of it in Hackworth County. The world's a big place, and somewhere there's got to be a place for us."

"I'm ready, Marlow," she said softly, coming over to kiss him, "ready to go find our place."

"Somebody told me there's land for sale and farms for rent up in Cleburne County. My cousin Horace lives up that way, and I was thinking of going up there and looking things over. Will you and the kids be okay till I get back? I won't be gone but a few days."

"We'll be fine. But, Marlow, promise me you won't fall for another escrow scheme."

"Betty, just reminding me is like a kick in the stomach," but grinning as he said it. "I promise I'll be careful. Besides, I won't have but a few dollars in my pocket, not enough to get into much trouble."

"No money? What do you mean?"

I mean, little lady, that I'm leaving most of the money we have with you. And don't you be snuckered by some fast-talking crook yourself while I'm gone. You're easier on a man's eyes than any woman I know."

Betty laughed and pulled him out of his chair. "I didn't know you went around comparing women. Just how many women do you know, Mr. Hardin? Let's go on to bed and you can tell me."

Cleburne County was a disappointment. Horace explained that cotton was dying out and cattle raising was replacing it. In fact, Horace confided, he was selling out for what he could get and moving up to Oklahoma. "You'all can go with me, if you want to. There's still a lot of idle land up there, I hear."

"Naw, I reckon not but I wish you well. I guess I'll go back home and figure out something from there."

Nothing could have prepared him for two things he learned when he got back to Hackworth: first, Dewitt and Howard Evans were dead, killed in a car wreck in Louisiana a week earlier; and second, his mother-in-law Sally Jenkins was warming herself by the fireplace when the surprised Marlow opened the door.

"Marlow, I am truly glad to see you, but I have to apologize to you by coming to your home uninvited the way I did."

"Momma just got here about an hour ago. She walked all the way here in this weather and got here shivering from the cold." Betty said with tears in her eyes.

"Mrs. Jenkins, there's nothing to apologize for," he said as he shook her hand. "You are more than welcome in our home. I can't tell you how glad I am to see you. But let's both edge up to the fireplace and warm up."

"I made some hot cocoa; that'll warm both of you up," Betty said, pleased and relieved by Marlow's comments.

"Have you met your grandchildren yet?" he asked.

"I saw the darlings just for a few minutes before they sort of ran off and I guess hid in their bedroom."

"They're good children, Mrs. Jenkins, good like their mother. And luckily they got their good looks from Betty and you."

"I need to explain to you, Marlow, what's going on and why I'm here. You know about Harmon and what he said years ago when y'all got married."

"Yes, ma'am, I was sorry he felt the way he did. I know he's a hard man, but good and hardworking. I know, too, that he thought he was doing what was best for Betty, and I respect him for that."

"I was taught to obey my husband, and I did for all these

years. But finally, it was just too much for me to bear. I know God didn't mean for me—or him—to be cut off from our daughter, grandchildren, and you, Marlow. So this morning I did what I never had the courage to do before: came to see you all."

"Mommy, you don't know how much I have prayed for this day. And I'll keep on praying until Daddy comes around too. Johnny is like him in certain ways. They're both missing out on some good times."

"Betty speaks for both of us, Mrs. Jenkins," Marlow added.

"Marlow, it would please me if you would call me Sally."

"And I'll be pleased to do so, uh, Sally, if it's not being disrespectful. And let me say, too, that you are more than welcome to stay here as long as you like. Our house is your house, as the Cajun folks say over yonder in Louisiana."

"Thank you, Marlow."

"But speaking of houses and Louisiana, I need to tell both of you a couple of things. First of all, you've probably both heard that Dewitt and Howard Evans both died in a car wreck down there somewhere. I recollect Howard saying the last day I went in to talk to him that he was getting ready to go down to New Orleans."

"Yes, we heard. What else do you have to tell us?" Betty asked.

"Well, that same day Howard told me that we would have to move out by the end of the year. Which suited me fine. I wouldn't want to deal with them anymore anyway. Sally, Betty's probably told you what happened. That's why I went up to Cleburne County, to see how things looked up that way."

"And how are conditions up there?" Betty wanted to know.

"Not too good. Cotton farming is dying out and cattle raising is taking over. And I'm not a cattleman. My cousin Horace is selling out and moving up to Oklahoma. He sorta wanted us to go with him, but I told him no. So that means we'll probably have to make do around here somewhere. I don't mean to speak ill of the dead, but now that the Evans brothers are gone, things could be a lot different—and maybe a lot better—in Hackworth County."

"Does that mean we still have to move out of this house, now that the Evans brothers are gone?" Betty wondered.

"That I don't rightly know, to be honest about it. Generally speaking, a renter can stay on for one or two months into the new year, and right now I think it's best if we stay put for a few more weeks. Howard told me to move out but didn't put anything in writing. Right now, from what they told me in town, nobody knows for sure what's going to happen with all the Evans money, land, and stuff. They owned nearly this whole end of the county, and word is that neither brother left a will. I guess they thought they would live forever. Maybe they're down there drawing up a mortgage on Hades like the old joke said."

"Marlow, don't joke about things like that!" Betty scolded.

Limbo lasted a week, then one morning a car stopped in front of the house and two men came to the door. One was accountant Andy Johnson, the other a slender man Marlow didn't know. Betty, Sally, and the children went into one of back rooms.

"Andy here tells me you are Marlow Hardin. Do you by chance remember who I am?"

"No, sir, can't say as I do," said Marlow, peering at the man's features.

"It's been a long time, Marlow, but way back we went to Bethel School together for a year or two before we moved into town. I'm Gene Evans," he said, smiling and holding out his hand.

"Gene Evans?" Marlow responded, shaking his hand. "I do remember you now. But I thought you were—"

"Dead maybe?" Gene laughed. "Well, you might say that in a way I nearly was there for a few years. But now I'm back, had to come back to take over the family business after Dewitt and Howard passed away. I'm the only survivor. As you know, Dewitt and Howard were both bachelors."

"Gene, I'm sorry about your brothers. But come in; it's too cold to stand outside. Y'all pull up a chair and tell me what I can do for you."

"Marlow, we won't take much of your time. We have several more stops to make this morning. But here's what I need from you. Andy here tells me that Howard misled you about a deed to some land, sixty-something acres over by Plum Creek, I believe. Is that right?"

"That's right. I thought it was in escrow until I got it paid for."

"But there was no deed after you thought it was paid off. Is that right?"

"That's right. Mr. Johnson here said he checked the records and found no deed. But why are we going over all this again? I don't see any reason to now. It's like beating a dead horse."

"Here's the reason, Marlow," Gene said, handing him a large manila envelope.

"What is it?" Marlow asked warily.

"Open it and see."

It was a deed to the sixty-odd acres of Plum Creek land.

"I don't understand."

"But I do, Marlow. Howard kept private records of his

dealings. He recorded your payments but denied their existence when the time came to deliver the deed.

"Andy never saw the records, but he knew they existed. He and I found them at Howard's house."

"But what does all this mean?"

"It means, Marlow, that the land is yours free and clear. I never accepted the family philosophy of cheating and double-dealing. That's why I walked away from the Evans enterprises and went through my own private hell."

"Gene, I appreciate what you're doing, but I have to tell you something: I never made the last payment on the land. I was so bumfuzzled and mad that day that I walked out with the money still in my pocket. We still have it, that's to say, most of it. Some we've spent on some things we had run short of."

"I gathered as much. Keep it. The land is yours regardless. The records show you paid fifteen hundred dollars, and God knows how hard you worked to raise it. That's enough for me. Now we'll be going, but I hope we can be friends and maybe do business together. And by the way, stay here on this place if you like. I'll treat you right on loans and farm equipment. No telling how long it will take, but I plan to make the Evans name as well known for honest dealing as it was for its mistreatment of folks."

*****

Several years later with in-laws Sally and Harmon Jenkins, Marlow and Betty were celebrating the completion of their new house on the Plum Creek land. Their children Johnny, Molly, Susie, and Emmet were splashing one another down by the creek.

"Well, Betty, sometimes it's still hard to believe that we're really living on the land and in the house we wanted. For a long time, it looked like a lost cause. But now I want to say something in front of you all, Betty, Harmon, Sally, something I've never said before: it was my good ole dog Blue, now long gone, and this beautiful daughter of yours, Harmon and Sally, that kept me from going off the deep end when things looked the blackest. If Blue hadn't died when he did, and Betty hadn't kept me from going back to Hackworth with that shotgun, maybe none of these good things would have happened. I don't know whether or not I would have used that shotgun, but neither do I know whether or not I wouldn't have. But thanks to those two and the Good Lord, I didn't have to find out."

"Well, Marlow, we're glad it turned out the way it did," Harmon offered. "I believe things happen for a reason. Now in the spirit of the moment and to all present, I need to say something I've never said before. I might not be here either enjoying this family gathering if Sally here hadn't put love of family over my stiff-necked pride. The other thing is that Betty knew best, too, when I thought she was wrong about you, Marlow. Now I have to say, and happy to say it, that she picked the right man to be her husband."

"Thank you, Daddy, I'm happy too," Betty said. "But now it's time to move on to better things. Marlow, go call the children. Dinner's ready."

WEB OF INTRIGUE

by Phyllis Murphy

Dorcas Lee Turgleton had few prospects that summer of 1921. At eighteen years of age, she had learned not to complain or worry too much about fate. Tabulating her deficits, she had to settle on whatever opportunities came her way.

The oldest of three children born to Earl and Palmona Turgleton, she was only five when her parents died of the Spanish flu in 1918. The attending doctor quarantined Dorcas Lee and her siblings until each recuperated. Then each child was farmed out to live with relatives. Fortunately, they lived close enough to visit often and later even rode the same bus to school. Aunt Lavondra and Uncle Parnell took in Dorcas Lee and treated her like one of their own biological children. However, she was old enough to know that she was a strain on their resources. Feeling guilty at being an added burden, Dorcas Lee did her best to be as cooperative as possible and worked hard on the farm for her board and keep.

A tall and robust girl with reddish-blonde hair, she soon outgrew the hand-me-downs from her cousins. Making the best of a situation was her forte, so she learned how to sew using whatever scraps she could find. She did such a good job that she was soon sewing and mending for the entire family.

She enjoyed the bumpy rides to school on the rickety bus where she could gaze out the window or visit with friends and family when she was in a sociable mood. School proved to be happy respite from physical labor on the farm and she enjoyed being with friends and receiving good grades in most of her subjects.

By the time Dorcas Lee graduated high school in 1921, she had grown to her full height of six feet. Athletic and strong, she could have been a star linebacker on the football team had she been born a male. Using her physical prowess, she worked tirelessly in the fields and around the house. Uncle Parnell marveled, "That girl's as strong as a mule and don't ever get tired."

With Amazonian strength, she split logs, built fences, and drove a team of mules better than most men. However, her physical prowess intimidated many of the eligible young men. She was a sweet-natured girl who hoped to have a beau one day like the other girls her age, but none ever showed interest. Their masculine egos were offended that she could outrun and outperform them in every sport or test of strength.

Aunt Lavondra felt sorry when boys called on her own daughters but ignored Dorcas Lee. It just wasn't fair that such a sweet and pretty girl could not entice anyone. Most women her age were being courted or already married, but Dorcas Lee remained unattached throughout the summer.

Everyone counted it a blessing when Walter Farkmore began calling on her late in the summer. Standing five feet seven with a sinewy physique, he would have been a handsome man had he ever smiled. Only thirty-one years old, he looked older because of the mournful aura surrounding him. His beloved wife Violina died a few years earlier after giving birth to their third child, and the sadness weighed heavily on his soul.

At eighteen, Dorcas Lee hoped for the kind of romance she read about in novels. The lackadaisical attention of Walter matched her own pallid enthusiasm. Although she tried to add zest to their relationship, nothing seemed to work. Even her sparkling banter and jokes were reciprocated with brooding silence. "Boy, he's dull," she thought before resigning herself to either spinsterhood or marriage to a man who had all the energy of a corpse. "Oh well, he's as interested in me as I am in him," she rationalized. "So, if it doesn't work out, there won't be a great loss."

"Dorcas Lee, now don't you be too hard on Walter," chided Aunt Lavondra. "After all, he's still mourning the passing of Violina. Give him a few years, and he'll warm up to you. Besides, he owns the best land in Aeolian County. And that's something to consider!"

Dorcas Lee listened and sighed. It was true that Walter owned forty acres of land bordering the Cahaba River, whose muddy waters deposited silt on his acreage, enriching the dark soil and yielding a harvest of the finest cotton in the region. Sill she could summon little enthusiasm at the thought of being stuck with such a dullard, regardless of the quality of his crops. Why couldn't Walter be like the landed gentry she read about in novels, she lamented. They complimented their sweethearts, but Walter never seemed to even notice her when she made an effort to look nice. Why for all the attention he paid her, she might as well be a sack of oats.

Sensing that her Aunt and Uncle wanted the best for her, Dorcas Lee nodded her head when they praised Walter's good points. "Well, you ought to give it a lot of consideration if he ever asks for your hand in marriage. He's a good and decent man and his kids need a mama," they said.

Dorcas Lee sighed, "If he asks me to marry him, I'll say yes. I ain't all that happy about it, but I don't exactly have a calling card filled with any other offers."

Aunt Lavondra hugged her. "Now don't go saying those words to anyone. You know how people around here gossip and if word got back to him, it would cause a ruckus."

Dorcas Lee nodded in agreement. "Yes," she said with resignation in her voice. "I'll keep my thoughts to myself."

Across town, Rosandra McCall was watching the courtship of Walter and Dorcas Lee with envious eyes. The same age as Dorcas Lee, Rosandra hailed from the contentious McCall clan. When not engaged in family feuds, squabbles, and spats among themselves, they bickered with neighbors over imaginary slights, deriving perverse pleasure in making mountains out of molehills and creating unnecessary conflict.

An attractive and flirtatious young woman, Rosandra gained the reputation of femme fatale because of her dark-haired beauty and the numerous times she sabotaged relationships. Never attracted to a man unless he was enamored of another female, her greatest satisfaction occurred when she stole an unwitting young swain away from his virginal sweetheart. Her *modus operandi* was to promise her unfailing devotion if only a young man would switch his allegiance to her. No sooner had she gained the attention of an enamored suitor than she quickly lost interest in him. Skulking back in humiliation, the young men profusely apologized to their spurned sweethearts. When word spread of her exploits, Rosandra learned to be more covert in her machinations to avoid being labeled a "Jezebel" or something worse. Ironically, her tarnished reputation as a rural Mati Hari only heightened male interest.

Naturally, when Rosandra found out that Walter was

courting Dorcas Lee, she set her sights on breaking up their union: her competitive instincts sharpening in anticipation of a battle. She was at the age when she knew it was time to settle down. Consumed with self-love, she had no place in her heart for romance; one man was as good as another. Her priority was to find a compliant husband who was stupid enough to manipulate. Like a lioness, she was intent on beating her rival and enjoying the thrill of the hunt.

She fixated on marrying Walter to gain access to his land since she wanted to live in style and figured that Walter was her key to a better life. "Walter may not be the most exciting man around, but his land is valuable. I'll convince him to sell it to the highest bidder and then we'll buy a fancy house in Elysium." She laughed just thinking about the envy she would provoke among all her country cousins and friends.

For a moment, though, her eyes clouded when she thought about the prospect of being stepmother to his brood of brats. "I'll feign sickness and pretend I'm too exhausted and stricken with nervous spells to raise children. Then I'll farm out his kids before we move to a big house in town," Rosandra thought, flashing her eyes and smiling in malice. "Imagine all the fuss people will make when they find out they've got more mouths to feed. I'll stir up such a mess." Then she laughed. "I'll especially enjoy making Dorcas Lee look like a fool when I humiliate her!"

Rosandra began weaving a plan as shrouded as a Black Widow's web. She knew a full-throttle blitzkrieg would scare Walter away, so she would have to be subtle in her diabolical scheme. "I'll have to act fast before they get too serious and decide to hitch up! Now let me think," she pondered. Like a lightning bolt out of heaven, she was struck with a devious plan that was sure to succeed. Recently she had heard a sermon about how the tongue could unleash a torrent of iniquity. Just as the Devil quotes scripture, so she searched the Bible for passages to concoct a malevolent scheme. With any luck, she could turn innocent speech into a deadly poison. Gossip spreads quickly with the same force as wildfire. All it takes is a tiny match to bring down an entire forest. Rosandra laughed in delight. "I'll use my wits to spark a deadly fire and take down that tall tree named Dorcas Lee."

Using artifice, Rosandra planned on gaining Dorcas Lee's friendship. It was easier than she anticipated since they attended the same church and Dorcas Lee was so witless. She would encourage Dorcas Lee to confide secrets to use against her and twist an innocent confidence into an insult that would reach Walter's ears with the force of a musket ball. He would retaliate by blasting Dorcas Lee right out of his life. Seizing the opportunity, Rosandra would offer solace and comfort to Walter. When he laid his weary head on her shoulders, he wouldn't know what hit him until after they were married.

Putting her plan into action, Rosandra summoned her considerable charm and charisma to win Dorcas Lee's attention by flattering and fawning over her and exclaiming about her pretty dresses when she sat beside her in church. She insisted that Dorcas Lee spend all her time with her.

A trusting girl with a pure heart, Dorcas Lee could not fathom evil in others and assumed that everyone's motivations were as pure has her own. Therefore, she was flattered with all the attention that Rosandra showered on her and considered it quite an accomplishment to have Rosandra as a friend. Dorcas Lee wondered why the other girls smoldered with bitterness when

Rosandra sashayed by them. Perhaps they were jealous of Rosandra's beauty. She had such a pretty figure and beautiful hair with piles of curls set off by silver barrettes.

Within a few weeks, Rosandra convinced Dorcas Lee to socialize at her house. Dorcas Lee smiled happily as she walked home in the afternoons. She considered herself fortunate to have a friend as pretty and popular as Rosandra who was surrounded by so many male admirers. Perhaps some of Rosandra's charm would rub off on her.

Dorcas Lee began confiding to Rosandra concerning her lackluster love affair with Walter. Her face blushed as she whispered about the lack of chemistry between them. "I know Walter is a good father, but he is just so hard to talk to," Dorcas Lee admitted. He's still hurting over Violina's passing, and I'm worried that he'll never cheer up. I love his children, but will they ever accept me as their mother when they still miss Violina? Aunt Lavondra says to give him more time. I know he's a good provider 'cause he works so hard on his property. It's just that I'm not sure if he has the ability to love any woman except Violina."

Rosandra pretended to listen compassionately and even offered some advice: "Well, just give him time and try to be patient," she said soothingly while patting Dorcas Lee on the back.

Within a few weeks, word reached Walter's ears that Dorcas Lee was complaining that he was a "boring sad-sack" who was not fit to marry because he had buried himself alive with his dead wife. The only reason she would consider marrying him was because of the land he owned. Infuriated, Walter could hardly believe his ears. And to think of the times he had visited Dorcas

Lee on her front porch. He had even brought her to his house to meet his children. In church, he kept her in his sights and always smiled at her even if they didn't sit together. And here she goes mouthing off to everybody about his faults. Well, he would show her. From now on, he'd have nothing to do with her! Now she'd realize what a mistake she had made!

Walter wondered why he was suddenly so inflamed by Dorcas Lee when he hadn't felt all that affectionate towards her. Oddly, after she rejected him, he suddenly thought about her all the time. In the middle of the day, he'd pause to conjure up her pretty face and alabaster white teeth that gleamed when she smiled. He envisioned her graceful carriage and the way her modest clothing draped over the outlines of her body. And then, suddenly, he'd strike the soil with his shovel and bark at his startled kids to get busy.

Finally, he had to admit that he was bereft without her. He missed her sweet smell like the lilacs that bloomed in his garden. He regretted that he had never bothered bringing any flowers. She would have laughed when he complimented her by saying she smelled like them. "I didn't give her a chance to like me," he thought. "I was so selfish about my own problems. I never thought about making her happy. Well, I might as well forget that!" he exclaimed to himself. His loud voice echoed around the fields as his children looked at him in wide-eyed wonder. "She'll regret that I ain't paying her no more visits!" he yelled.

After a week, Dorcas Lee began to wonder why Walter had stopped calling on Saturday afternoons. "I guess he's busy on the farm," she decided. As the weeks passed, she wondered why his absence bothered her so much. She thought about his light brown hair shining in the sun and the casual way he tossed his head when he laughed. She remembered the way his muscles strained inside his shirt when he held the reins and how close they sat in the wagon when they visited his children. Then she blushed and wondered why in the world she thought of that.

One day, Uncle Parnell complained, "What's the matter with Dorcas Lee? She ain't got her mind on her work and she's been kind of grouchy lately. She ain't acting like herself."

Aunt Lavondra smiled and said, "I think you better go visit Walter and see what's going on. Her moods are tied up with him these days and she don't even realize it."

A few days later, Dorcas Lee was wandering aimlessly around the house looking at flowers when she saw her uncle hitching up the wagon. "Where are you going, Uncle Parnell?"

"I'm going to pay a visit to Walter to see why he ain't comin' around no more. You wanna come with me?"

Feigning disinterest, Dorcas Lee spent a long moment pretending to make up her mind before she said, "Well, I reckon. Just give me a few minutes and I'll be right out."

Aunt Lavondra smothered a knowing smile when Dorcas Lee reemerged from her room wearing a new dress and bonnet, her face flushing in excitement, making her look as fresh and pretty as a rose in bloom. The fresh sachet of lilacs she kept in her pocket wafted around her.

Uncle Parnell and Dorcas Lee rode in silence, each absorbed in their own thoughts. Uncle Parnell had always felt sorry for Dorcas Lee. She'd been so young when her parents died, and life had not been easy for her. He wanted her to be happy and was upset that Walter had dumped her without ever offering an apology.

Dorcas Lee sat beside her uncle lamenting the fact that she

was just too tall and big-boned to ever get a man. "I reckon I'll always be a spinster," she thought sadly.

As they drove up to Walter's house, both were surprised to see a Model T parked by the house.

"Why, that's Tom McCall's car. Wonder what they're doing over here?" queried Dorcas Lee.

"I guarantee you Rosandra's got the McCall gang all worked up about marrying Walter! I knew she was up to something when she suddenly started being your friend!"

"What are you talking about?" asked Dorcas Lee, suddenly apprehensive.

"You'll see!" fumed Uncle Parnell. "Dorcas Lee, you better be ready to fight for Walter if you still want him 'cause I got a feeling that vixen is trying to grab him for herself."

When Dorcas Lee and Parnell entered the house, tension filled the room. Walter looked bewildered at all the commotion. His house was crammed with Rosandra and all her relatives, intent on talking their way into his life. He was astonished when in walked Parnell accompanied by Dorcas Lee. What was going on?

Parnell shook Walter's hand, nodded a reluctant greeting to the McCall family, and came right to the point: "Walter, I got business with you. I'm here to see if you're still interested in courting Dorcas Lee since we ain't seen you in a few weeks. Now, if you're thinking of switching affections to Rosandra, that's fine, but you're making a big mistake. Dorcas Lee is a pretty girl and she's got a good character. She's strong and will make a good worker on your farm and a good mama to your kids. Then pointing to Rosandra, he added, "And that Rosandra stirs up problems quicker than a swarm of hornets!"

"Why do you say that?" Walter asked. "Rosandra and her

family were the only ones with the courage to tell me the truth. She told me the only reason Dorcas Lee wanted to marry me was for my land. And besides that, Dorcas Lee said I was duller than a sack of manure and smelled just as bad. How do you think that made me feel?"

Rosandra smiled archly. "Yes, I did tell Walter that because I didn't want him jumping into a loveless marriage with a conniving witch. I'd make a better wife than Dorcas Lee any day."

"Now wait a minute!" exclaimed Walter, suddenly on guard. "Rosandra, I appreciate you tellin' me about Dorcas Lee and her greed, but I ain't studying to marry neither one of you!"

Suddenly, Dorcas Lee pounced on Rosandra, grabbing her by the collar and screaming at her. "You no good hussy rat! You twisted what I said and turned it against me so you could have Walter for your own!"

Parnell grabbed Rosandra's hand before she started hitting Dorcas Lee. "Uh, I wouldn't do that. First of all, you owe Dorcas Lee an apology for libeling her. Second of all, you are a scheming girl who only wants Walter for his land. You put words into Dorcas Lee's mouth that belong to you own evil heart. Dorcas Lee ain't got a mean bone in her body. Now, If I was you, I'd hightail it out of here before Dorcas Lee gets a-holt of your hind end!"

By now, Dorcas Lee was so mad she was about to explode. "You nasty girl! I oughter tear your hair out! You pretended to be my friend just so you could gossip to the entire community about things I never said. Walter's my man and I want to marry him!"

Walter began to laugh at the ridiculous situation. For the first time in months, he actually felt light-hearted and alive. The tension in the room mounted as the McCall gang sat on one side of the room fuming at Parnell and Dorcas Lee. Walter's children watched the unfolding events with all the excitement of witnessing a circus act. What an entertaining afternoon it had been, culminating in a free-for-all. They held their breath in anticipation, hoping the two women would start fighting.

Walter regained his composure and sent his children out of the house. Then he calmed everyone down and ordered the feuding sides to be quiet.

Parnell was the first to speak. "Walter, I ain't lying. You hitch up your wagon and go around the county asking everyone about Rosandra. They'll tell you that she's broken up more couples than Carter has pills. I'm telling you that if you want to settle down with her, you might as well be marrying a bobcat."

Suddenly, Rosandra began denying everything. "Now, Walter, don't you listen to him. He's just mad because Dorcas Lee has ruined everything, and he doesn't want you and me to get married."

"I figure we can settle this once and for all about who's telling the truth," said Walter. "I'll go hitch up my wagon and all of us will get in it. We'll stop at every house along the way and just ask the neighbors what they think."

"No!" screamed Rosandra, her face contorted with fury. "You're not going to do that! You are going to throw Dorcas Lee out the door!"

"Why are you suddenly so defensive?" asked Walter. "Seems to me you've got something to hide, Rosandra."

Then turning to Dorcas Lee, Walter's face softened, and he spoke gently. "Dorcas Lee, tell me exactly what you said."

"I said I didn't know if you could ever love another woman because you are still grieving over Violina, said Dorcas Lee with a quivering voice. It had been a long afternoon and she suddenly felt like crying.

"Dorcas Lee, I do love you. And I intend to prove it. 'Cause if you'd like to marry me, I surely would like to marry you."

"Yes, I would," said Dorcas Lee.

Walter noticed that her outburst had unleashed something in her that he admired. "She's a beautiful woman," he thought. "I wonder why I never noticed that before now."

The McCall gang spent a long time at Walter's house trying to persuade him to marry Rosandra, but they knew it was futile when they saw how Walter and Dorcas Lee kept staring at the floor and blushing to keep from looking at each other.

"True love wins! Now get Rosandra and go home!" exclaimed Walter to the McCall's in exasperation, looking as if he wanted to throw the entire bunch out the door. "We got to get ready for a wedding soon!"

Love has a way of blooming under even the most improbable conditions. Dorcas Lee blossomed as a wife and mother, accepting Walter's children as her own, and bearing him four additional children. Their love thrived as richly as the crops in the fertile soil beside the slow-moving current of the Cahaba River. Uncle Parnell and Aunt Lavondra loved Dorcas Lee as their own and their blessings multiplied a thousand-fold. People in the community learn a lesson about how gossip and innuendo can hurt people and they endeavored to tame their own tongues.

Rosandra also fared well as conniving people so often do. She married a banker from Tuscaloosa, and they thrived in high society. The McCall gang is still engaged in vitriol as bitter as sulfuric acid. Their words and actions continue to punish themselves and they still haven't learned their lesson.

JULIA

by Harold Raley

As he walked along elm-shaded Washington Street to his early morning English Class at the Female Academy, Professor Andrew Blackwell, 25, recited "She Walks in Beauty," timing his steps and whispered verses to the iambic rhythm of Byron's sweet stanzas. Today he would begin class with a dramatic recitation of the poem, then under his guidance the young ladies would analyze its structure, aesthetic imagery, and characteristics of Romanticism.

Although he kept a proper distance from his students, he knew that many of them were already romantically infatuated with their handsome young teacher. Most of the girls were bright and attractive, and only those from elite, wealthy Springfield families could afford the Academy's steep tuition. Already a plan was forming in his mind to choose a girl from among the wealthiest and most beautiful to be his bride. One must be practical in practical matters, he reminded himself. Literature is one thing, real life, quite another. It was a lesson learned from his own family's experience. In earlier times the Blackwell's were counted among the Virginia Tidewater aristocracy, but they lost nearly everything in the War Between the States and had struggled long and mightily to survive its ravages and rebuild their fortune. Andrew was still a Romantic by temperament, but a realist by experience. In any case, he was in no hurry to decide; for the time being he was content to enjoy the prospects of the feminine world at his disposal.

His pleasant concentration on the poem and his prospects was broken by a feminine voice inside a wrought iron fence that enclosed the grounds of a three-story white brick mansion set half a block from the street. Just inside the fence stretched double rows of lilacs still in riotous red and lavender splendor. First frost was late that year.

"You walk so fast," said the voice behind the exuberant lilacs. I don't like it when people walk fast. Stop and tell me your name. Talk to me. I'm lonely. I have no friends to talk to and play games with. Will you come this way again? I hope you will. I would like for you to be my friend."

"I cannot see you. The lilacs are too thick. Who are you?"

"I'm Julia. That's my name and there's my house," she said, thrusting her head between the lilac clusters and pointing to the mansion. "Do you like it? Isn't it pretty?

Her beauty almost took his breath away. Even Byron's poetic gem paled in comparison, and the pretty girls at the Academy fell incomparably short. She pressed herself against the fence in full feminine glory: burnished gold hair that hung in caressing curls to her trim waist, sky blue eyes, skin white and pure as a fleecy summer cloud, and features and form exquisitely proportioned like those of a pagan goddess, though erotically softer. At first glance she looked to be perhaps eighteen but with an indefinable childlike aura that rendered her ageless, provocative, irresistible.

"My name is Andrew, Andrew Blackwell, Miss Julia, and most certainly I shall come this way again, Lord willing, this afternoon perhaps, tomorrow morning for sure. And indeed, I like your house. It is very pretty."

At once his pragmatic, calculated scheme to avail himself of a bride evaporated like morning dew, replaced by a new amorous imperative. In an instant he was in love with beautiful Julia. Now he would not have to choose a lady for his life, as he had so coolly planned; fate chose for him. He had studied to teach English and Latin but always with the feeling that he stood outside his academic knowledge, molding it to his purpose and advantage. Now, suddenly, he had reverted to who and what he really was: a romantic in the twilight of the Romantic Age now restored to its old glory as Julia filled the horizons of his life and resurrected ineffable ideals of love and beauty. He recalled Shelley's verse: "The world's great age begins anew; the golden years return."

At that moment, though, a middle-aged woman emerged from the mansion and elbows akimbo called out imperiously: "Julia, come away from the fence and come inside please! Haven't I told you not to speak to strangers in the street, and much less to unacquainted gentlemen?"

"Yes, Mother," she called back, head down. "I must go," she whispered. "The Lord is good. Andrew is good. Andrew will be my friend," she cried out happily as she turned to run to her mother, leaving Andrew in a state of indescribable euphoria but puzzled by her odd comments.

"Don't run, Julia!" the woman called out. "Remember what I taught you: walk, walk like a lady."

"She walks in beauty," Andrew whispered Byron's verse as Julia slowed and walked with rhythmic womanly grace toward her mother. He thrilled to the archly romantic coincidence of seeing the poem personified before his very eyes and in real time. A rising tide of love and happiness swept over him. His fondest hopes were unfolding magically before him. He had found his love, or it had found him, and he believed at that supreme moment that he was destined to possess everything joyful, lovely, and beautiful.

It was middle October of 1880, Andrew's first year at the Springfield Female Academy. His assigned classes had filled quickly on rumors that not only was Professor Blackwell single but heartbreakingly handsome besides. Mrs. Hortense Wilson, Principal of the Academy and vigilant guardian of campus morals and decorum, was pleased with the talents and gentlemanly bearing of the newly appointed University of Virginia graduate. But for those same reasons was determined to see to it that his charming manner did not lead to unpleasant consequences.

"Mr. Blackwell will bear watching," she cautioned her inner circle of trusted faculty. "Even should he turn out to be the fine teacher and proper gentleman that his references describe, and we expect, through no fault of his own he could prove too attractive for the good of our girls. Report to me immediately any hint of improper behavior—his or the girls'—in or out of the classroom."

Today his classes were more inspired than usual, and Professor Blackwell outdid himself in poetic mastery. At the conclusion of each class the girls crowded around his desk to ask specific questions and insinuate subliminal messages. Byron's love poetry was a pretext for their own romantic sentiments. Even in his afternoon Latin class their perplexities with cases and syntax were colored by concealed feelings. In the first weeks of class Andrew had pretended innocence of their hidden messages. Today, as always, he answered their questions, but for the first time was truly indifferent to their suggestive overtures. "She walks in beauty," he thought to himself, already savoring the possibility of seeing Julia on the walk home to his lodging in Mrs. Faraday's boarding house. Would Julia be there again amongst the lilacs, as he hoped; or not, as he feared. Why had he not seen her earlier in the semester?

There was no sign of her that afternoon and no sound or movement in the mansion. He was dejected. The briefest glimpse of Julia would have sent his spirit soaring; her absence plunged him into momentary despair. His feelings ranged far beyond his control; once he fancied himself their master, now he was their puppet. Too restless and perturbed to read or sleep that evening, he donned hat and coat, and cane in hand walked through Julia's neighborhood again. He did not expect to see her, but just to be as near as possible to her was exhilarating. The mansion was dark, but his mood brightened at the sight of it.

With all the casualness he could muster the next day, he asked colleagues about the mansion and its occupants. To cover his real motives, he added questions about other residences on Washington Street. They told him about other families, but only history professor Bernard Talmadge knew anything about the residents of the white mansion.

"The family name is Moorland, I believe, and as far as I know, the only members in the residence in question are a widowed mother and her daughter whose names, if ever I heard them, I cannot recall," Talmadge informed him. "I have seen them on occasion at our church and greeted them in the Passing of the Peace, but I know precious little more about them."

"I take it then, Professor Talmadge, that you are of the Episcopalian faith?"

"Fortunately, I am so affiliated, and since you ask, may I inquire, sir, as to your religious allegiance?"

"It is also my Mother Church, but I must confess that since moving here from Virginia this past August and with few links to the community, I have been lax in resuming my devotions."

"Then, Andrew, if I may address you familiarly as a fellow believer, Mrs. Talmadge and I would be delighted to have you join us in worship this Sunday at St. Luke Episcopal. I can pick you up in our carriage and save you the considerable walk."

"If you are certain that it would pose no great inconvenience."

"No inconvenience at all, but a pleasure to have your company, and if we can persuade you, perhaps you will do us the honor of taking your midday meal with us. I am told that you call it dinner in the South."

"We called it so where I grew up, and I accept both invitations on condition that at the first opportunity you will allow me to repay your hospitality in an appropriate manner."

"Agreed!" Talmadge said vigorously as they shook hands.

In truth Andrew was only mildly interested in the invitations themselves, but happy for the chance to see Julia under proper circumstances and meet her mother formally. But as he passed by the mansion that afternoon and saw no trace of Julia or anyone else, he had the horrifying thought that perhaps they had moved away.

I have a letter for you, Professor Blackwell," Mrs. Faraday told him as soon as he reached the boardinghouse. "It has a Virginia postmark. I hope it's good news. Is everything all right?"

"Let's hope so," he answered, pocketing the letter unopened to the disappointment of the ever-curious Mrs. Faraday.

The letter was from his mother in which she expressed her concern for his life in Illinois and her hope that he was attending church:

Dearest Andrew:

As you know, I was apprehensive about your taking employment in Illinois. I worried that being subjected to the evils of that place, the very home of the Great Aggressor who brought so much grief to our homeland, you might be tempted astray in your loyalties. By all means, son, stay true to the Church and its teachings. I realize that despite the War and all the sufferings, the northern aggressors inflicted on us, life must go on. You tell me that there are good, decent people in Illinois, and I take some comfort in your words.

Nevertheless, Andrew, I have not lost hope that you may yet relocate near us and marry a nice Virginia girl. But if that is not to be and you remain there, do at least choose a good girl of our faith up there in the north and be to her and the children God may give you a man of firm moral character and truthfulness unlike so many today. You know that I pray daily for your health and wellbeing in that distant place and hope that we shall see you back here in due time. James and Franklin are well, though Franklin complains that the University is not to his liking, and I fear he may drop out soon. According to him, you set a bad example for your brothers with your impressive academic accomplishments. Not everybody is turned the same way, he says.

Alice and her cousins are as busy as bees with preparations for her wedding to Malcolm this coming June. She will be sad if you cannot attend the ceremony and festivities, but she understands the problems of time and distance.

I thank the Lord that He preserves me in health. Your father is as well as can be expected under the circumstances.

With undying love, Mother

The same coolness as always towards Father, he sighed. But how truly remarkable the convergence of this letter and my conversation with Professor Talmadge turns out to be, thought Andrew. Now I can reassure Mother without hedging the truth that I have resumed my religious devotion and at the same time make the proper acquaintance of Julia and her mother. Providence is working in my favor.

So it was that finally Andrew saw Julia again. Seated with her mother a mere three rows ahead of the Talmadge pew, she was a vision of loveliness, her golden, ribbon-bound hair aglow in the prismatically filtered sunlight streaming through the stained-glass windows high along the east wall of the sanctuary. Once during the service, she turned, as though aware of his intense concentration on her, to give him a smile before her mother scolded her with a whispered order to pay attention to the sacred business at hand. At the same time, the sharp featured Mrs. Edith Talmadge caught their glances and smiled knowingly at Andrew. At the Passing of the Peace, he made energetic efforts to shake as many hands as possible so as to reach Julia and Mrs. Moorland. Julia pulled back at first in embarrassment and only shook his hand and muttered words of peace in imitation of her mother who echoed his words and frowned slightly at him in apparent recognition.

After the service Andrew excused himself momentarily from the Talmadge's and hurried to overtake Julia and her mother already leaving the church grounds.

"Please forgive my forwardness, ma'am. I should like to introduce myself formally. I am Professor Andrew Blackwell of the Female Academy and this is my calling card," he said, proffering the card.

"Thank you, Professor Blackwell," she answered, putting the card in her purse. "I am Mrs. Agnes Moorland, and this is my daughter Julia. We're happy to meet you, I'm sure. Now we must be on our way. Good day to you, sir."

"Before you go, Mrs. Moorland, may I presume on your kindness by requesting your permission to call on your family of an evening convenient to you?"

"And the purpose of your visit, may I ask?"

"To pay my respects and to discuss a matter of importance with you and the male members of your family."

"Sir, there are no immediate male members of our family and none to be included in family matters."

"Mrs. Moorland, I apologize if my comment offended you in any way. It was not so intended."

As they spoke, Julia smiled but avoided eye contact with Andrew. Mrs. Moorland looked aside, sighed, and was silent for a moment before responding.

"No offense was taken, Professor Blackwell. And yes, you are welcome to call on us. And better sooner than later. Would this Wednesday evening at eight be a suitable hour for you?"

"Indeed, it would. Thank you, Mrs. Moorland, Miss Julia. I look forward to it."

"You know where we live, I believe. We shall expect you. Now I say again, sir: good day to you."

The next three days were an eternity and his classes, an endless tedium for Andrew. When at last Wednesday evening came, he left early for Julia's house and was obliged according to his frequently consulted fob watch to kill twenty minutes before knocking. Mrs. Moorland herself opened the door. There appeared to be no servants or other help in the mansion.

Mrs. Moorland took his cane, propped it in a corner by the door, and offered Andrew a padded chair of regal proportions facing her and Julia seated on a divan. After an exchange of platitudes Mrs. Moorland got up to fetch tea and chocolate cookies, cautioning Julia to partake sparingly of the sweets. Several more minutes of desultory conversation followed about the weather and the unusually warm season. With Julia present, Andrew was unsure how to bring up the reason for his visit. Then as they finished their tea, the problem resolved itself in a completely unexpected way.

"Mother, is that enough grownup talk?" Julia asked Mrs. Moorland. "Now may I take Andrew to my room to play? I want him to see my dolls and toys."

"Yes, Julia, you may take Andrew to see your room. Come with us, if you will, Professor Blackwell. You will understand things better and get the answer to the question I think you intended to ask me."

The three of them climbed the stairs to the second floor. Julia ran before them and opened door at the end of a hallway.

"Andrew," she called back happily. "This is my room! We can play here! You can be the daddy and I'll be the mommy. This will be our house. Don't you like it?"

It was a child's room painted in gay colors in the center of which stood an elaborate three-story dollhouse complete with miniature stairs, fireplace, beds, tables, closets, clothes, verandas, porches, gardens, carriages, and at least a dozen exquisitely carved dolls of both sexes, adults and children, dressed and undressed, sitting, sleeping, dining, or engaged in household activities. Andrew stood, petrified and speechless, as the realization of the horror spread over him.

"It's . . . It's very beautiful, Julia," he stammered, as his eyes began to tear over. "Beautiful."

"Darling, you play while I talk a bit with Andrew, Mr. Blackwell. He'll come in later, won't you, Andrew?"

"Yes, I will. Go ahead and start, Julia. I'll be in directly."

"All right, but hurry!" she said happily.

Both adults were struggling with their emotions.

"Professor Blackwell, you understand now what I could hardly tell you earlier. I love Julia with all my heart, far more than I would a normal daughter. And now you understand why. She is as innocent and guileless as an angel, and you are not the first man captivated by her beauty. But for obvious reasons she can never marry and lead a normal life."

"Mrs. Moorland, has she always been this way?" Andrew asked, recovering somewhat from the shock but not his sadness.

"No, when she was seven, she had what the doctors called an encephalitic condition. Afterwards, her body grew normally but her mind did not. She has remained a child but in a woman's body. After Colonel Henry Moorland, my husband and Julia's father, died at Gettysburg in the Rebellion, I took her to the specialists I could afford. None offered any hope. Julia was only two when he was killed, so she has no memory of him. But he was skilled in woodwork and made the dollhouse and all its furnishings for her. I have told her the story so often she thinks she remembers him."

"I do not mean to be indelicate, but is she in some sense aware of her condition?"

"I think not, I hope to God not, for her sake you understand. Yet sometimes I wonder. There have been moments, terrifying moments for me, things she has said . . . Not long ago I took her to the wedding of a girl about her age. For a moment there Julia got the oddest look on her face, as though she had a sudden understanding. I resolved then and there that I would never expose her to a similar situation. My greatest fear, Professor Blackwell, is that something will happen to me, and she will be left alone and defenseless like the child she is and must always remain."

"We promised her that I would go in and play with her, Mrs. Moorland. She is waiting. What shall I do?"

"What your heart tells you. It's your decision, sir."

He thought for a moment, then said: "If Julia plays as a seven-year-old, then I shall do my best to play as her eight-year-old companion. After all, the Scriptures tell us that we must become as little children if we would enter the Heavenly Kingdom. Maybe it is we who can take lessons from Julia."

"Professor Blackwell—Andrew—I am so sorry about all this. I can only imagine how great a shock and disappointment it must be for you. Under normal circumstances I could not think of a better man for a son-in-law. But you are young and must get on with your life. In time you will meet and marry another girl. And it is completely right for you to do so. Julia speaks of you with great fondness, no doubt in a normal woman with sentiments that would respond to your own. But given the circumstances and for the good of all concerned, I think it best, as surely you do, for you to end all contact with her. Perhaps you could take a different route to the Academy, and for my part, I shall find another church for us to attend."

"Mrs. Moorland, your counsel is painful but prudent, and I shall conform my behavior to it. But let me add one more thing before I join Julia at play: if ever you need assistance in providing care for her, I promise, as God is my witness, to come to her aid insofar as my means and circumstances permit. I shall always cherish Julia, if not as once I hoped, hereafter as God allows in his Providence."

Then for an hour Andrew and Julia played with the dollhouse and its residents. After that, he never saw her again. But when Mrs. Moorland passed away in 1895, he honored his promise by seeing to it that Julia had proper care. By then he had long since exchanged the teaching of literature and Latin for banking and building in Chicago, becoming a wealthy man in the process. Before he left Springfield and the Female Academy in 1883, and without returning to the cynical plan of earlier times, he met and married a bright and beautiful girl from one of his classes, just as Mrs. Moorland foresaw. One can only speculate how his wife reacted to her husband's abiding concern for Julia.

The story concludes with three more facts: first, Julia died in Springfield, October 16, 1914. Second, for many years thereafter on the anniversary of her passing and regardless of the early or late advent of first frost, red and lavender lilacs adorned her tomb. And third, inscribed on her headstone is Byron's immortal verse: *She walks in beauty.*

SO MUCH DEPENDS ON A
BLUE FORD FAIRLANE

by Phyllis Murphy

Life is a voyage in which I steer a ship over deep waters, ever vigilant to repair miniscule cracks in the hull. Vigilance and self-preservation are gifts that enable me to take action like a lone fisherman paddling away from a maelstrom. On rare sky-blue days, I row gently towards idyllic islands of hope.

I was christened Frances Assisi Harthcourt in April of 1935, under the watchful eyes of my parents, Pastor Wycliff and Marion Harthcourt, who hoped I would emulate my namesake by being benevolent, pious, and scholarly. My older sister, born five years earlier in 1930, was Jane Addams Harthcourt in honor of the social reformer and suffragette. Our parents encouraged us to honor God through faith and good works, and we tried to comply.

The sharp edge of the Great Depression cut like a blade through the fertile soil in the township of Elysium in Aeolian County where we lived. Thankfully, neighbors worked hard and welded together during these difficult times to form intricate networks of caring and generosity. Everyone scrimped and saved, filling cellars with rows of canned goods like elixirs to ward off sickness. We were more connected to the cycles of nature back then, so we accepted the vicissitudes of life with grace.

My father, the minister of Elysium Methodist Church,

fostered optimism. Always civic-minded, he helped keep the local First Merit Bank solvent by depositing his meager salary into an account. A short, compact man with the stubborn countenance of a rural Churchill, his bulldog tenacity fostered courage. "If Pastor Harthcourt thinks its's o.k. to put money in the bank, then we better do the same, muttered men in huddled conversations as word spread that the bank could be trusted.

News spread almost telepathically when even one's thoughts seemed amplified like a preacher before a congregation. Naturally, when a rumor spread that Bonny and Clyde were planning on robbing the local bank, Father and other men held sentinel on the perimeters of town, shotguns in hand. Although charitable to anyone who needed help and even grudgingly tolerant of local chicanery, citizens had little patience for thieves outside the community. Like early settlers protecting their land against invaders, men readied themselves to capture the renegades.

Sheriff Gorsham scoffed that outlaws would not bother finding their way to Elysium. "Why would criminals risk their lives for the piss-ant sum in our bank vault?" he grumbled. Eventually he quit trying to talk common sense to the populace. Like Isaiah crying alone in the wilderness, he could find no one to heed his clarion call. Since practically everyone in town had spent their entire existence in the community, they assumed Elysium was the center of the universe, heralded by trumpeting angels in the clouds. Therefore, they reasoned, their township drew scofflaws like nails to a magnet.

Father persuaded the sheriff to take the matter seriously by saying that the "scent of money has tempted many a scoundrel to rush into iniquity's paths." For a week, citizens lined up from one end of town to the other, hoping to see some action. Opinions varied on whether the outlaws were modern-day Robin Hoods or vicious fugitives who needed to be gunned down in a blaze of bullets. Many dual-minded citizens wavered between the two opinions as variously as they walked from one end of town to the other.

Even the most sanctified fantasized about the financial windfall of selling souvenirs if a shootout occurred. "Imagine a showdown in Elysium," they murmured with mounting excitement. Father compared them to 'money changers in the Temple,' saying "It would not be right to profit from tragedy." He also thought it wrong for Elysium to be the site of bloodshed. "Why, if a shootout occurred, it would negate the very symbol of our town as a pastoral utopia." People just shrugged and looked confused. They were used to Father's tendency to pontificate on arcane topics. Only Judge Brent understood the allusion. "Wycliffe," he said chuckling, "not many people know Greek mythology around here. Keep this up and you'll be headed for jail as a heretic."

A week passed with no sign of the gang and eventually everyone went home. One man summed up the situation by stating: "They heard we was ready for them, so they stayed in Oklahoma," pointing in the direction of western hinterlands. Many went home disappointed. Their lives paled in comparison to the dashing exploits of fugitives. A few spent wistful hours in daydreams as they imagined whiling down dusty roads in stolen cars under cover of night. Young men awoke from sweaty dreams of loose women brandishing weapons as casually as they drank from hip flasks. What fame and glory they could achieve if only they had the courage to break the surly bonds of respectability! Sensible folk kept their musings private, knowing that if they told another soul, word would spread until kinfolk whipped the debauchery out of them with leather straps.

In a few days, people went about their duties, working as if to the steady cadence of a metronome. Father put down his gun and returned to the ministry. With monastic devotion to scholarship, he translated the "Good News" to his flock. We prayed there would be enough money in his salary as the congregation hurriedly plunked down a few cents in the collection plate before passing it down the pew. Over Sunday dinner, we thanked out Heavenly Father that sufficient money was left over to pay for our needs. Like people in times of famine, we leaned on God to deliver us.

Other preachers might have exhorted the congregation to give with cheerful hearts, but Father knew how hard money was to obtain. Just the thought of giving money with a jolly countenance seemed about as dignified as savage pagans dancing at a sacrificial ceremony. "Why they might as well be tap dancing at the funeral of their own mothers!" exclaimed Father. Money was a precious commodity, and all financial transactions should be conducted with grave dignity. "There is no reason to act like we are buying tickets for a carnival ride when contributing hard-earned money in service to the Lord," Father often intoned. "Give what you can and don't make a show of it."

We lived in a dilapidated two-story house which had been in our mother's family for over a hundred years. Her wiser siblings gladly gave Mother the deed to the house, relieved to be rid of the ramshackle money-pit. It perched at the edge of town, as patched together as a crazy quilt, surrounded by five verdant acres which we labored to keep clipped and mowed. We designated the back acres to apple and pecan trees, a chicken coop, and a large garden. As children we enjoyed playing under an arbor overlaid with trailing tendrils of fragrant flowers and wisteria.

From an early age, Jane and I fetched tools and carried supplies to replace wooden floors, rotten siding, and leaking roofs. Mixing up loads in the cement mixer, we dumped and smoothed shovelfuls of the dense, caustic material into sagging foundations of the cellar, working from early morning until sundown with aching shoulders. Our hard work taught us the importance of cooperation, so we hardly ever fussed in sibling rivalry. The only time our fortitude faltered was when we had to work in the cellar—the humid darkness heightening our fears of slithering creatures hiding among the shelves of canned goods.

When weather allowed, we'd climb on the roof with Father to replace rotting joists and rafters with fresh lumber that we hauled up on a pulley. We'd throw rotting wood to the ground before patching beams and nailing on metal roofing to reinforce the sagging roof. Being on the roof was almost as terrifying as crawling under the foundation, except on those rare days when we enjoyed the vantage point of our surroundings. On a clear day, when we balanced ourselves to stand upright on the roof peak, we pretended to be sailors looking over vast seas to infinity. However, the happiest times were when we were safely inside the house after a day's work. On rainy nights, we listened in satisfaction to the pounding rain on metal slats as we drifted into dreams, thankful that were sheltered and dry. Despite Father's admonitions to seek spiritual domiciles, we all rejoiced in ceilings that didn't leak.

Meals were a priority in Mother's life as she prepared

cornbread and vegetables with heaping portions of beans or peas for protein since meat was scarce. Occasionally, Mother fried chicken or fish, feeding leftover scraps to the pets, or composting it in the garden so no food was ever wasted. Father brought slabs of salted pork to hang in the smokehouse for special occasions. Our victuals were meager, but we never went without. As Father and Mother reminded us, "God will provide." And he did.

One redeeming quality of our house was that it was spacious. Jane and I shared a bedroom so that the other two second-floor bedrooms could be rented to boarders. Mrs. Lydia Marfickle, a retired schoolteacher, lived in one room, and her nephew, Bartholomew (Bart), lived in the other. Father and Mother shared a larger, ground floor bedroom convenient to the downstair fireplaces. Both tenants were excellent boarders: punctilious about paying a few dollars in rent for shelter and three daily meals. Fastidious in their habits, their peculiarities only added to their luster.

The boarders contributed to our tenuous finances which were as unstable as our rickety house. Father depended upon maintaining harmonious relations with the congregation so he could continue his tenure. Common work hazards of ministers including being dismissed for even the suspicion of moral turpitude; falling out of favor when a congregation wanted new leadership; or being relegated to part-time status if a congregation could not afford a fulltime pastor.

Mother insisted that the house was an incentive for the congregation to retain Father's services since they did not have to pay for a parsonage. Father did not have the heart to inform her that the cost and effort of renovation far exceeded any realty value. Despite this, we continued to renovate, reasoning that if we ever had to move to a different location, the house could be rented to additional tenants.

Although Father would gladly have sold the house, he never mentioned this to Mother, knowing the mere suggestion would break her heart. The homestead was her only family legacy, and every piece of furniture or battered dish contained a story behind it. She cooked with the same pots and pans and served our meals on the same chipped dishes her ancestors had used for decades. "I'll buy new dishes one day," she said after scrubbing them in a large white dishpan, the soapy bubbles floating like multi-colored spheres in the steam. Appraising them, she held the wet dishes in her hands to look at the faded floral motifs before dipping them in rinse water for us to dry and place in the cupboard. "These dishes will do nicely for now." While she appreciated their value, all we saw were the chips and tiny fissures eating away at the enamel. "What does she see in these old things?" we wondered.

In the spring of 1940, Father installed an inside bathroom—a luxury at the time—to help secure future renters. Despite the upgrades, the house was a constant source of worry and frustration. As soon as one item was fixed, another problem took its place. "This is my penance to pay," Father sighed in exasperation as something else sagged in disrepair. Jane and I puzzled about why he needed any more punishment when the worst thing he'd ever done was swear in Latin.

Borrowing heavily from movie plots and novels, we concocted elaborate stories to explain why Miss Lydia and Mr. Bart never married. Jane fabricated a tale about a tragic love affair gone sour in Miss Lydia's youth when her stern father refused to give his consent for her to wed a dashing young man. Little wonder that poor Miss Lydia taught school for forty-six years before retiring to solitude. Any day now, her silver-haired Lothario would arrive in his Packard to sweep her away to a new life in New York City to marry and live happily in high society.

I cooked up an equally far-fetched story about Bartholomew and his lady friend, Vermetta Altheried. In this elaborate scenario, they were transformed into glamourous ornithologists on an expedition to find rare species of birds. During one journey, they got lost in a swamp where they survived on seeds and edible plants. The lovers ignited savage passions by dancing the tango until being rescued and taken to safety. After an elaborate wedding, they journeyed to the South American rainforest where they gained fame and riches by discovering new species of birds and deposits of rare minerals. Using their riches to rescue orphaned natives, they returned to their Mediterranean mansion to raise a brood of children. Jane and I naturally wove ourselves into the story as babysitters and personal assistants.

Bart and Miss Lydia were considerably less interesting when viewed in the cold lenses of reality. Both lived such a regimented schedule that each day was interchangeable with the next. Bart rose at six each weekday morning to dress in his daily uniform of starched shirt and black suit. His thin black tie hung to the third button of his shirt meeting pants suspended high on his waist like a thin, frumpy scarecrow. His heavy black shoes thumping down the wooden staircase signaled us to wake up and begin the day. The floors creaked as he walked into the kitchen where he sat for his daily breakfast of two poached eggs, toast and black coffee, followed by a tall glass of tepid water. After spending exactly ten minutes in the bathroom, his morning toilet routine was complete.

Promptly at 6:40, Bartholomew walked into the living room, sat on the couch, and read the morning paper. At seven he rose, quietly bidding my Father goodbye, and then drove his brown Oldsmobile to the home of Vermetta who rode with him to the courthouse. After parking in a designated spot, they exited the car and climbed a flight of marble stairs to a small corner office where they worked.

Bartholomew was the County Tax Assessor and Vermetta, his devoted secretary, about as well-liked as tax collectors could be at the time. During their tenure as public servants, they worked together as a highly functioning machine. Vermetta typed and filed with frightening proficiency while Bart tabulated sums and sent out tax notices. All records were maintained with meticulous accuracy.

I imagined Mr. Bart at work, sitting under the window at his desk, adding and cross-referencing columns of numbers from early daylight until afternoon shadows and the chiming clock signaled the end of the workday. A serious, slender man with a narrow face accentuated by a Roman nose and arching eyebrows over deep-set brooding eyes, he looked like a biblical prophet about to proclaim God's messages. It was always surprising to see his thin lips turned upward in a surprisingly mirthful smile of innocence proving that he was a good-humored ascetic.

He and Vermetta had been engaged for more years than they could recall. When asked about their upcoming nuptials, Vermetta explained that she had to take care of her parents, but they intended to be married one day. Plain and angular, Vermetta was about as animated as a Roman death mask. The joke around town was they were too independent to get hitched. Vermetta was happy living with her parents, and Bartholomew was equally content living in bachelorhood. Jane and I giggled that they were so similar to each other that it would be like marrying a mirror image. Perhaps being too much alike kept them apart like repulsing polar magnets.

Miss Lydia, a pleasantly plump woman in her sixties, whiled away the hours in her upstairs bedroom, reading and painting watercolors of birds as sunlight splattered through blinds and lilting music wafted from her room. Every afternoon, she immersed herself in the lurid plots of soap operas. On weekends during pleasant weather, Vermetta, Bartholomew, and Miss Lydia sat in the backyard observing birds alight in the feeder in a fenced-in aviary that we build to keep out cats and dogs.

The highlight of their year consisted of a week's vacation to the Florida Keys where they joined members of the American Birdwatching Society to view coastal species. Each watcher recorded sightings in notebooks to share with club members. One year, Vermetta won a birdbath for her prize-winning journal of all the birds she had seen. Jane and I learned coloration, diet, nesting habits, and mating rituals by reading their journals illustrated by Miss Lydia's watercolors.

Life churned by with all the regularity of water flowing through a turbine. After our daily ministrations, the trio invited us for high tea on Saturday afternoon. Jane and I dressed in our Sunday finest, careful to make pleasant conversation while balancing cups of tea and saucers of delicacies on our laps. We politely excused ourselves before the lengthy radio concert or interminable opera production they listened to each Saturday evening.

A new set of worries besieged us on December 7th, 1941, when the attack on Pearl Harbor necessitated U.S. troops to join Allied

Powers in World War II. We bought war bonds and did not complain about using ration stamps for flour and other necessities. The shortages of food and other stapes did not bother us, but the men leaving for the frontlines did.

Later, returning veterans shared military experiences, suppressing unspoken horrors that they kept hidden in their hearts. One man complained about his phantom limb itching so violently that he nearly went crazy, finding relief only when his wife pantomimed the motion of rubbing ointment on his missing arm. It was a reminder of how something no longer existing can be replaced by devastating emptiness.

Neighbors gather with the families of two young men killed in the war as Father presided over the funeral and consoled the families. Once, when I fetched Father for supper, I found him kneeling quietly over the soldiers' graves in communion. Father told me that occasionally while preaching, he'd see the dead heroes revived as children sitting beside their parents, a spectral reminder of how the heart can delude us.

The war ended and life drummed steadily onward. Jane and I matured from children with scraped knees to teenagers who rode our bikes to friends' houses. I envied Jane her tall, reed-thin body which accentuated whatever she wore with insouciant elegance. Except for her graceful bearing, Jane might have been described as somewhat nondescript with straight brown hair and features a little too symmetrical to be arrestingly pretty. I would have gladly exchanged my curly locks for her lank hair if only my metabolism burned calories as quickly as Jane's did. Although I heard ladies at church whisper that I was pretty as a silver dollar, I would have preferred being as thin as a fashion model, proving the adage that few are satisfied with their blessings.

I discovered the power of beauty to manipulate people with a flutter of long eyelashes and dimpled smiles, taming my curly hair into long, golden braids festooned with ribbons and flirting shamelessly with anyone to gain the sweets that were proffered to me in hope of winning my heart. Jane said I was completely Machiavellian, which alarmed me enough to look up the word in a dictionary. My saving grace was I was more interested in friendship than romance. Hopeful suitors eventually quit trying to court me and settled on friendship instead. Occasionally I even shared my candy with them.

With typical Shakespearean embellishment, Jane lamented that everyone in our house "creeps in this petty pace from day to day." I had to admit that compared to the movies, we lived a fairly dull existence. Miss Lydia was still ensconced in bird watching and listening to her radio schedule. Bart and Miss Vermetta continued their chaste courtship and vigilant work ethic as civil servants. Mother and Father spread the gospel in the community while Jane and I kept our daily schedule of schooling, socializing, and repairing the house. During one reconstruction project, Father asked the philosophical question: "If we replace every beam and timber in this house, is it still the same house?" I said "yes." Jane thought for a while and said, "That's a quandary. I am not sure. On the atomic level, it is quite different. I will have to study Descartes." Puzzling over her reply, I assumed that "Descartes" referred to the "the carts" of supplies that came in handy in our house restoration. I wondered why she laughed when I reminded her we had just bought a new wheelbarrow.

Almost a blueprint of Father, Jane was an odd balance of kindness and intelligence. She took in injured wildlife and homeless strays, patiently tending them in a barn stall that she converted into a makeshift veterinarian clinic. As a ten-year old, she ran into the street to rescue a mangled puppy run over by a car, nursing him back to health with information she gleaned from a medical textbook and her own blend of patience. Father complained that he never knew what kind of creatures he would encounter in the barn, but everyone could see his pride in Janes's accomplishments.

Jane was a girl who actualized the values she cherished. She had strong affinities for the excluded. Never one to back down from an argument, she championed the underdog even if it affected her popularity. More than one chaste affair or close friendship ended because of her unconventionality. Most girls would have been devastated, but she considered it a trade-off. "I have to do what is right. If friends are that shallow, good riddance" was her usual way of dealing with the disapproval of peers and suitors alike.

Jane and Father discussed scriptures with such intensity that they'd sometimes have to be reminded to eat supper. Mother and I occasionally listened in on their conversations, but rarely interjected our own opinions. As Jane matriculated in school, she and Father discussed ideas far beyond our interests.

How is it that the years pass, and we find ourselves at pivotal points in life? By 1948, Jane was an eighteen-year-old high school senior, and I was her thirteen-year-old kid sister. Despite the five year age difference, we were very close. Tensions rose later during the Korean War and the spread of communism as we prayed for young men and women to return home safely. Still, it was a time when small-town life was a buffer to growing threats from an increasingly dangerous world. We tried not to fret about apocalyptic weapons in the "Cold War," but like many of our neighbors, we dug a makeshift fallout/storm shelter, reasoning that it was good to be prepared for emergencies. How could we know that one can never completely insulate oneself from trouble? Despite all preparations, unexpected problems have a way of changing the landscape as effectively as fault lines in an earthquake.

Jane was excited about attending college on scholarship. But life contains no guarantees as I was to find out soon enough. Like a heroine in a monster movie, one only has to turn a corner to encounter danger. So imperceptible were the changes in Jane's behavior that we hardly noticed tiny cracks as delicately patterned as gossamer webs. As Jane's graduation date loomed ever closer, her moods darkened. She spent more time alone with only pets as company. During spring evenings when the sweet aroma of clover saturated the air, I went to the barn in search of her. Jane had always been a companionable sister, so I was hurt when she turned away from me. Although she continued helping with repairs, Jane was preoccupied and silent and only stared at us when we coaxed her to talk.

Mother and Father rationalized that Jane was maturing into adulthood and needed to gain independence so that she would not get homesick once she moved away to college. They reassured me that she would be back to her old self once the established self-sufficiency. Still, I wasn't completely satisfied that Jane's behavior could be attributed to growing pains. She had never gone through such an extended period of isolation. Even Miss Lydia and Bart could not coax Jane out of her self-imposed exile.

I missed the camaraderie I had with Jane. More than ever, I needed an older sister to offer guidance about certain topics that

I dared not discuss with Mother. Jane was dangling in the air on a seesaw counterbalanced by a heavy weight. When would she regain her footing on firm ground? All the unknowns perplexed me; how often would I get to see Jane after she left? Would we ever be as close? Would Jane continue to change so much that she turned into a different person? I was beginning to figure out the enigma of replacing the beams in a house to form a new structure or to transform the old. Was Jane transforming herself? Did that mean that eventually I'd feel comfortable with the "new" Jane? Not having solid answers made us all apprehensive.

Jane's emotional conflicts were exacerbated by physical problems. A few months prior to graduation, she began to fast, which caused her naturally skinny frame to become alarmingly emaciated. On the evening of graduation, she was so gaunt and pale when she gave her valedictorian address that we were inundated with people calling to see what they could do to help Jane regain her health. We made excuses and tried to convince ourselves and friends that Jane was just going through a "spell of nervousness" from which she'd soon recover. As the weeks passed, Jane continued to retreat into a shell. Jane had always been fanatical about orderliness. A few years earlier, she had remodeled the attic into her bedroom with every piece of furniture and article in pristine order. Her closets and chests were immaculate; each picture hung straight on the walls. She pressed each garment so every seam was straight and arranged every book neatly on the shelves. However, as the summer progressed, her room became disordered with scattered clumps on the wooden floors and her closets looked as if a bomb had exploded in them. I was surprised to find that she was locking her room when I knocked on the door and wriggled the doorknob.

Jane began to wear the same wrinkled, musty-smelling clothing day after day, neglecting personal hygiene. Her lank hair hung in tangled locks to her shoulders and was darker now because of oily build-up. One day, Mother unlocked Jane's bedroom and was aghast to see the disturbing disarray. She gathered everything in her arms to lauder, crying in horror at Jane's soiled bed sheets.

As summer progressed, we heard Jane pacing back and forth in her room like a restless phantom late at night. One day in June, when howling winds bent branches to the ground as if reflecting Jane's inner tempest, we found her in the barn using Father's tools to build a casket. "I'm dying," she said in a solemn voice, looking at us with dull, unseeing eyes. "I don't know who I am anymore, which is ironic because I'm already dead." Then she chuckled sardonically. It was both reassuring and unnerving to see that her sense of humor was still intact through her tormented psyche.

"Jane, you're still you," Father said in a shaking voice. "You're going through changes, but you are still Jane. We're going to help you." And with those words, he enclosed her in a warm blanket and half carrying her, walked back to the house. Miss Lydia and Bart illuminated the path with lanterns like guardian angels.

Father and Mother scheduled an appointment with Doctor Meadows, a psychiatric specialist in Birmingham. All of Jane's tests showed that she was in good physical health, though anemic and underweight. He gave Jane a diet plan and exhorted her to begin eating correctly. "You are demonstrating neurosis because of severe nutritional deficiencies," he pronounced solemnly. "Go home, rest, and eat." Handing Mother and Father several prescriptions, he explained dosages and feeling regimens with the ominous warning that Jane might have to be hospitalized if she didn't "buck up and return to common sense."

Within a few weeks on the new diet, Jane improved but still showed signs of paranoia. Without a definite diagnosis, we were stumbling about in the dark with no direction. Needing professional guidance, Mother and Father call Dr. Meadows who referred us to a renowned psychiatrist in Tuscaloosa. Surely we could reassemble the old Jane if we could identify the source of her problems. Jane was hospitalized at a psychiatric hospital in Tuscaloosa for weeks of testing. Dr. Paulson, her consulting psychiatrist, was a rotund, bearded man in his late fifties with a shiny bald spot that separated graying, curly hair on either side of his head. Both a physician and a pharmacist, he worked at the state psychiatric hospital and taught at the university. He was the author of several psychiatric studies and was renowned for using pharmaceuticals and therapy to alleviate mental illness in patients.

After extensive testing, Dr. Paulson called us into his office one rainy Wednesday in late July. Sitting in chairs surrounding his desk, we breathed in the stultifying air which even the large, oscillating fan could not cool. Ominous clouds outside the windows oppressed our spirits as though we'd been sentenced to a lifetime of dull, cloudy afternoons. Dr. Paulson entered the office, sighed quietly as he closed the door, walked to his desk, and sat down heavily. He adjusted his spectacles, looked at us for a long moment, and then began examining the contents of Jane's folder.

It is odd how much one notices during those long minutes before heartbreak. I'd always thought traumatic events would be signaled by wrenching groans and cries; but the worst agonies are silent. I surveyed the office and noticed framed diplomas on the walls and bookshelves crammed haphazardly, which revealed a surprisingly endearing trait of untidiness. His stark office was sparsely decorated with straight-backed chairs; bookshelves lined the walls and folders were piled on his desk. A wall of large windows that fronted his office revealed dark skies overlooking the surrounding college campus. Even the wall seemed to pulsate in sorrow. Finally, my reverie ended when Dr. Paulson cleared his throat to break the silence.

Looking directly at us, he rubbed his bald pate in a self-soothing reaction before clasping his hands together on his desk. "We have spent two weeks conducting tests," he said in a deep baritone. Then sighing heavily, he examined his hands, grabbed a pen, and made more notes on Jane's chart. The tension in the room was as suffocating as a boulder on my chest. I thought my heart would explode before Dr. Paulson gazed at us sadly, shook his head, inhaled deeply, then exhaled a long sigh. "I am sorry to tell you that your daughter has all the symptoms of Paranoid Schizophrenia."

And with that pronouncement, Father collapsed on Mother, his shoulders heaving, gulping all the air out of the room as he sobbed in unleashed misery. Mother held his head to her shoulder as she cried quietly. I sat there dumbfounded before I broke into tears. Somehow, the metallic taste of mucus filling my throat and tears falling down my face was cathartic. Finally, we had a diagnosis. Surely things would improve once Jane started treatment.

After a few minutes, I calmed down enough to ask, "Can we please pray together?"

Dr. Paulson said, "Of course." Then he turned off the lights and we all stood and clasped hands together in the darkness. For a long moment we waited until Dr. Paulson began to pray in a resonant voice for healing and strength. Although we were heartsick, a spiritual presence comforted us with a strand of hope that we clung to in order to move forward through our ordeal. Years later, a Park Ranger turned off the lights in a cave and the darkness was so stark that we could not see our hands in front of our faces. In that void, I felt powerless and afraid. Then I realized Dr. Paulson had turned off the lights to represent our need for God to light the way. The darkness was a way of showing humility in our quest for spiritual light.

After the prayer, Dr. Paulson turned on the light. The tears in my eyes created an optical illusion of a starburst in the glowing lamp as we took our seats. "We will do everything we can in our treatment of Jane," said Dr. Paulson. "She has a very serious mental illness. There are medications which can alleviate her symptoms, but in all probability, she will have this disease for the remainder of her life. She may remain on a plateau, improve, or regress, but she will never again be the same girl you once knew. If you can accept her transition, you will help her progress."

"Now for the good news. Jane has a very strong will to improve and high intellectual capability. With medication and therapy, she has the potential to lead a successful life. Over the following weeks and months, just realize that she will probably get much worse before she eventually improves."

By this time Mother and Father had calmed down enough to listen. As if emerging from a dark tunnel, they wanted to find the best track to recovery. After asking a litany of questions, Father vented in frustration: "She has a full scholarship to attend the

University, with her future all mapped out. She wanted to work in the medical field. Why would God strike down someone with such gifts—someone who had such potential to help others?"

"Mr. Harthcourt, I am so sorry. It will take months before we can determine Jane's progress. I have seen patients progress before episodes of psychosis overtake them. I have seen patients with severe symptoms regain their equilibrium. You must believe that with intervention and medication, Jane might very well improve. Then again, I must warn you not to get discouraged if she goes through a difficult period. People with this condition often go through stages. And always, we must have faith that Jane can use her illness and her recovery as a tool to help others. Whatever the outcome, it is perfectly normal to feel anguish and anger. We will all work through this, but it will take stamina and time."

Dr. Paulson gave us a schedule of treatments for Jane and explained medications, rehabilitation, hospitalization, and expected results, answering all out questions and attempting to alleviate our fears with a pragmatic approach. Sometimes God appoints guides to lead us out of obstacles. Our shepherd happened to Dr. Paulson who became our trusted ally and friend. He advocated for patients and their families as he taught us that mental illness should not be stigmatized. Eventually, we received family counseling to cope with the situation. Angels come in all sizes, genders, and colors. Ours happened to a short, flabby, bespectacled man with an oversized intellect and heart.

Jane was placed in a security ward of the state mental hospital to receive extra attention. I'll always remember an impermeable odor of defeat when I walked down the hall to the visiting area. Strong disinfectants couldn't completely mask the pervasive scent of despair that clung to the walls and floors. Nor could we avert our eyes from some of the patients who seemed so forlorn and hopeless.

Each Saturday afternoon, we met with Jane in one of the small, glass-fronted partitions off the main visitation area. For the first few weeks, a nurse accompanied Jane, but eventually she shuffled alone into the room wearing a long flannel robe covering her pajamas. Because of medications that affected her gait, Jane shuffled like an inept cross-country skier.

Jane gained weight during her hospital stay as a side effect of medication and inactivity. Although bloated and medicated, Jane still maintained perfect posture. We were relieved that she was again hygienic; her hair was freshly shampooed and combed into a pretty hairstyle. She smelled fresh and clean, and the medications had miraculously changed the texture of her hair waves she had always coveted. At night she slept soundly, and the nurses promised that soon Jane could take regular exercise in the gym.

There were times when she regressed into sullen silence. We'd try to engage her in conversation, but she just stared at the floor until the visitation was over. After a difficult visit, we'd say our goodbyes, huddled together to watch Jane being led through security doors to her ward. Then we'd wander numbly to our car for the long ride home in silence. During those first long months we kept our concerns hidden from one another. In the silence, I felt mired in immobility as only the scenery appeared to move on the long trips to the hospital and back again.

Two years passed with regular Saturday visits. Mother acquired a job as a clerk in the courthouse, which greatly helped with medical bills. Father was upfront about Jane's situation to the congregation, explaining in detail her experiences and prognosis. We were forever grateful to their assistance when members helped out with our financial burdens. A few moved to other congregations; some murmured that Jane was a hypochondriac, and more than once I had to laugh at the irony when people insisted that the sickness was all "in her head." But most accepted the situation with kindness and grace. The illness had made Father more compassionate and approachable. He still preached about moral fortitude with a need for love, patience, and forgiveness, using Jane's ordeal as an example of how God's love offers respite when we are most vulnerable.

People in the community heard about Father's patience and understanding. Within a few months, the heavy-laden began coming to the church Monday through Friday to discuss their problems with Father in confidence. He listened with the solemnity of a judge and offered sage advice to anyone in the community who needed guidance, always informing them that he was not a professional counselor, only a man with common sense. Knowing that people just needed to speak their minds to someone outside their immediate family, he arbitrated disputes, persuaded people to seek medical and legal help, or just listened objectively.

To avoid any suspicion of misconduct, Father insisted that a church member sit directly outside the office door to avoid controversy if he counseled a woman. After listening to ninety-six-year-old Daphne Pellner complain about her lack of privacy, he insisted that witnesses observe them so that no one could accuse him of taking advantage of her. She was so flattered that she told everyone in the community. Forever after, she flirted shamelessly with Father and always brought cookies to share.

Eventually Father became so overwhelmed with counseling and ministering to the expanding congregation that the elders appointed an assistant pastor to assist him. "Zeke," as he was nicknamed—shortened from Ezekiel—was a young man with a master's degree in Counseling and Theology. His wife as adept in helping Mother with church duties. Eventually, Zeke set up a counseling service in the church basement. Father was greatly relieved that professional services deterred any possible lawsuits. When a few old-timers insisted on talking to Father, he took time to listen to his friends. One old farmer paid him the highest compliment by saying "Pastor Harthcourt don't condemn me to hell for being honest."

We no longer lived in anguish as Jane made incremental progress. With God's grace and community support to bolster us, we quit obsessing about a strict schedule for Jane's recovery and began accepting the rocky course that our lives had taken as if we had wandered up treacherous cliffs, bruised and battered, to gain a wider perspective. By the time I graduated high school in 1953, blue skies emerged, and the future looked brighter. If occasionally, we longed for the "old Jane," we allayed expectations like one packs away mementos in a cedar chest, later to be taken out and examined.

I was apprehensive about attending the local university because it meant leaving home. Now that Jane was institutionalized, I felt a greater responsibility to my parents by fulfilling all their expectations. I worried about how my absence would affect them. Without analyzing my actions, I assumed the burden of being the "perfect" daughter so they could focus on Jane. Knowing I represented the family legacy, it was up to me to get a degree, marry, and raise their grandchildren. Jane cast a long shadow as I attempted to live up to her academic aptitude. I studied and made good grades while appearing to be the perpetually happy and "perfect" coed. Only later, did I realize how arduous it was to be an idealized version of myself instead of being authentic. I was so dependent upon making others happy that I neglected my own needs.

Jane moved to a less restricted area of the institute. Since I lived in a dormitory in close proximity to her, I visited frequently. Occasionally she was stilted in conversation and drifted into some other realm before snapping back to reality. My parents brought her fresh clothing each Saturday, so she always looked attractive. She read the books we brought and once again began conversing with Father about a wide range of topics.

Sometimes she slipped into hallucinations which created revisionist memories. "You remember you broke that rooster's neck when he scratched me, Father?" she said one day. "You killed him. Then threw his body into the creek and the water turned a bloody red color. I remember walking to school and seeing the rooster floating downstream in a crimson current." As proof, she offered up her arm. "See? I still have the scar from that rooster's talon."

We never knew what to say when Jane went off on these tangents. Oddly, her stories contained elements of truth. It was correct that on our way to school, a rooster had tormented us for years and once scratched Jane. However, Father never broke the rooster's neck. He cherished good neighborly relations, loved animals, and hated any sort of violence. He would never have instigated hostility by killing a neighbor's prize rooster. It would be as improbable as Father joining a group of professional wrestlers to think that he could harm someone's pet. However, when we tried to reason with Jane, she got flustered and insisted on the veracity of her own memory.

"That rooster knew my thoughts. He was the devil. You slew him to protect me!"

"Jane, I never killed a rooster," Father quietly retorted. "I remember that the neighbor had a very territorial rooster named Champion who harassed every creature that crossed his path, but I never killed him."

It did no good to argue with Jane who clung obstinately to her own reality. Eventually, Mother and Father placidly listened to her long monologues, nodding their head in agreement to everything she said. After listening to her version of the epic rooster debacle, I laughed and admitted, "Well, Jane, I was scared to death of that rooster. I obsessed about that bird during my entire third grade year until the neighbors eventually penned him up. So in a way, he did control our thoughts. He was a grouchy old coot, wasn't he? And then Jane and I laughed. My affirmation was as refreshing as a cool mountain stream, and she gazed at me in gratitude for a long time. Just validating her statements helped level the table upon which she could balance the scales of truth.

"What color was Champion's feathers?" I asked. Jane smiled, took a deep breath, and as if looking at a painting, she described every subtle hue of his feathers; how his talons glistened in the sun, and the shape and texture of his bill and red crest with great clarity. At one point, she pantomimed his majestic bearing, peering intently at us like Champion. We all burst into laughter. "Why, Jane, now that you mention it, I can see Champion as if I were right there next to him. He was a proud strutting rooster!" laughed Mother. "How in the world did you remember all that?"

Jane's illness enhanced her memory to photographic accuracy. She recalled details of the past such as our first residence: a little two-bedroom shotgun house that we lived in before moving into the house Mother inherited. As she described every vivid detail down to the pattern of the linoleum floor, we were relieved to know that none of Jane's cognitive abilities had diminished. If anything, she noticed things in sharper detail than ever before.

Eventually, Jane was discharged to live with Mother and Father during my sophomore year in college. Still uneasy around crowds, Jane sat in Father's office during church services and rarely spoke to anyone. Mother and Father knew Jane needed to associate with people, so it was a setback when she locked herself in her room with the shades drawn. Jane shrugged off their concern. "I like solitude," she explained. Then seeing the look of concern on their faces, Jane added, "Just give me time."

Sally, the associate minister's wife, encouraged her to attend volunteer sessions at the church on Tuesdays and Thursdays to no avail. Jane preferred reading in her bedroom. Within a few weeks, she started walking to the local library to check out books. The exercise and fresh air were tonics to her spirit, and we all sighed in gratitude that she was getting out of the house.

Twice a week, I drove my battered old Mercury to take Jane to psychiatric consultations with Dr. Paulson, so we could talk on the way. Occasionally, I even got to join Jane's counseling sessions. Dr. Paulson listened as Jane related small victories, frustrations, and occasional delusions as he asked pertinent questions that cut delicately through her hallucinations with the precision of a surgeon's scalpel. And as though dissecting a specimen, Jane cut through layers of illusions to excise fantasy from reality.

Jane realized with growing lucidity that the whispered voices she heard were auditory delusions. Like a forcefield, the voices confined her to a region of paranoia during the worst part of her sickness. Their constant threats eroded her confidence as her cells of reason were blown off course by menacing winds. As Jane gained confidence, she challenged their insinuations and demanded that they break their hold on her. Although the voices still murmured, they were consigned to the corners of her brain where they hid and observed, gaining volume when she was stressed or tired. Once conquered, they never again controlled her thoughts or actions as he exorcised their demonic hold over her. She once said, "I see and hear shadows, but I tell them to jump into some wild hogs and jump off a cliff—alluding to the scripture in the Gospel of Matthew.

Slowly, with painstaking effort, Jane crawled out of torment into a world of clarity and reason. Still medicated, she did everything a little more slowly than others as if constrained by invisible chains. If Jane had an especially difficult day, she talked to Sally, who had training as a nurse and often clasped Jane's hands and talked her into equilibrium. Occasionally, Sally sat up all night with Jane, waving off our family's heartfelt appreciation as the sun rose and sleep overtook Jane.

Eventually, Jane became more sociable and moved to the back of the auditorium during church services. The sunshine, filtering through panes of stained glass, illuminated the church with soft nuances of colored light as we prayed for God to reassemble out lives and make us stronger. Sensing empathy, Jane began to interact with members. On Tuesdays and Thursdays, she accompanied Sally to Bible study and Lady's Benevolent sessions to prepare food and sort clothing.

Jane needed plenty of physical exercise as part of her recovery, so she and Mother began going on long evening walks. Father and Jane worked in the yard, planting a variety of flowers whose petals bloomed in profusions of fragrance, color, and patterns throughout the seasons. Mother, Jane, and I spent summer days in the hot kitchen, cooking and canning the food we harvested. And, as always, we repaired the house.

Jane started journaling her ordeal and sharing her writings with Dr. Paulson, who was so impressed that he contacted editors who published her memoirs in professional journals. Eventually the publishers of popular magazines took notice and recruited Jane to write articles on mental illness which gained such attention that she became a sought-after writer who was asked to speak at mental health seminars. Getting her driver's license was another huge victory in Jane's quest for independence, although it took months of practice before she had enough confidence to drive long distances. She joked that someone needed to be with her in case she went into a fugue state and ended up in Alaska.

Dr. Paulson had negotiated with the university to reinstall Jane's scholarship so she could register as a full-time student. We rented rooms in a modest boarding house close to campus. Life bloomed with verdant possibilities, and I started breathing easier again—small breaths at first—and then larger gulps of air. I hadn't realized how long I had been holding my breath. I sometimes felt as if Jane and I were trapped in a box and felt guilty at consuming any air that Jane might need. Perhaps in the back of my mind I was saving my breath in case Jane needed resuscitation.

I walked to classes with Jane as often as possible, but our

schedules were not always aligned, and we had to go our separate ways. One beautiful autumn day, I looked across campus and noticed Jane walking alone to class, far enough away not to notice me. She looked so brave that I stared at her in admiration. I realized how easily we ignore those who are "different" and how much courage it takes for outliers to keep their eyes focused on the goal when they are so often "unseen."

Although she had a supportive network of professors, family, and therapists, Jane still longed for acceptance, but it was difficult to make new friends. She was older and more serious than her fellow students. It would have made such a huge difference if she could have made one true friend, but Jane was too guarded to approach others. I was especially disillusioned with students at the campus church who excluded Jane. How could Christians express unconditional love when they avoided people in their own congregation?

Feeling increasingly responsible for Jane, I began spending all my free time with her. I enjoyed Jane's company, but at times I wanted to be as carefree as people my own age—to laugh and socialize in a group. I'd feel especially isolated in class when students joked and bantered so freely. To channel my frustrations, I submerged myself in studies with the goal of becoming a school counselor. Although I wanted to become a psychologist, it would have been very difficult for a female therapist to set up practice with enough clientele to make a profit. I was also practical enough to realize that I might not be hired as a therapist in a mental health clinic since women were stigmatized as being "too emotional." In the 1950s, the prevailing attitude of many administrators was that women were not objective enough to diagnose and counsel patients accurately.

One summer, I took a job in the campus library and attended classes during the day. I enjoyed the more informal atmosphere of the summer semester, but the sweltering heat was so overwhelming that I had to fan the bottom of my blouse to keep it from sticking to my skin. The fans made a droning sound as I walked into the cooler air of buildings. I'd go to the bathroom to splash cold water on my face, enjoying the way it cooled my fevered skin.

One July day when the heat and humidity approached three digits, I met Arvin MacNama in class. He had a square, friendly face with glasses that framed wide, light blue eyes. His large, weathered hands and lined face revealed that he was used to hard work on his family's small farm. Although not handsome, he had such a winsome smile and engaging personality that we became fast friends. I found out that he was studying to be a school administrator with the goal of being a high school principal. Although I felt no zing of instant attraction that I read about in romance novels, I was happy to be with Arvin who was personable and well-spoken. Soon he accompanied me to class and started studying with me in the library. We made an attractive couple, and I enjoyed the approval of others when they smile at us.

Though hesitant to get too close to anyone, I was forthright about Jane's problems to alert Arvin that my sister had mental health issues. If Arvin wanted to pursue me, he needed to know about any potential genetic complications before getting too involved. To my surprise, he didn't seem overly concerned. "Every family has problems. If we never took chances, we'd never do anything except worry," he said as if discussing the weather or a perplexing case of tomato blight. Arvin, I was to learn, held to the philosophy that whatever "will be, will be." I almost laughed when he said this as if he would suddenly break into a chorus of "Que Sera Sera" to the lilting accompaniment of Doris Day. With his matter-of-fact sensibility, Arvin possessed a bedrock of common sense and self-assurance. "There is no reason to worry," Arvin reassured me. "God will help guide us."

Arvin, Jane, and I attended church together, sitting in the pew like well-watered plants whose roots intertwined deeply underground. But during services, Jane would sometimes become drowsy and droop her head in a gesture that reminded of a plant wilting from a lack of nutrients. I'd read that certain fungal plants take chlorophyll from the roots of adjoining trees and thought that Arvin and I could help Jane survive by putting down roots so she could soak up whatever essential elements she needed.

Jane liked Arvin because he treated her with respect and kindness but was not overly conciliatory. Often, he teased her out of her worries by joking that she had supernatural powers. "Ask your voices which horse to bet on in the Kentucky Derby if they have such insight!" he laughed. At first, I was mortified that Arvin could be so insensitive, but Jane delighted in his jokes. He could jolly her out of her deepest funks as she laughed in delight at his humor. My heart, which had been so constricted in worry and fear, began to thaw in the warmth of his kindness. As compelling as a spring day after a winter's freeze, he used the tools of laughter and kindness like an expert carpenter repairing a fine piece of delicate furniture. As the summer progressed into autumn, I knew that Arvin would become part of my family.

When Arvin graduated in the spring of 1956, he got a job as a history teacher in a high school a few counties to the south. In his absence, I continued my studies, happy that my life was heading in the right direction. Arvin and I wrote frequently, and he visited as often as his old truck would allow. We had an unspoken "understanding" even if we had not formally announced our intentions.

I assumed that Arvin and I would eventually marry, so I felt a little guilty that I enjoyed my freedom without him. As much as I looked forward to Arvin's visits, I wanted to soar in the sky like a hot air balloon before tethering myself in marriage. Sometimes, I resented having to fit the image that my parents and Arvin projected on me. I tried so hard to conform to their perceptions that I struggled with my own identity. At times, I wanted to be like brave characters I read about in novels who had zany, outrageous adventures. If I watched a late-night movie on television, I envied heroines who dallied with debonair men. In comparison, my life was as straight as a plum line to conventionality. At night, I dreamed of being a married woman with children, waking up and feeling stale and thirsty. Between trying to please my family, being a loyal companion to Jane, and a worthy girlfriend to Arvin, I felt like a puppet being manipulated by an unseen choreographer.

I envied the popularity of other girls as I saw them experiencing life with exuberance. As a pastor's daughter, I had been raised to be circumspect. In a burst of independence, I felt compelled to have fun before settling down for good. I made friends with a gang of friendly girls, and we danced to rock and roll, sipped soft drinks with peanuts at the bottom of the glass, and spent hours talking about our dreams for the future. Eventually, we started going out in the evenings just to talk and laugh. I didn't want Jane to feel slighted, so I made excuses that I was working late. Although I felt guilty about lying, I knew that having Jane around would only dampen the fun. I'd be so worried about her that I couldn't relax. To be honest, I wanted to throw off the mantle of worry and responsibility and just be carefree.

I'd come home in the evenings to find Jane happily working on homework, writing, or enjoying her solitude in the company of a good book which helped assuage my feelings of guilt. Still, occasionally when I was with friends, guilt threw a pall over my personality until my friends coaxed me out of my funk. So impenetrable was my need to keep family secrets that I didn't divulge anything confidential.

One rainy night at a local hangout, I met Ben, a slender young man with shiny dark hair, large brown eyes, and a New York accent. He was as foreign to me as an archeologist searching for ancient African artifacts. I learned that his family had moved south a few years earlier so that his father could teach economics at the university. While he enjoyed his time at the university, Ben was eager to graduate and study writing at Columbia University as a graduate student. His goal was to become a freelance journalist, traveling the world over in search of interesting subjects. Life in a small town had been a peaceful interlude, but he anticipated the bright lights of big cities and the enchantment of foreign lands. My life paled in comparison and I felt a mixture of envy and melancholy knowing that we would likely discontinue our friendship once he left.

Ben was a thoughtful listener who offered good advice when I told him all my concerns about Jane and the future. As close as we were, our lives were so disparate that he might as well have been an alien from Jupiter. On the day Ben graduated, I hugged him tightly and wished him well. He invited me to his parents' home for a reception, but I declined.

"Well, it was nice knowing you, Ben. I'll read your articles in the magazines." As he walked away, he turned around and smiled, waving goodbye. I watched until he got in his car and drove away. I was in love with Arvin, but a little bit a little of my heart ripped when Ben left that day. We corresponded for a while, but after a few months, I quit replying to his letters. Although I wanted to keep in touch, I didn't think Arvin would approve of my correspondence. Over the years, I kept up with Ben's travels by reading articles he wrote in major publications and wondered about his life. Would he remember my name since our friendship had been as ephemeral as the rising vapor of an early summer dawn. He had represented freedom and exotic adventures. Sometimes when I felt restless and boxed in with domesticity, I looked out windows and thought of him.

With only one year left to finish my studies, I was restless to complete college and start a new phase of life. After graduating, I worked full time as a clerk so Jane would not be alone as she completed her degree requirements. When I visited home, I welcomed visits from Arvin who fit right in with my family as easily as a hand inside a glove. One Sunday afternoon, Father gave his consent for our union after Arvin asked for my hand in marriage. Mother, Jane, and I started planning a small August wedding. Once Jane graduated with a degree in journalism, we packed up and moved back home with Father and Mother to await my happy nuptials.

It has been said that it is almost impossible to return home again. During my last summer at home, I'd walk with Jane in the evenings and the scent of honeysuckles revived such poignant memories that I wanted to go back to childhood when life had been so innocent. I had the odd dichotomy of nostalgic longing for the past while impatiently awaiting a new phase of life. I enjoyed talking to Bart and Miss Lydia but had to mask my irritability with them for leading such predictable lives. Why couldn't they, for once, do something completely out of character? And then, I'd look at them and think how much I loved them.

One bright August Saturday, Arvin and I were married with Father officiating at the church ceremony. Surrounded by well-wishers, we enjoyed the reception afterwards in the church hall. After a quick trip to Mobile for a honeymoon, we moved into a small rental house equidistant from both our families. "They're just close enough to visit, but not too close that they'll be staying over too much," laughed Arvin, who didn't savor the thought of having a house filled with relatives all hours of the day and night. The month ended on a good note when I accepted a job as guidance counselor at a nearby high school.

Our weekends were busy with work, but we found time on weekends relaxing with family and attending church before the grinding cycle of work. Arvin drove to his job as a high school civics/history teacher with long afternoons spent coaching seasonal sports. It was not unusual for him to put in a sixty-hour work week with all his extracurricular duties. I was glad to have my own car as a I drove the round trip from school to home each day. Truth be told, after a day of interacting with teachers and students, I enjoyed the welcome reprieve of an empty house. Arvin arrived home exhausted and hungry to a clean house and warm meal.

Sports and coaching became an integral part of our routine. I traded sitting on stadium bleachers watching football on chilly autumn evenings to gym bleachers during basketball season as my ears rang to the staccato of players dribbling the ball on court. While sitting on field bleachers during spring baseball, I inhaled the sweet aroma of newly cut grass and enjoyed the lengthening days that reinvigorated everyone. I could almost see the sap rising as young hearts opened up to the first blooms of renewed life.

After a few years, I felt as if I'd been married all my life. Arvin and I were respected members of the community, content to navigate our way over smooth waters so even-keeled that we neither tossed nor strained against the current. After supper, Arvin often sat at the corner desk in the living room, adding up weekly expenses and deposits. One day he announced that in a few years, we'd have more than enough to put a down payment on acreage to build a house. He had even picked out the plot of land where he wanted to live.

I was irritated that he'd arbitrarily decided on the site of a potential house without consulting me, but as usual, I held my tongue, not wanting to cause discord. With typical assertion, he announced that we could start planning a family once we settled into our new place. I noticed that the operative word was "planning" instead of just "having" a family. Why did everything have to be thoroughly planned ahead of time instead of allowing unpremeditated spontaneity? It was annoying that we planned our lives with the accuracy of a professional bowler throwing strikes; even though I begrudgingly admitted that he was right. I agreed that it would be better to wait since parenthood would alter our lives significantly and I'd probably have to give up my job. Delaying would give Arvin time to find a replacement to assume some of his coaching responsibilities so he could devote more time to raising our children. But that night, after nestling down in warm quilts, I felt stirrings of impatience. We had already been married five years and I was twenty-eight years old—at a time when most women my age were already on their second child. Was my biological time clock ticking towards obsolescence? Were we become "Miss Lydia and Bartholomew," too comfortable with monotony?

Arvin budgeted for necessities and put the rest in savings. Prognosticating our future, he charted the trajectory of our lives with all the precision of a rocket scientist. If I occasionally longed for an impromptu vacation or restaurant meal, I kept it quiet, not wanting to create a stir. I had learned self-denial too long to upset the balance of power in my family. But keeping the peace became a heavy tribute to pay. Although conscientious, I was never as compelled to account for every penny as Arvin who urged me to balance my checkbook and save every receipt. In a blatant display of self-assertion, I insisted on keeping stray cats. Fortunately, he did not hold this against me as my menagerie grew to eight cats and three dogs. He probably figured that having pets was a good substitute for my maternal yearning and did not complain when I paid for their upkeep.

Our frugal lifestyle did have its rewards. One day, after complicated calculations, Arvin proudly showed that we had enough money to secure a mortgage. For the next few weeks, we pored over house plans before settling on a modest ranch style with three bedrooms and two baths, which was *de rigueur* in 1963 for the upwardly mobile. We bought twelve acres close to my parents and hired a contractor to build the house. When it was finished, we moved in our belongings, inhaling the intoxicating scent of fresh wood and paint. The house and I were like ripe wombs just waiting to be impregnated with new life. I bided my time and did not worry too much when I failed to become *enceinte*. I assured myself that I would have plenty of time to conceive. But after more years passed, discouragement mounted.

I consulted numerous doctors who put me through batteries of painful tests which proved nothing was wrong with me. "Perhaps I just needed to relax and quit trying so hard," said well-meaning doctors. When they encouraged Arvin to be tested, he balked at being the culprit, so I bore the blame for our infertility. By now I was in thirties in an era when I was practically "geriatric" in terms of childbearing. Added to the stress of infertility was the pressure to keep my family legacy perpetuated before my child-bearing years ended. Jane was approaching her forties, an unmarried woman, and not a good candidate for maternity because of her illness.

In the last vestiges of the "baby boom" era, it seemed that everywhere I looked, young married women were either pregnant or surrounded by children. It was hard not to be envious when I watched them cuddling newborns or casually barking orders to their offspring.

Then one morning I awoke to intense nausea and an odd prickling in my stomach. When a metallic taste bubbled up in my mouth, I visited the doctor who announced that I was pregnant. Overjoyed but apprehensive, I was battered with exhaustion during my entire pregnancy. Between the nausea and permeating weariness, I continued assisting students to apply for colleges and scholarships, arranged for military recruiters to visit the school, and helped students fill out applications for employment. I'd look at seniors with all their lives ahead of them and think about how the gulf of time and experience separated us. Although transitioning to adulthood, they seemed so young and innocent. Wasn't it just a few days ago that I was a young, pretty girl venturing out into the world? How had I turned into this bloated woman whose body ached with new life?

I resigned at the end of the school year, said my heartfelt goodbyes, and went home to await impending motherhood. I enjoyed my career and friends but having bravely soldiered on to the end of the school term, as huge and ill-tempered as a hungry warthog, I was relieved to cocoon myself for the next few months, knowing that I would feel better after delivery.

Although the air conditioning was dialed to an Artic freeze inside the house, I still sweated profusely. While most women would have luxuriated in their voluptuous condition, I was repulsed by my awkward shape. Almost as helpless as an invalid, I had to wallow sideways before I could stand up to go to the bathroom. While washing my hands, I tried to avoid looking at my face since it brought tears to my eyes. I had always been vain, so it was hard not to cry at the sight of my swollen features. Surely, all this extra weight would disappear once I gave birth.

Arvin tried to help, but I could tell that he was disenchanted by my mood and appearance and restless to get out of the house. A compulsive worker, he was at odds at being pent up for days and sighed so often in exasperation that I ordered him out of the house to his great relief. My mother-in-law, Agnes, came to my aid. She was a hard worker with a good disposition who cleaned the house, cooked, and spent long hours keeping me company. As she crocheted baby blankets, she sat by my bed to keep me company and was so solicitous that I felt guilty that I wanted to be left alone. Eventually, I feigned sleep long enough for her to leave my side so I could read to my heart's content.

In mid-September, I awoke to uncomfortable pangs and knew it was time to go to the hospital. Arvin called my parents on the phone before nudging Agnes awake in the next room and stood by the door, waiting patiently for us to trundle to the car before locking the house. I sat in the passenger seat, staring nervously out the front windshield, while Agnes sat in the backseat.

After a protracted delivery, I gave birth to a golden-haired baby girl name Margaret Lucille. "Lucy", as we called her, was a lively and happy baby with such a sunny disposition that she only cried when she was hungry or needed a change of diapers. The pregnancy and its aftermath had been so arduous that I was exhausted with fluctuating hormones that played havoc on my emotions. The doctor advised that I needed help, so Mother and Ages stayed alternating weeks during the first few months until I felt up to the task of fulltime motherhood.

Lucy thrived on a regimented schedule just like her father. The delicate aroma of her soft skin drew me to her as I marveled at her dimpled fingers and chubby legs that curved inward when she slept. I observed her as she discovered the world with piercing eyes and outstretched hands that reached for everything.

Too soon, it seemed, Lucy was dressing for her first day of school. As I accompanied her to kindergarten, I was more anxious that she was. Unlike other children, she did not cry when parents were ordered to leave. She simply smiled and waved cheerfully as I departed. I returned home to a house that felt as hollow as my heart, busying myself with activities until it was time to retrieve her from school where she chatted happily about her day.

Throughout her schooling, Lucy was seemingly free from any angst or conflict. Affable and outgoing, she never lacked for friends and was always the leader of any group, arbitrating disputes, laying down rules, and quietly dispensing advice. She enjoyed the discipline of scholarship and was happiest when absorbed in some task. Teachers praised Lucy when I talked with them during conferences, but my intuition probed for the meanings behind their words. I could tell that they were trying to say that Lucy was a little too self-assured. One teacher even said, "She can be a little controlling. Perhaps she needs to relax and just be a child. A little failure or slipup once in a while can be good for her character." Alarmed, I insisted that the teachers make Lucy apologize if she overstepped her boundaries. Almost reluctantly, they had to admit that she voiced regret and admitted her own mistakes so adroitly that she made the injured party feel envious at her facility with language. Ever vigilant, I watched for signs that Lucy might be applying too much pressure on herself. I worried that she might have the genetic predisposition of Jane. I should not have worried. For all her perfectionism, Lucy sailed through life with the stability of a tank.

I understood how teachers received a measure of validation by guiding their students, so I knew how disconcerting they must feel when it seemed that Lucy was two steps ahead of them at all times. I had empathy with them because as a mother, I envisioned times when Lucy would come to me for guidance, but to my dismay, that rarely happened. Minor mishaps and mistakes bothered her about as much as a breeze ruffling her hair. If she encountered difficulties, she wrote a checklist of her problems on the left-hand column with solutions on the right-hand side of the page before she made a decision.

A vivacious child, she insisted on riding the bus home from school so she could socialize with friends. Bounding into the house, she described her daily activities, voiced her opinions about friends, and then went to her room to do homework before coming into the kitchen for a snack. Even her book satchel was orderly as she took out books and supplies to do homework, carefully arranging everything back when she finished. In all her years of schooling, she never turned in a late assignment or had an overdue library book.

When she played, she strove for self-improvement. I'd watch her from the kitchen window as she dribbled the ball and aimed for the basketball net and ponder how any child could be so irritatingly mature. Seeing me, she'd wave and shout, "Mom, I'm practicing to make the team!" An affectionate child, she'd hug me at bedtime as I read stories to her. I wanted her to need me in a more primal way and was ashamed to admit that I enjoyed her minor illnesses when I could nurture her with medicine and attention. How I wanted to be needed instead of feeling like a shiny, unused tool hanging on the wall.

In my forties, I considered returning to work, but decided to spend time assisting my parents and in-laws. Agnes moved in with us after her husband died and her rheumatoid arthritis worsened. She was a God-fearing and kind mother-in-law who treated me as her own daughter. I admired her tenacity to continue crocheting despite the pain in her knobby hands and wrists. However, she persistently filled ever molecule of air with sound waves that emanated from her voice. Only afternoon naps interrupted her incessant chatter. Arvin now spent long hours at his job as a high school principal and Lucy was busy with friends and school activities which meant that I received the onslaught of her verbal tsunamis. I was the gracious hostess who encouraged relatives and friends to visit often so they could assume the responsibility of bantering with her.

Just for a change of venue, I looked forward to driving Agnes into Tuscaloosa for visits to the doctor. After the appointment, she was always content to sit in the car while I took an inordinate amount of time walking along grocery aisles to examine every item in mute appreciation. Like a human cash register, I memorized the prices of everything in the store. In addition, we also looked forward to our visits to the weekly Ladies Benevolent meetings and Bible studies at my parents' church. Car rides provided a much-needed reprieve as I tried to tune out Agnes' incessant prattling while she spewed words like exhaust fumes from a car muffler.

Through strenuous effort, I had retained a relatively slim figure by cutting down on food and taking long daily walks, but now that Agnes was living with us, I had to wait until late in the afternoon when Arvin arrived home before I could exercise. Since that time was devoted to supper and family, I eventually quit exercising and also began snacking more to sublimate my frustration at being tethered to the house all the time.

My tight clothing reflected the accuracy of the increasing numbers on the bathroom scales. I did not think anything was out of the ordinary when I had a physical checkup; but the doctor was concerned about my listlessness and weight gain, so he conducted extra tests. Imagine my shock and dismay when he informed me that I was already two months pregnant at the age of forty-two. Speechless and aghast with worry, I kept my composure until I returned home. How in the world was I supposed to find the strength to tend to an infant, maintain a house, and take care of my family when I was as swollen as a blimp with the energy of a slug?

I waited until bedtime to inform Arvin. "Oh, Arvin, I am so sorry. I don't know who this could have happened. And imagine a house full of nosy relatives coming every day to tend to Agnes and me." Arvin, nonplussed as ever, assured me that everything would be fine. The last thing he wanted was to come home to a house full of well-meaning but intrusive family members that he would have to entertain. He arranged for additional rooms to be added to the house and hired live-in help before the news got around that I was expecting.

Neighbors and relatives were upset when they found out that we had hired help. Not only were they resentful that we could afford a maid, but they also expressed frustration that we did not ask them for help. We soothed ruffled feathers by explaining that Agnes and my family had chipped in for the maid. We emphasized that because of my age, I would need a long period of rest before I would feel up to resuming the demands of hosting social visits.

That is how Miriam came to live with us as a nursemaid. She was an attractive woman with warm mahogany colored skin whose smooth complexion belied the fact that she was in her fifties. Good-natured and hard-working, she rarely divulged any personal information as she cooked, cleaned, and tended to our needs. Miriam lent a receptive ear when Agnes wanted to talk. "I like Miriam," whispered Agnes one day with a smile, her crocheting needles clicking as she looped them through the blue yarn of a baby blanket.

Jeroboam was born in early winter on a rainy Wednesday afternoon. The delivery had been so excruciating that I had surgery performed afterwards to ensure that my childbearing years were over for good. I was not about to be like Sarah in the Bible who gave birth at a ripe old age.

"Jerry," as we nicknamed our son, developed into a sturdy, ginger-haired boy with bright blue eyes that focused on everything around him. From infancy, he was as even-tempered as his older sister whom he adored. I was thankful that Lucy doted on her baby brother, showing him off to her friends and including him in her activities. I underwent back surgery when Jerry was two years, and the months of rest and therapy that I required made me count on Lucy and Miriam more than ever to babysit.

Arvin was proud of both children and spent as much time with them as his work schedule allowed. Between Arvin, Miriam, Agnes, and me, the adults of our household outnumbered the kids. It was not until Jerry grew older that he found out what an anomaly this was. With so many grownups in the house, he grew up with plenty of attention and was content to play quietly in the house or outside if the weather allowed. As I gained stamina, I spent hours pushing him back and forth in the swing while he pretended to be a plane high up in the clouds. Sometimes, he would run around the yard flapping his outstretched arms, yelling, "Mama, I'm a bird!" and running so fast that it almost seemed as though he could take flight. How Jerry made us laugh with his antics!

We wanted to keep our children under our wings as long as possible, but childhood is fleeting. Too soon, Jerry was in school and Lucy was living at college to return home on weekends and summer vacations. We reluctantly adjusted to her absence as we stayed busy attending Jerry's school events and having his friends over so they could play in the yard and ride bikes up and down the long driveway of our house.

We lived frugally so we could afford Miriam who was an indispensable part of the family. We laughed that she was the warden of the inmates at our house. Miriam was sandwiched in age between Agnes and me but was more robust than either of us. After a busy week of housework and nursing, she drove her car to her sister's house on weekends, arriving back at our house on Sunday evenings in time to watch her favorite western TV show in her bedroom.

Our lives hummed by as pleasantly as a Sunday concert in the park with few crescendos or discordant notes. Lucy graduated with a nursing degree and married a pharmacist. They secured jobs in Elysium and moved in with Mother and Father. In fervent gratitude, Father put down his tools when my son-in-law hired professionals to renovate the old house, turning it into a lovely estate. Lucy's children filled up the second-floor bedrooms and attic space that Miss Lydia, Bart, and Jane vacated.

As I finish this narrative, it is 1995 and I am in my fifties. My parents continue to work at the church as volunteers, Father studies and holds counsel in his office, and Mother works with the Ladies Benevolent group. Although Zeke has taken over as pastor of the church, he listens as rapturously as the rest of the congregation when Father feels called upon to preach. Jerry joined the congregation when he graduated as a psychologist from the university and took over Zeke's duties as a professional counselor.

Miss Lydia passed on about ten years earlier, leaving behind a legacy of watercolors which are hung throughout the house as a reminder of her love of birds. Bart and Vermetta married and moved into Vermetta's house where they enjoy sitting in their backyard, listening to the warbling of songbirds that perch in trees and birdhouses and watching them eat from the bird feeders. Birds flick their wings to shoot tiny sprays of water in the bird bath that Vermetta won so many years earlier. When I visit, I observe intricately woven nests containing hungry hatchlings waiting for their mother and father to deliver food. The parents remind me of Mother and Father's devotion to raising Jane and myself. I speculate that the strands of hair that I see embedded in the nests might be some that I have shed. It is a reminder that I contribute to life long after I have departed. As I listen to the birds, I appreciate their abilities to communicate the songs of life so beautifully. Why can't people appreciate life as much as birds?

Life has ironic twists. Jane moved to Tuscaloosa where she married a widower, Benjamin Prendolph, Sr., a professor of economics at the university. In an odd circuitous routing of fate, he is the father of my old college friend, Ben, Jr., the renowned journalist and world traveler. Ben and his family moved to Tuscaloosa a few years ago where he is a journalism professor. At Jane's wedding ceremony, my son met Ben's daughter, Maria, and they are planning an August wedding. Ben and I laugh at all the confusing family ties and are still trying to figure out how we are related.

Miriam retired a few years ago to live with her sister in Tuscaloosa. I share meals with them whenever I have business in town. Recently, they joined us at Mother and Father's house for a family reunion to prepare for the upcoming nuptials. The family was visiting in the living room when Jane suddenly stood up and exclaimed: "Well, since both sides of our blended family are here, I have an announcement. Father! Remember when you taught me how to drive the blue Ford Fairlane when I was five years old under a purple sky?"

Father looked alarmed, swallowing hard and staring intently at her. Jane's moods had been so stable for years that we dreaded the prospect of illness striking again. Everyone in the room paused to absorb what Jane had just said. Sensing everyone's incredulity, Jane spoke heatedly, "You don't believe me! Well, I'll prove that I am speaking the truth! Follow me, everyone."

We all got up reluctantly; the older ones of us bracing our hands on the armrests to pull us up to a vertical position and followed Jane into the back yard. She had arranged seats for all of us under an arbor. We all sat down in disconcerting silence. "Look up everyone. What color is the sky?" Under beautiful April skies, we looked up and saw that the top of the arbor contained a crisscrossing pattern of purple wisteria which tinted the sky a lovely violent hue. Chiding us, Jane said, "I told you the sky was purple. When Frances and I were children, we played under this arbor." Then she laughed, "I'm not crazy, you know!" We all laughed in relief and burst into applause.

"Wow, it really is beautiful," Maria said in amazement as Jerry squeezed her hand.

"Now for the blue Ford Fairlane." Jane walked into the trees surrounding the arbor and came back rolling an antique child's car that she had refinished back to its original blue sheen. "I bet you had forgotten this, Father. Remember you taught me to drive when I was five." Everyone stared at the antique car that had been restored so lovingly to its original state.

"Where in the world did you find this car, Jane?" asked Father. "I'd completely forgotten about it" Pausing, he looked as if deep in thought. I imagined she was conjuring up memories of world long forgotten.

"Now I remember," he said in wonder, as if turning the pages of a book that revealed the secret to a mystery. "I played traffic cop and taught you to steer the cart with your little hands. We played a game where I made you stop at intersections and use your hands to signal right or left turns." He smiled and added: "I thought it would help you later on in life when you started to drive. It's funny, but I remember thinking that I wanted you two girls to stay little and never go driving off, as I showed you how to steer safely." Father wiped his glistening eyes with the handkerchief that he folded in his hands.

Jane said, "Thank you for teaching us how to drive. I found the car when I was exploring the barn one day, looking at my old veterinarian's office where it was hidden in a corner. I fixed it up and hope the grandkids enjoy it. And now I have something else to show all of you. When I had my breakdown, I made a casket out of wood." Then, removing a tablecloth, Jane revealed the casket which she had reassembled and finished in a bright shade of yellow. Inside the casket, she had planted petunias in shades of purple and yellow. "Ta da! I turned the casket into a planter! What could be more symbolic of my life? I took something tragic and turned it into a thing of beauty."

We laughed at Jane's startling confession as we stared at the flowers waving in the evening breeze, inhaling the perfume of the evening while the sky darkened to purple above us. Someone lit citronella lamps to ward off mosquitos and we heard the distant singing of night birds as we talked.

My thoughts wandered to all the people in my life who are no longer with us. I closed my eyes and offered silent thanks for Dr.

Paulson as I remembered how he prayed with us on that anxious day in the darkness of his office. When I opened my eyes, my tears make a starburst pattern in the illuminated lamps which nourished my soul with hope.

I looked at the house where I had spent my formative years. It had been restored to its original state and I thought about the enigma that had puzzled me for so long. If you fortify an old house with all new wood to replace the old, is it still the same house? It has taken me a lifetime to figure out that I am like the house. Someone constructed me out of the elements; and one day, my physical body will be gone. My spiritual essence will replace my structural frame so that what is missing is replaced with something that will always exist. And then I will reunite with the carpenter who formed me to live in a mansion that I will never have to repair. Hope endures because God's love is the only force that is eternally constant.

NORMA

by Harold Raley

Reeling from hunger and exhaustion, Norma Trahan, 50, finally made it back to her tent attached like a pimple to the back of an abandoned drug store that still announced in faded lettering the miraculous effects of Doan's Little Liver Pills. The left front wheel of her junk-filled grocery cart had jammed a few blocks back, making it twice as hard to push. Just one more small problem in her list of larger disasters. When you're down, everything stomps on you, she thought. Not that she wasted a lot of time complaining about it. She was too busy trying to stay alive to question why the world seemed stacked against her.

She anchored the cart's right wheels in a deep crack between the concrete and the wall, pulled back the tent's entry flaps and collapsed on her bed of frayed blankets and water-stained cushions piled atop newspapers and black plastic bags. The night was chilly, but Blackie had warmed a spot as he waited hopefully for her return with a morsel for him. Lately her run of bad luck forced him out to prowl the night for his own food despite many cat years lived and few left. Their common misery bonded them, but now their lives overlapped only briefly.

Today—a Thursday unless she had lost count—had been another dry run. On her side of town church kitchens that sometimes fed her would be locked until late Saturday or early Sunday morning. The restaurant owner two blocks over drove her off his property again with angry threats, and there were no meat scraps, stale bread, vegetable residues or rotting fruit in the smaller grocery's two garbage bins. At the larger market she found shiny locks the new management had installed on the disposals. Today she and Blackie would probably go hungry again. In recent weeks they had fasted more often than an ascetic monk, and not with spiritual intent.

By reasonable human measures, she was too beaten down to get her hopes up for anything better. Maybe I should just give up and die, she thought in a recurring combination of self-pity and anger, maybe just end it myself. My life is an insult to God—if there is a God. But something within, something beyond her understanding, rebelled against the idea of taking her own life, and she scolded herself for the umpteenth time for letting the notion slip back into her thoughts. She had no illusions about herself. Her life was crap, and no one would miss her or give her passing a second thought, probably not even old Blackie. But although she had little will or reason left to fight for her life, a remnant of humanity balked at snuffing out its spark. I did not give myself life, she said aloud to Blackie, and I have no right to take it. I fought a tougher fight in prison all those years ago, she explained to the old cat. But I was younger then and thought I might still make something of my life. Now all that's gone by the board. So here I am, too stubborn to die and too screwed up to live.

Blackie had heard it all many times before, and since she had brought him nothing to eat, he yawned, stretched, and padded out silently for his nightly prowl.

Not that her circular argument settled the dilemma. It was an old stalemate that always ended back where it started. Anyway, tonight she was too tired to rehash it. A few seconds later she was asleep, and having exhausted her possibilities, dreamed the impossible.

*****

Now it was hard for her to remember happier days, but there was a time long ago when Norma Wainwright's spirit was exuberant and her future shiny with love and hope. She was nineteen and Wilson Trahan twenty-one when they met and fell in love. She was a pert, redheaded waitress and occasional cook in a Columbus, Indiana café and Wilson worked as a mechanic for the local Ford agency. But Wilson's overriding passion was modifying engines and competing in regional drag racing. And he was good at both. Two years after high school racing was bringing in more money than his regular job. They met at a party after his latest win at the county fairgrounds. Wilson was tall, tan, and handsome, and girls flocked around him in flirtatious enthusiasm, hoping to be his pick. But from the moment they met he had eyes only for pretty Norma. They soon paired off and became a chief topic of conversation. Engagement and wedding plans soon followed.

Her parents, Carl and Darla Wainwright, liked Wilson but were not thrilled with his racing ambitions. He was working his way up to regional competition and beyond. The prize money was enticing, they admitted, but car racing was a dangerous business. Better a steady job as a mechanic, they told Norma, than a husband risking life and limb on the racing circuit.

Norma understood their misgivings, but she was too much in love with Wilson to worry about what might happen. Okay, so life is risky, she said without real concern, but you have to take your chances.

They married in June of 1983 and a year later in 1984 their son Travis was born, and little Susie arrived in July of 1985. That fall they moved from their crowded apartment near her parents to a three-bedroom home five miles west of Columbus to give Wilson room for his shop and three cars. By that time Norma's homemaking instincts were replacing her girlish idealism, and she was beginning to share some of her parents' worries about Wilson's passion for racing. He had a reputation for risky maneuvers, anything it took to win. Her worries grew when Wilson announced that he was quitting his job at Ford to concentrate full-time on racing. Norma backed him as the devoted wife she was, but privately she had forebodings.

At first, Norma went to all his races, but after the move it was not always possible to leave the children with her parents or Wilson's married sister Edith McDougal, especially if it meant staying overnight. Wilson's father Spencer Trahan, at loose ends since his wife's death, was not an option.

One day in October Wilson came in waving a letter informing him he had been officially accepted to race at the Hickory Motor Speedway down in North Carolina.

"Honey, it's my big break!" he yelled, whirling her around the room in his excitement. "This letter is what I've been hoping for! And I'm here to tell you, honey, I'm gonna win that sucker!"

"Is it a long way down there? How long will you be gone? You know I can't take Travis and Susie that far."

"I know, honey, and I'm real sorry we can't all go. But it's only a couple hundred miles. I'll be back in three or four days—and with a pot full of money for us!"

"I hope so, but I'll settle for just having you back safe and sound."

Norma had to settle for a lot less. A car length behind the veteran leader guarding the inside lane with a half mile to go, Wilson made a daring swing outside to pass him. His engine could have done it, experts said, but the angle was too sharp and his momentum too great. His car flipped, hit the wall, and burst into flames. The emergency crew got there too late. Wilson died instantly from his injuries, his face so disfigured that his casket was buried unopened, and Norma and the children were unable to tell him goodbye. A lot of her was buried with him.

No one could replace Wilson. The men she met were substitutes who served only to remind Norma how much she missed him. They filled her time, but Wilson still ruled her life. Her parents doted on the children with the best of intentions, but with unintended results. At their persistent offers after Wilson had been gone for several months, she began leaving them overnight, "so you can reconnect with friends your age," Darla told her, hoping she would eventually find someone else. Norma went out, drank, and tried to forget, then drank more as the memories lingered and her alcoholic craving grew. Overnight became several nights.

Wilson's cousin Ed Martin was the chief architect of her downward spiral. Tall like Wilson and physically similar but without his drive and ambition, he stuck around after other men rotated in and out of her life. She accepted him not because she loved him but because he reminded her of Wilson. And Ed resented the difference.

The worst part of living was being sober, and since alcohol was not enough to deaden her pain, Ed introduced her to stronger stuff: weed first, then cocaine, and toward the end of their run heroin and meth. They quickly burned their way through Norma's bank account. After four delinquent months, the bank repossessed her house. She moved the children permanently in with her parents and mostly stayed there herself until she could no longer stand their hysterical complaining. She cut loose completely from family and drifted south with Ed. They ended up broke on the Nashville streets. Because she had not been on the hard stuff very long and her looks were not shot completely, Ed ordered her to prostitute herself for money and handouts for them to live on while he scrounged up what he could and dealt drugs. She refused with a remnant of dignity, and Ed beat her. She loved her children with all her heart, but her will and body belonged to her addictions. She was as helpless as a dove caught in an eagle's talons.

That phase of her life ended a few months later when Ed stabbed a man to death over a soured cocaine deal. Norma witnessed the murder and testified truthfully at his trial—and received Ed's curses for her effort as they dragged him away. But her honesty did not help in her own trial. She was tried as an accomplice in the homicide. Ed got life and she, twenty years, both sentences without possibility of parole. In that era many states, Tennessee among them, were coming down hard on drug dealers and users. She was locked up in the Nashville Prison for Women.

For a while after lockup, she tried to feed her several addictions, but without any way to get money or do significant favors behind bars, it was a lost cause. Prettier women were available to offer sex, and her parents had cut off all aid and communication after informing her that they would raise Travis and Susie but that she was to have no more contact with them or her children. Shut off without other close friends and relatives, she had two options: to kill herself if she could or quit drugs cold turkey and hope to resume her life in the far future. With an uptick of will she took the turkey route, and the addictions took their revenge: hour after hour, day after day, week after week, her hellish pains and cravings continued, accompanied by night sweats and spasmodic muscle contractions. Then, slowly the withdrawal torture began to subside. There came a pain-free moment, then another as the peaceful intervals grew and the cravings lessened. She would never recover completely from the drug damage, but finally she believed she could make it. At least I never got hooked on cigarettes, she joked later to a cellmate.

Because of her experience as a cook and waitress she was assigned to work in the prison food facility. There she would remain as the years dragged on. Sobriety eased her physical distress but sharpened painful memories. Daily she thought of Wilson and tried to imagine Travis and Susie as teenagers, then adults, and finally married maybe with children of their own. Letters to her parents returned unopened.

She was bewildered the day she walked out of prison in 2009. Despite what logic told her, she had let herself hope that the family might be here to meet her. They weren't. She remembered what the world once was but could not understand what it had become: strange styles, bizarre automobiles, news and shows she couldn't relate to. She had lived in slow motion for twenty years; now everything zipped by impossibly fast around, over, and beyond her. The constant bombardment of noise was unnerving. Prison was terrible, but in some ways the outside world was nearly as bad. She could not adjust and recover her balance. There were days when she almost wished she could return to the comparative security of prison steel and concrete. At least there everything was decided for her and she knew what to expect.

Norma returned to Columbus and spent most of the small fund she had saved over the years trying to locate her parents, children, and relatives of either family. Spencer Trahan had disappeared with a trace. One man thought he had moved to Florida. Edith had vanished. She learned that her mother had died nearly fifteen years earlier and her father Carl was now a mindless shell of himself in the memory section of an assisted-living center. He stared blankly at Mary when she asked him about her children.

"Who . . . is she?" he asked the nurse.

"She's your daughter Norma, Mr. Wainwright. She's asking about her children, your grandchildren. Their names are Travis and Susie, I believe. Isn't that right, Ms. Trahan?"

"Yes, ma'am, Travis and Susie. They would be twenty-four and twenty-three now."

"Tell her to . . . leave," he said angrily. "I . . . don't know her or the people she's . . . talking about. Leave me . . . alone!"

A neighbor of the Wainwrights told her she thought Darla's sister and brother-in-law had taken Travis and Susie to Muncie after Darla's death but could give her no more information. Norma knew she had an aunt but had never met her and could not remember her name if Darla ever mentioned it. The sisters had parted ways after a bitter dispute. It seemed to be a pattern with Darla. Norma walked the hundred miles to Muncie, but it was a sizable town, and her search and her money both ended in frustration. But on the outside chance that eventually she might run into Travis and Susie and having no better place, she stayed on in Muncie. At first, she tried to find work, but jobs were scarce in a declining economy. She had no references, and when prospective employers found out she was a convict, they wanted nothing to do with her. After multiple humiliations, she decided the uncaring street was less painful than unforgiving humans.

So, at fifty, her life had spiraled down to this: destitute, hungry, and asleep on a pile of trash she called a bed, Norma dreamed an impossible dream.

*****

Acting on directions revealed to her in the strange dream, the next morning Norma suspended her normal circuit around town, drank as much water as she could from a plastic bottle, removed the glob of tar that had locked the left front wheel of her grocery cart, and rolled it south toward a house outside the city limits near the White River. She had never been down that way, but the dream was so vivid that she remembered exact details and was sure she could find it.

She did, but nothing else. The house she saw in the dream—a farmhouse in its happier age—was now a deserted wreck of rotting boards, broken windows, and missing shingles. Would this be a better place for me than my place in town, she asked herself, but quickly rejected the idea. It was even farther from possible food sources than the derelict pharmacy. Besides, she was terrified of snakes and spiders, and being so close to the river, this old house probably has plenty of both, she decided. Dejected now that the fleeting euphoria of the dream had passed, she rested on a rickety bench under an elm tree at the edge of the yard and considered her next move. She hated to beg openly in the streets, but there seemed to be no other option. After a while, she sighed, forced her stiff knees and tired legs into movement and started pushing the cart back toward Muncie.

That's when she noticed the cellar door all but invisible under weeds and shrubbery. She tugged and pulled until it yielded, and stale, moldy air rushed out to engulf her. Eager but fearful of snakes and spiders, she descended the rotting wooden steps but found nothing except a few ancient newspapers from the fifties.

She felt like cursing in frustration but what good would it do? What good would anything do for her? She climbed the steps and again started pushing the cart back to town.

But on second thought, since she had gone into the basement, why not check out the attic to make doubly sure she had not overlooked anything? For she would not come this way again. She wheeled the cart back to the bench and went back inside, careful not to trip on broken porch planks. The ceiling around the fireplace looked solid enough, but the wall ladder to the attic was in the kitchen ten yards and several broken ceiling boards away. The last thing I need is to fall through the attic and break a leg or arm. Nobody would ever find me here. Her arms quivered in exhaustion as she pulled herself up and onto the attic floor, thankful that it did not collapse under her weight.

More disappointment. The attic was empty except for an odd wooden housing covering the junction of the kitchen stove flue and the chimney. Odd, she thought idly. Why a wooden housing in the first place with the risk of fire it posed? It seemed totally unnecessary. Hey, she thought suddenly, didn't I see the flue junction down in the kitchen? She went back to the ladder and looked. Sure enough, the flue was connected near ceiling level in the kitchen. Now her excitement was building. She pulled on the exposed boards; several came loose, and she peered inside.

And there they were: the dark, shapeless things she had seen or sensed in her otherwise vividly clear dream. Now in the dim light she saw that they were two huge, bulging leather suitcases. Already cracked from age, the fragile leather tore even more as she tried to open them. Then through the larger cracks she saw the money. Bundles of money, a world of money, a fortune, thousands, maybe tens of thousands. Am I still dreaming? She rubbed her eyes to make sure she was awake. "My God," she said in a whisper, "My God, My God! Am I dreaming? Is this real? But I can feel it! I am rich! I can eat again! I can live again! God in heaven! I'm rich! I'm rich! My God, I'm rich!"

Because of their weight and her famished condition, she had no choice but to drop both suitcases to the lower floor and hope they wouldn't burst. She was anxious to leave the place. It looked like no one had been there in years, but now that she had found the money, she was afraid its owner—or owners—might even now be on the way here to retrieve it. The old leather cases survived the drop, and as quickly as she could climb down, she wheeled the cart over by the door and muscled them into it with a strength born of equal parts of elation and fear.

But Norma had been kicked around too much to let the sudden rush of joy push her off the deep end. Reality came back with a vengeance to temper her euphoria. Was she really rich after all? she asked herself as she hurried as quickly as she could back into Muncie. Was the money genuine or counterfeit? She stopped and peered again at the money to assure herself that it was real and not a lingering figment of her dream. The money was real to her touch. But who left it there and who might come back at any moment to reclaim it? And what about all the fingerprints I left all around that old house? Damn! Maybe I should go back and set it on fire. That would destroy the prints. But I don't even have a match on me. And if I burned it, people would come running and catch me. No, I can't do that. Nothing hasty or drastic. I've got to think this thing through carefully. And there were other major problems: there was no way she could spend any of the money even if it turned out to be legal. All she had seen were hundred-dollar bills. I might be able to pass smaller denominations, but who would accept hundreds—real or phony—from somebody like me? The first time I tried to pass one, the police would pounce on me like Blackie on a rat. And where will I keep it while I figure things out? And who can I trust to tell me how to deal with it? She asked these and a long list of other questions as she rolled the cart and rag-draped suitcases back into town. The cart was top heavy with the load, and she had to be careful not to let it tip over and reveal the precious cargo she was pushing. One false move on my part and the money's gone, she kept reminding herself over and over. And nobody can help me. Can't trust anybody. Can't run the risk. By the time she got back to town, she no longer owned the money. The money owned her.

But before anything else, she told herself, I have to find food right away or I may faint right here in the street. Something, anything, even if I have to break down and steal something. If I fall out here in the street, then the money will be gone for sure. She thought of a poem her class had read back in high school, something about an old sailor stranded way out on the ocean with water everywhere but not a drop to drink. She couldn't remember the exact words, but she was in a similar fix: money in gobs but not a penny to spend. She couldn't remember whether or not the old sailor had survived, but she understood how he must have felt.

For the first time in days, she got lucky on the way back home. Glory be, maybe my luck really is changing, she thought as she seized a half loaf of unspoiled bread from one of the small grocery garbage bins, and next to it a broken jar of mayonnaise. Maybe Blackie won't eat it, but it will keep me going until I can figure all this out. And if I can, then Blackie and me will have us a feast! She wolfed down a slice, the most delicious bread she had ever tasted, then—first checking for glass shards—another dipped in the mayonnaise, and another. The old saying was true: hunger makes any bread delicious. Strength started returning to her quivering limbs. Step one done, she said, holding up a clinched fist in triumph. Praise God, I'm alive! I made it! Now to figure out the rest.

*****

Seven hundred fifty thousand dollars and still counting. But Norma was not sure it was accurate, and there was much more in the other old suitcase. Between slices of bread and the problems facing her that Friday, she could not keep her mind on the counting. It was tons of money, and correct or not, more than she could wrap her mind around. But was it real money? It looked genuine, but was it? So far, she had seen only hundreds, but there were other stacks in the smaller suitcase. She was hoping for at least a few fifties, even better some twenties. Those I can figure out how to handle, but I'm afraid of the hundreds. I'll have to rack my brain to find some way to spend some of it. But what if it turns out to be counterfeit? It looks real and the series numbers I've checked are only twelve or fifteen years old, not like it's been here forty or fifty years. But whose money is it? Or was? Is it from a robbery? Probably is. But who would just walk off and leave it? Maybe somebody died or was killed or locked up and never had a chance to come back for it. Probably it is money from a robbery. Must be. And if it is, where does that put me? Probably right back in prison. People like me are not supposed to have this kind of money. But I'm sure as hell not going to turn it over to the police. They'd either arrest me on the suspicion that I stole it or keep it all for themselves—or both. I found the money and I'm going to keep it. And it's up to me to figure out what to do with it. One thing's for sure, I can't tell anybody, can't trust anybody. It's all up to me. For once in my life, I have to do some smart thinking. If I don't, or can't, I'll end up worse off than I am now, if that's possible.

Along with bundles of hundreds, the smaller case contained nearly ten thousand dollars in fifties. A little better than the hundreds, but I need some smaller bills, she thought as she dug toward the bottom, in her haste not bothering to count any longer. And there near the bottom she found a few dozen bundles of twenties and similar bundles of tens. She heaved a sigh of relief and gave thanks to whichever Cosmic power deserved her gratitude. Maybe I can do it. Even if it's phony, they're less likely to spot a ten or a twenty than a fifty, much less a hundred. Anyway, hunger had a greater force than legality. Norma was not a thief by nature, but experience had taught her that legal stuff is for people who can afford it.

The big problem—at least the first big problem—was she looked too disreputable to pass money of any kind. You have to look a little prosperous to spend money, she thought, shaking her head at the irony of her situation. I've got to dress up a little at least so people won't think I'm too poor to have any cash on me. But how and where do I start? The longer this money stays in the tent, the greater the risk of it being discovered. I've got to hide it and quick. And that means right off the bat that I've got to clean up, find me a passable dress, and fix my hair if that's still possible. I wonder if it has any red left. Probably all gray by now. It's not what you are that counts; it's what you appear to be, at least at first. So, let me see, let me think. But be careful, careful, old girl. You've got one chance, stay calm, think clearly. It's all or nothing, so don't blow it.

She stuffed each suitcase in a plastic and hid them under the pile of rags and newspapers, smoothing the bulges as best she could and adding other rags and plastics from the cart to help disguise it. Okay, I guess, she assessed her work, but it can't stay here like this for long. Too risky. But then who would ever think of robbing a bag lady? No telling who. if only they knew. But for right now this is the safest place I can think of under the circumstances.

Blackie dropped in to watch her pile on the rags and plastics, maybe asking himself in cat reasoning what in the world his strange companion was up to this time. I'm not forgetting you, old pal, Norma said to him. All this is for you too. Blackie didn't react. He had been lied to before and didn't take many things seriously. The only stuff that impressed him was what he could eat.

Then Norma went out again, looking back nervously several times, thinking that if Blackie were a dog, he would guard her things. Cats don't really give a damn about people or their property, she thought. Why if thieves came in, he'd just sit there licking his paws while they made off with all her money. But he is what he is, and you can't expect him to be what he wasn't made to be. Anyway, I need to get myself ready as soon as I can.

Even though all the churches were closed on Friday, she remembered that one of them, she didn't recall or care which one for that matter, sponsored a resale charity store stocked with donated clothing and household items. This late in the day all the workers probably would be gone, and if her luck held on two other fronts—no cruising police patrol and after-hour donations piled in the collection shed—she might, just might, find herself a passable dress, and possibly a decent pair of shoes. And who knows, maybe even a hairbrush to go along with a comb she kept in the tent.

But it was not to be. Several cars were still in the parking lot, and through the windows Norma could see church volunteers still busily restocking for Saturday. She watched for a bit before turning back in disappointment. The merchandise was cheap but not free. She had been turned away before, but now that she was beginning to think she was rich in her own right was in no mood to beg for the things she needed to claim her fortune.

On the way back to her tent, she saw a woman bring out two bulging plastic bags and set them on her porch. Clothes she wondered. She was about Norma's size. She waited; the woman went inside and came out again with a box before going back in the house. Then Norma approached cautiously to look. Both bags and the box had a "Goodwill" label. Norma was excited; it is clothes, and the box may contain shoes. Maybe, just maybe, this will work out. She knocked on the door.

"Yes?" the woman cracked the door and asked.

"Ma'am, I happened to see you set those bags and the box on your porch, and I notice they're labeled Goodwill."

"So, you came on our property and read them?"

"Well, yes, ma'am, I did. You see, I need some things myself and I thought maybe you could—"

"The answer is no, and you'd better get off our property before I call the police. Those are donations for poor people, not for the likes of you," the woman said, her voice rising in anger.

"But, ma'am, I'm a poor person too. Wouldn't I qualify?"

"You're poor because you choose to be. I've seen you around here before, rolling that trashy grocery cart around full of junk. I'm sure you took it without permission. I'm trying to help honest people down on their luck temporarily, not people who choose to live on the street and turn the city into a garbage dump."

"Marge, what's going on out there? Who're you talking to?" a male voice called out.

"Nothing and nobody that concerns you, Bob. You stay out of this. I'll take care of it."

The man appeared anyway and stepped out on the porch, holding the newspaper sports section. The woman glared at him.

"What's the problem here?"

"I told you, Bob, nothing for you to bother with. But if you must know, this woman came by to beg, and I told her to leave, or I'd call the police."

"What are you looking for, lady?" he asked Norma.

"Bob, I told you to stay out of this. I'll—"

"I know what you told me, Marge, but she doesn't look like a threat to me, and it won't cost us anything to listen to her."

Norma looked from one to the another, uncertain of what to do.

"Tell me, what were you looking for?" the man repeated.

"I don't mean to bother you folks. It's just that I need to dress as best I can, and I don't have any decent clothes. And I saw this lady set these things on the porch and thought maybe—"

"What is it you have to dress up for, if I may ask you?"

"I need to go to some stores. But I can't go like this."

"Probably to steal something . . ." the woman said under her breath, but loud enough for Norma to hear.

"No, ma'am," Norma said with a hint of pride in her voice. "I am what you see, but I don't steal things."

"If you have money to buy things in stores, why are you living in the street?" he asked.

"Well, it's a long story, sir, that I'm sure you folks don't want to hear. Hey, listen, I'm sorry I bothered you. So, I'll just be on my way."

"I didn't ask you to leave. I just wanted to know a couple of things."

"Bob, don't—"

"Cool it, Marge. I see no reason why you can't denote one of those old dresses of yours to this woman. It doesn't sound to me like she's trying to scam anybody."

"But you don't know that for a fact."

"No, I don't, and that's why there's always a risk involved in trying to help somebody, isn't there? But if they abuse the favor, it really is charged to their account, isn't it? So, lady, I'll open one of bags and you pick out a dress."

"But, Bob, as . . . as dirty as her hands are, she'll soil the others."

"Well, so what? Anybody that buys used clothing ought to have sense enough to wash it before they wear it. Wouldn't you say? Come on over here, lady, and take your pick before I get tired of all this and toss the whole mess in the trash bin."

No mention was made of shoes, and Norma didn't ask. She chose a gray dress that seemed nice enough to serve her purpose. Then she left quickly before sullen Marge had a chance to unload on her husband and drop more insults on her. The dress is the main thing I need, she thought. The rest I can work out if only I can cash one of the tens at the grocery self-checkout. Tomorrow's the big test. If the bill clears, I'm home free. And if not? She chose not to think about it. She had too many other things to take care of before morning.

Late in the day she took an old washcloth and went over to a carwash that had a faucet with ringers for cleaning car rags.

Sometimes, management or customers left a soap bar next to the ringers. A new, super wash two blocks away had taken away nearly all the customers, leaving the old facility idle except at peak hours. It would probably close before long as other businesses had done around the neighborhood. The lone teenager at the far end of the vacuum line was too absorbed in spiffing and caressing his glossy red mustang to notice the grimy old woman washing her face, arms, and neck. I can't do anything with my hair here, she thought, glancing at the boy. I guess I'll straighten out the tangles with the comb if I can, then roll it up and put a rubber band around it. Maybe that'll be enough. The shoes, well, who looks at shoes? I'll just wear these old things I've got on. They're cracked and ugly like everything about me. But then there are a lot of ugly people around and hardly any of them as rich as me—if it turns out that I am rich. She had not taken a full body bath in years, but one of these days . . . she promised herself.

*****

Arms and legs trembling the next morning, Norma walked into the big chain grocery wearing the gray dress, her hair untangled and done up in a ball, and carrying three tens in a change purse. (The smaller market did not have self-service checkout). She could bear the tension no longer. Do or die, she had to try. She grabbed the first pack of franks she came to—meat she and Blackie could share if the transaction went through—and got in line to pay. She watched as the people ahead of her went through the process. When her turn came, she thought she had the hang of it. She worked her way through the steps, pressed the pay option, and selected the cash icon. She inserted a ten; the machine sucked it in; and then as quickly spat it out. Norma was crushed and terrified at the same time. So, the money is counterfeit after all, and now I'll have hell to pay for trying to pass it.

The employee in charge of the checkout noticed her distress and came over to help.

"Having trouble, ma'am?"

"The machine won't take my money."

"Let me see the bill."

Norma was lightheaded with fear as she caught the counter edge for support. The girl spoke, but at first Norma did not understand what she said.

"Huh?" was all she could manage.

"I said the corner of the bill was crinkled. Now try it."

Again, the machine swallowed the bill, and this time dropped some coins and a few seconds later proffered two lovely bills: a five and a one for a total return of $6.47 in change. But what the transaction really meant was that Norma had a chance to live again.

She was rich but still not out of the woods and a long way from being able to deal with department stores and big places like that, much less a bank. In fact, she was not sure she would ever be able to have a checking account. How would she be able to explain the source of so much money? In any case, she would have to use the grocery checkout a few times until she built up enough cash to buy a list of things. The next time she came she would try a twenty, or maybe a fifty. No, not a fifty she said on second thought. Don't get in a hurry and draw attention. You've been poor a long time, old girl, she told herself. Hold it down, keep a lid on it. Be calm. Go slow, deliberate, be patient. You've got time and you've got money. Don't try to rush either one.

She ate one of the frankfurters and walked with a stronger stride to the thrift shop where she paid two dollars for a pair of comfortable tan shoes. Back at the tent, she laid a frank beside the sleeping Blackie. The aroma woke him, and he attacked the frank as though his life depended on it, which practically it did.

"I promised you, Blackie," she reminded him, "and here it is."

Blackie stood, stretched, and circled his tail around her leg. Maybe it was his way of saying thank you, something he did not often have cause to do. He could probably count on his claws the people who had done anything positive for him.

The next day a public notice sign appeared in front of the old building, announcing that the property was to be put to other commercial use, part of a campaign to renovate blighted areas of the city. Norma was already anxious to get her money in a safer place, and the notice increased the urgency. By afternoon she had converted enough tens and twenties to have four hundred dollars in refunded cash, which was all she dared to exchange in a single day. Then it occurred to her that there was no reason to bother with the checkout ploy, at least not with the tens and twenties. They had proved to be legal tender. She would not try the hundreds for the time being. For the moment, the bundled big money was as safe as she could make it, but she was still skittish. On the brighter side, she had more than enough in change to rent a motel room with a real bed and bath, and—if she remembered how—to eat an honest-to-God sit-down dinner. Among other things, she bought a new purse, cosmetics, clothes, and two metal suitcases with wheels and stout locks. By flashlight that night she stuffed them with money and put the old suitcases back under rags and plastics instead of pitching them out in the alley. Better not to leave them out in plain sight, she thought. Just in case. You never know. Best to be as careful as I can.

Not that these precautions were enough to calm all her fears.

Somehow, some way, she had to find a way to deposit the money in a safe place. Sure, she could rent herself a nice place, but landlords are snoopy, and she would have to be gone for hours at a time. But time was short for major changes, and discovery was possible any day. People may have noticed the transformation in me, she fretted, and if they start putting two and two together it could add up in their mind to money. And money attracts thieves and violence—and cops. Damn! It's hard work being rich, Norma thought. But hard and all, rich is a hell of a lot better than poor.

Norma had not driven a car in over twenty-five years and was not sure she ever would again in today's crazy traffic. But she needed a driver's license to establish an identity and residential address if she hoped to get things in order, especially the money. And I'm thinking owning a car would be the only way I can out of Muncie with all this money. I think I still have my birth certificate, social security card, and, I hope, our marriage license, she said to herself. I'll have to dig through my box of old papers to see. I can toss out all the junk, or just walk away from it when I'm finished here. But there's no way I can roll these suitcases to all the places I have to go to get things done. But where can I leave them? I have to have a car, but how can I buy one? Maybe from a private person who won't ask questions if I have cash money. But then what about insurance and all that stuff? Problems, problems, and more still to come. Will I ever get through all this mess without losing my mind and my money, or going to jail?

*****

Weeks passed and a few people realized that the trashy old woman who used to push a grocery cart around with all her junk had disappeared, about the same time they bulldozed the old pharmacy building to make way for a new supermarket, if the rumors were true. "Thank goodness all that ugly mess is gone," the locals agreed, "And good riddance to that old street hag. All that trash was hurting our property values."

*****

"Who's the new family that moved into the new house next to you guys?" a neighbor lady asked her friend as they strolled past the property on their morning walk in a quiet upscale neighborhood in Pensacola, Florida.

"It's not a family unless you call one person a family. She's a single woman named Norma Trahan. Lives there with just an old black cat named Blackie. It's as ugly as sin, but she adores him. You know how people are about their pets. She says she's a widow, I'd say about fifty or so."

"So, a lot older than we are. Right?"

"Ha! You wish." Naw, she's somewhere around our age group, I'm pretty sure."

"So, how does she strike you? Think she'll fit into the neighborhood?"

"Well, she seems nice, a little on the reserved side, but that may be because she's new here. But I can tell you one thing: she has money."

"Money? How do you know?"

"You can just tell, you know, by the way she acts and carries herself. And it's not like she's trying to impress people. In fact, she didn't talk much about herself at all. But I liked her right from the start."

"Maybe she had a rich husband, you think?"

"Maybe, or maybe wealthy parents or grandparents. She strikes me as old money. Not showy and stuck up at all. Just comfortable being who she is if you know what I mean."

"I understand. Well, let's invite her to our bunko group. She sounds like our kind of people. I'm looking forward to meeting her."

*****

By degrees Norma was becoming herself, returning to herself, discovering herself. Her life was not perfect and would never be, but she was learning to accept its limitations and enjoy it as much as she could. After driving her old Chevy to Florida, she hired a detective, Al Samuels, who found out a lot. First, not surprisingly, her father had passed on, and there were no outstanding problems with his estate. Indeed, for all practical purposes there was no estate. The cost of his care and funeral took all that was left. She was relieved. Let him and Mother rest in whatever peace they find on the other side, she asked of God. Despite the hardheartedness they mistook for Christianity, she said, I choose to love them anyway.

Second, the matter of the old farmhouse and its owners where she found her fortune, though intriguing, was destined to remain a mystery. All Samuels could find out was that there was nothing except eccentricity and miserliness associated with its former occupant, a Mr. Isaac Hempstead, who lived like a hermit and had no family that anybody knew about. It was rumored that he had money, but authorities found nothing of value when he died in 2004 at ninety-five. The property now belonged to a distant cousin, but as far as Samuels could find out, the property had been deserted since the old man's death. (She hadn't explained her interest in the property to Samuels.)

But his third discovery was major: he located Travis and Susie, both living in Indianapolis with their respective families. Her heart raced when she saw their pictures. Travis bore a strong resemblance to Wilson and Susie looked like her grandmother Darla. Norma prayed earnestly about what she should do. (As she returned to herself, she also returned to God, not the angry deity she had dreaded as a child, but the Redeemer who had walked step for step with her through the valleys of degradation.)

She decided to write them at the addresses Samuels gave her, then waited, growing more anxious and jittery by the day. She resolved that she would accept as the best course whatever their decision might be, either to respond as she hoped, or to ignore her, if they chose. After all, long ago she had forfeited the right to be a part of their lives.

A week later, on the same day, she got two letters with Indianapolis postmarks. For an agonizingly long time, she left them unopened side by side on the kitchen counter, fearful of what they might say. Finally, when the suspense became unbearable, she opened them with trembling hands.

"Dear Mother," began the first.

"Hi, Mom," began the second.

Her tears flowed in remedial abundance, cleansing decades of hurt and misery. Later, when her eyes were dry, she picked up the phone and dialed the numbers Travis and Susie had listed.

Finally, against all odds, Norma the addict, the convict, the social reject, not only had survived but had come all the way back to life.

NOVEMBER HUNT

by Phyllis Murphy

Clark walked out of his house early that bright November morning with a hunting rifle and a knapsack containing a sack lunch and thermos of iced tea. He locked up and made sure the screen door fit tight against the frame so it wouldn't bang in the breeze. It was a beautiful, cloudless day with temperatures in the cool range, so he wore a jacket. Yellow, red, and orange leaves still clung to trees, although there were fewer each day. Fallen leaves in brown splashes lay scattered on the ground.

He wore his oldest overalls, the light blue denim soft from weekly washings, smooth against his legs. His white shirt was fatigued with wear and frayed at the cuffs. It had once been his church shirt but now was relegated to daily use. Every Saturday afternoon, Rayanna, his middle daughter, hauled his clothes in a wicker basket to her house to wash. He imagined the overalls and shirt spinning in the washing machine, clinging like allies against the violent cycle of rinse and spin. After the clothes were washed, Rayanna hung them on the clothesline if the weather allowed. Clark enjoyed watching them being clipped to the clothesline in a row, hollow and forlorn like soldiers recuperating after battle. He'd chuckle and think "These clothes have been through the ringer, and it show. Like me, I guess."

He measured the day carefully like someone scooping sugar to pour into coffee. Usually, his morning routine consisted of getting up, washing his face, brushing his teeth, shaving, and getting dressed. He ate a bowl of cornflakes and afterwards, sipped coffee. Although he listened to the news, he had a tendency to detour into memories like a hot man seeking shelter on an oppressive day. He knew that dwelling in the past isolated him, as if he were stranded on a road while everyone else drove off in a rush to get somewhere. Even the cars that passed in front of his house signaled that he was viewing life from afar as he sat on the swing, gripping the chain that screeched in metallic rhythm as he rocked back and forth.

He remembered a recent sermon by a young preacher who described heaven as a place of no strife. It made Clark wonder: "That's fine, but how do you cope when each hour is so full of the past?" He thought, "Sometimes preachers don't know what they're talking about."

On this Monday in November, Clark had a destination. For weeks, he carefully planned this day in detail: the supplies to pack and the time he needed to leave. He made sure to wait for his daughters and their families to go to work. When the coast was clear, he would drive his truck to the old farm, walk to the pasture and hunt—something he hadn't done in years. Had his daughters known of his plans, they would have put a stop to his plans. The illicit trip made him feel daring.

It used to be a routine in the autumn when he and the dogs set aside entire days to roam the woods, camping out at night, looking for small game to bring home. The solitary excursion gave him time to think. He loved the autumn sunlight. When he bedded down for the night, he was in awe of the magnitude of stars above him. This trip into the woods would celebrate all the times he had hunted in the past, and he would make the most of this day before putting the rifle in the closet for good and shutting the door on another part of his life.

Clark called for Peppy, his constant companion these days—a spotted dog who'd shown up on his doorstep a few years earlier. Clark opened the truck door, motioning for the dog to ride in the passenger seat. He smiled to think of all the times when hound dogs, bred to track down 'possum, 'coon, or squirrel, accompanied him. Those dogs had been so excited about catching prey that they ran ahead on the trail with their long noses held close to the ground. If they treed a raccoon, they'd yap for hours before Clark shot the animal to take home for food and pelts. Peppy, with his short, upturned ears and compact body was more like a shepherd dog, running around in circles if he saw a squirrel as if herding sheep to safety. But he was good company—with a perpetually happy disposition and wagging tale. It had been a long while since he and the dog had ridden in the truck. Clark rarely drove anymore, so they both were in a mood for adventure as he started the engine and reversed the truck onto the country lane.

As he drove, Clark thought, "Funny, how driving comes so naturally even after all this time. There are some things in life a person never forgets." He loved the utilitarian old truck with the stick shift and seats covered in sturdy cloth and vinyl that crinkled when he sat on them. The engine made a deep rumbling sound when he shifted gears before settling down to a steady hum. He felt expansive, looking through large windows and sitting high in control of his destiny, like the captain of a ship. It was different than riding in his daughters' sedans where he had to crawl in and fold his legs to sit down. A truck made a person feel elevated, but sitting in a car made him feel cramped, almost level with the road below him.

In one week, Clark would have cataract surgery to remove the "clouded membranes" from his eyes. "You'll be surprised how much clearer everything will be," the doctor said. The downside was that Clark's peripheral vision would be practically erased and he'd have to wear thick glasses to compensate for his visual impairments. "I guess I'll have to turn my head like an old owl just to see what's to the side of me," Clark joked at the time, trying hard to cover the wound to his heart and feeling somehow angry at the doctor. His narrowed vision was the reason that Clark's daughters persuaded him to give up driving. Having this option taken away saddened him even though he knew it was the practical thing to do. "Yep," he sighed. "My world is closing in on me. I won't be driving again after my eyes get fixed."

For many years, his daughters had been carting him to church, town, and appointments. Clark enjoyed these ventures, looking out the window at landscapes that triggered rabbit-trails of memories. On the way into town, he'd look at the scenery and say to whomever was driving, "That's where Old Miss Tabitha lived. I remember when we used to go to baptisms in her pasture pond. She always made sure people put on a long robe, so they'd be modest when they came up out of the water. Lived to be ninety-five and was mighty set in her ways, but she made the best apple pies and didn't mind sharing them." He could almost taste the buttery crust and the sweet fillings of those scrumptious delicacies.

Minutes would go by while he'd immerse himself in the past like wading in a cool shallow creek. He thought about the people who lived on old homesteads along the way and of how he had once shared conversations and jokes with them. "Back when I had things to do and places to be," he'd think. He remembered socializing with people after church on long-ago Sundays. Hildie would give him a look as a reminder that it was time to go.

Hildie always seemed so busy. Clark remembered her large, wrinkled hands worn smooth from all the scrubbing and cleaning to attack every pestilent germ. Clark joked that she'd rubbed all her top skin away by drenching her hands in disinfectant to kill every microbe. She believed in the mantra: "Cleanliness is next to Godliness" and had the cleanest cookware in the county. "Good clean dirt is fine and healthy, but I can't stand to have a messy house. It's slovenly and dissolute like a dance hall queen." Clark figured that women who didn't set a high standard in cleanliness might turn to bad things like gossiping, drinking out of hip flasks, and dancing with stranger, so he was grateful that Hildie put her efforts into keeping a clean, tidy house.

Occasionally, on the way to the grocery store or post office, entire minutes would pass before he looked around, as if waking from a dream, startled to find he was on the way to buy groceries at the local "Friendly's Food Mart," his hands folded over the hat in his lap. Little things like his hat reminded him of how times had changed. There was a time when every man wore a hat to town. "What happened to those days?" he'd think, fingering the shiny hat band. "I wonder when everything changed. At the entrance to the store were empty benches where his friends once sat. What had happened to all his old friends he used to banter with while Hildie shopped inside? Sometimes he sat along on the bench waiting for his daughter to finish shopping, but lately, he didn't like sitting by himself, so he went inside to buy his own groceries.

Life was like walking on steppingstones to a destination. Even though Clark dropped out of school when he was a youngster, he thought of life as a series of passages like being promoted to each progressive grade and then leaving school to begin another phase of life. It was a habit he'd picked up from being married to Hildie, a schoolteacher, who'd taught longer than the fifty years they'd been married. He missed driving Hildie back and forth to school and hearing about her day. She had a way of describing things so vividly that Clark felt as if he were hearing and seeing everything firsthand. He imagined the rub of chalk on the board, screeching children on the playground, the smell of pine floors and industrial cleaner, water splashing from drinking fountains, and the murmur of students reading aloud.

As he drove by the church, he thought about all the people in the congregation who had worshipped with him through the years. Many of them had been older than Clark and he still considered them permanent fixtures in his life. Over the years, people who'd seemed impervious as the old oak trees had weakened and died, and he'd become one of the elderly to take their place. Even the landscape had changed. It was hard to remember how the land had once looked before it was cleared to make way for new houses and roads. Life is as temporal as the flowers that bloom so vividly and then begin to droop. Then he smiled. Some flowers are perennials and rebloom after a fallow winter, just like the irises in his yard.

It seemed just yesterday that so many people were alive; and then over time, they were no longer around, leaving an empty pew where they had once sat. Years ago, he'd witnessed a preacher in the pulpit suddenly slump to the floor. How could this person have been such a pillar of strength one minute and dead the next? And where did people go after leaving earth? He hoped they were in heaven—even the ornery ones. Drowsing in the ground seemed so dull and pointless. "Maybe they're just resting," he thought.

He wasn't ready to join them anytime soon. Sometimes when his arthritis acted up, he thought he was tired of living, but not quite ready to die. Then he'd remind himself that he still had things to do. For one thing, he had to take care of the dog and watch the neighbors' houses to make sure no one broke in while they worked during the day. He wanted to stay around to see the seasons change: the glow of sunshine on autumn leaves, and the joy of looking out the window at bare branches pointing towards clear winter skies. Springs brought back memories of plowing, the promise of new life; and summers were a verdant reminder of growth: the time when he and his family had once worked in the fields before harvest.

Turning left on a side road, Clark noticed sunlight interspersing tree branches with splashes of gold, creating a shifting mosaic of light and dark in the woods. He'd always appreciated beauty even in the most ordinary of things—the way sunlight filtered through trees; dark summer clouds pouring rain; amber weeds blowing in the wind; the patterns on a snake; or the afternoon sun lighting up the side of a house. Appreciating beauty was like praying—a way to commune with God and a captured memory to stretch into a lifetime. Hildie once said, "Clark, you'd think an outhouse on a moonlit night was a beautiful sight." To which Clark had joked back, "Well, yeah, especially if I needed to use it and the path was lit up bright. I take a blessing for what it's worth.'

He passed the Drummond place—an old abandoned wooden cabin with a dog trot running down the middle, nestled in a clearing, the yard packed down with dirt and leaves from the trees. Clark remembered the three sisters and one brother who'd once lived there—an eccentric bunch who left the house only when they were driven to church. One of the sisters, Delcie, a bony woman with long pointy feet used to walk the quarter mile to his house in summers when Hildie was out of school. Clark enjoyed her company, even when she rambled on about her "miseries." She was a hunched, dried-up old woman who had been "born old" as people would say. Her pale yellow hair had faded to gray over the years and she wore it pulled to the back of her head in a thin bun. She'd never married, spending most of her time reading the Bible, rarely leaving the house except to milk the cow, bringing the milk back to the house in a metal bucket and parceling it out to her brother and sisters with their evening meal. Sometimes, Clark saw Delcie and her sisters sitting on the back porch churning butter, snapping beans, or quilting on a pleasant evening.

Clark and Hildie stopped once a week to visit with Delcie and her siblings. It was a sad day when relatives took them to a nursing home in town. Occasionally he and Hildie visited them at the rest home, but it wasn't the same. Clark didn't like the vinegary smell or fluorescent lights. The people sitting outside their rooms looked to lonely. He hated to see Delcie, who had been so active, permanently bed-ridden with illness. Even so, she smiled at Clark and Hildie, thanking them for coming and listening intently as they talked about friends and relatives.

Clark sighed. Getting old sure wasn't fun. He pulled into the long, narrow driveway of his old house; the dirt road straight as a ruler, woods on one side and field to the other. When he lived there, he'd walk the length of the driveway to the mailbox to pick up the mail every afternoon for Hildie to sort through when she got home from school.

One a month, he received a magazine entitled "The Enterprising Farmer," which he couldn't read because printed words were a jumbled-up mess of coded symbols that he'd never been able to decipher. He enjoyed listening to Hildie read the articles aloud to him from the magazine. Afterwards, she'd place the journals in a drawer of the vanity table in the back of the house. He could hardly believe how they had accumulated when his grandchildren stacked them on the floor to play school. There must have been over a hundred of them! Hildie said they needed to burn them as kindling, but Clark didn't want to get rid of them. "They have some good articles," he said, incredulous that Hildie didn't appreciate their value. Hildie had replied, "Clark, you've got to let go of things."

Most of the articles were about crop rotation; ways to improve yield; getting rid of pests; or fixing farm equipment which were not very useful to him on his small farm. But the article about getting rid of dog mange really came in handy. Hildie bought the ingredients at the local pharmacy for Clark to apply to a yellow hound dog named "Hugh," and it cured him of the mange.

Parking under the overhanging branches of the tree in the front yard of the house, Clark turned off the ignition, looked around, then got out of the truck and walked to the house. It had been a while since he'd visited the old homestead and weeds had overtaken the yard. Bushes blocked the front porch and the holes bored in the wooden columns by the carpenter bees were larger and more numerous. One of the front steps was loose with a nail sticking up from the plank. He would have fixed it with tools stored in the nearby shed, but someone had pried open the door a few months ago and stolen everything inside. The theft was especially offensive because Hildie's Pa had given him the tools. It made Clark feel violated and angry that someone stole something that was rightfully his. "There's some things a man has that nobody else has a right to take," he muttered. He figured the Yarkus boys were the culprits. They stole just for the thrill of it in the dead of night, bragging about it over hard liquor. Clark had a kind heart and would give people anything if they asked, but he had no compassion for people who stole from him. That made him madder than a rattlesnake.

He walked quietly up to the porch, careful not to put any weight on the broken step and holding on the porch column for support. Walking to the front window, he peered through the thin curtains into the front room. Funny how looking into a house from the outside made a person feel like an intruder. Something in the shadows moved furtively. "Is someone living in there?" he asked, his voice thin and unsure. Peppy, at his feet, began whining. Clark involuntarily shivered — "a possum walking over his grave" — his mother used to say. He peered into the room, but whatever it was had receded out of sight.

Neither he nor the dog wanted to find out what it was they had seen flitting across their line of vision. Maybe it was one of those "haints" he'd always sensed. Many years ago, he had divulged his gift of sensing spirits to Hildie who'd advised him to quit seeking things that were "none of your business" and "out of your control." It was best to leave some things a mystery, so they don't take 'a hold' of you and live inside your head," she said. "Such things have been known to drive people crazy."

"Hildie is right," he said, "some things just ought to be left alone." Peppy pricked up his ears, crooking his head sideways at the sound of Clark's voice. The trees whispering to each other in the breeze were so quiet that Clark's footsteps on the porch seemed amplified by comparison. "I wonder what the trees are saying," Clark pondered, looking upward at their canopies.

All his life, Clark had an affinity with nature and a quiet respect for what his Ma said were "the unseen spirits." As a young child, Clark sensed things that didn't belong to the "normal realm of life"—a bond he shared with his mother. He never talked about his experiences with anyone other than Ma and Hildie. They didn't scoff at him and were not given to gossiping or tattling to others. It was best to keep his testimony quiet to others would not think he was crazy. Besides, the state mental institute was only about thirty miles north, and Clark didn't want to tempt fate and be locked up in there.

He remembered a man in his community, Stanton Ferrell, who'd had "visions". One day in church, right before preaching commenced, Stanton stood up and proclaimed that for many months he'd seen Jesus walking in Vernon's Creek every Monday at dawn. Friends and family told him this not possible and even stood beside him every Monday during the bitterly cold March of 1922 to prove their point. For many weeks just at sunrise, Stanton, surrounded by family and friends, pointed and shouted, "There he is! Don't you see him? He's wading in the creek!" The sleepy-eyed and sullen people only stared in consternation at his intractability to reason. "Stanton! There ain't nobody there!" they shouted, attempting to stop him from jumping into the creek.

Stanton had been dispatched to the state asylum after almost dying of hypothermia one Monday. "I'm tired of having to drag that poor feller out of the creek. He puts up such a fuss that I've got bruises all over my body!" exclaimed Preacher Wycliffe Harthcourt who counseled the man's family "to get Stanton up that hospital as quick as possible before he kills himself and the rest of us!"

Within a few days, Stanton was evaluated in a court of law where he was deemed "mentally unfit" after narrating his watery communions with the Lord. Before announcing his verdict, the judge asked, "I don't understand something, Mr. Ferrell. Why does Jesus only come at sunrise on Mondays?" To which Stanton replied, "Well, because Jesus wanted to come "bright and early" in the day 'cause he had a lot to do, and since its his 'second coming', he came back on the second day of the week. I knowed he had things to tell me, but them nosey people kept interrupting Him." The judge replied, "Well, I guess that makes as much sense as anything else you've said," before pronouncing his verdict and slamming his gavel hard to keep from laughing out loud.

Shortly afterwards, Stanton was driven to Dyson Mental Institute to begin a new phase of life where he could "peacefully live in quiet reflection and benefit from intense psychiatric help" by court decree. Apparently, the treatment was a success; within a few months, Stanton was released to the bosom of his family, where he was watched like a hawk stalking a field mouse. No one in the community wanted any more episodes of hysteria in the freezing dawn.

Clark was a young man at the time and didn't want to bring up his experience with the "unknown and unseen." People would assume he was just stirring up trouble to get attention. Preacher Harthcourt believed in order and good sense when conducting services and was dead set against anything that smacked of consorting with spirits. "It's good to know about the

Holy Spirit, but some folks carry the mysteries of the 'spirit world' too far and conjure up things that need to remain quiet!" Preacher Harthcourt thundered, "We don't need any more of this kind of foolishness in our community," referring to Stanton Ferrell's claim to "A New Covenant with God."

As a young boy, Clark once saw a glowing, husky man sitting on a rock in the woods, pointing a stout arm at him. Frozen in fear and morbid curiosity, Clark was too scared to run or ask questions. Was the man summoning him? He thought all spirits were wraithlike, but this one looked like he'd never missed a meal in his life. What did he want Clark to do? For a long moment, Clark stared and tried to speak, until the feeling returned to his legs, and he ran home at breakneck speed. His Ma, normally not affectionate, pulled him close, rubbing the top of his head to comfort him. "Clark, it will be fine. Just let it be. These things happen to only a few. It's a way of showing you're favored."

For a long time afterward, when Clark experienced an otherworldly presence, he felt unworthy—someone who didn't deserve to be singled out for spiritual communion. He also wondered what message these spirits were relaying to him. Were they trying to warn him about some calamity he could prevent if he used powers of discernment? "I must be pretty dumb" he thought one night after hearing a voice say "Clark, it's over there—what you're looking for. It's over there!"

He was resting in bed, recuperating from a fever, but quickly jumped over to the window and peered out. All he saw were trees swaying gently in the moonlight. If only he'd seen an owl— which everyone knew was a harbinger of death—then he might have prevented something tragic. He stared for a long while to see if anything out of the ordinary occurred, but nothing happened. Eventually, he went to bed with foreboding that clouded his mood for many days. No one died and nothing bad happened, but he carried a sense of unease for many months afterwards.

As he got older, the voices and strange images faded and stopped over time. Then he fretted that he'd been disavowed because of not living up to standard. "I have failed. I could have done better," he thought. Then a new fear gripped him. Since he had spiritual perceptions, perhaps now he was in danger of being possessed by "the other side." Even the preacher was apprehensive about demons because he read from the Bible about them. He shuddered when he recalled passages where wild people tore their clothing and ran naked in graveyards, clawing at their bodies screaming in a "legion" of voices. Clark surely didn't want that to happen to him. He'd be so humiliated, running savagely in the dark, tearing up the graves of the departed and bringing shame on his poor family. They'd wrap him in canvas and throw him in the mental institute.

As the years passed and he continued to worry, Clark eased his mind by staying active. Sometimes, he'd walk on a long pilgrimage or work so hard that he wore himself out in exhaustion. Using goodness as a talisman, he attended church faithfully and became a hard-working, somewhat solitary young man who refused to do anything that might get him into trouble.

To ease his mind, he spent hours carving wooden dogs, cats, squirrels, chickens, chipmunks, snakes, raccoons, and livestock. It was a peculiar hobby, but it brought him a sense of peace and accomplishment. It also set him apart as "curious." People considered him somewhat eccentric but talented, nonetheless.

For a while, he thought about preaching, but knew that career path wouldn't work out since he couldn't read the scriptures and he was too shy to speak in front of a large crowd. Aside from carving, he enjoyed hard physical labor. It was a cathartic experience to smell and till the dark reddish-brown dirt that he plowed every spring, a soil so fertile that Clark cultivated a harvest of succulent vegetables and bales of soft, white cotton. He'd come home soiled and reeking of sweat to immerse himself in a tub of soapy water. Transforming himself from filthiness to a state of cleanliness made him feel hallowed and sanctified.

Back to the present, Clark said, "Come on Peppy, we've got things to do," as the dog quietly fell in step beside him. They walked silently for a while, both feeling somewhat disquieted like children who have witnessed something children shouldn't have seen. Clark quickened his steps to gain distance from the house. Halfway through the woods, Clark had to turn back and walk to the truck to retrieve his rifle, thermos, and sack lunch which he'd forgotten in his frightened retreat. He slung the knapsack on his back. Then he found an opening in the trees and followed a cow path down the hill to the pasture. It had been a long time since he'd been in the woods and the smells and sounds on the path rejuvenated him. "Sure is pretty out here," he said, jarring the quiet with his voice. He felt odd speaking aloud, as though he were in a holy place where he was supposed to keep quiet.

As he walked, he thought of the first time he and Hildie went on a picnic in these woods sixty years earlier, accompanied by her four sisters. He'd felt foolish walking around with all those girls, but Hildie and her sisters had insisted that he accompany them, much to the amusement of their family. It was quite a party with Clark, Hildie, her sisters, and dogs walking deep into the woods. Each sister took turns carrying the basket until they found a clearing to lay the tablecloth and set up the picnic.

He remembered the red cloth napkins in checkered patterns like handkerchiefs. He'd felt self-conscious wiping his mouth with such pretty things but tried hard to be polite and civilized around the girls. Clark still remembered the shafts of sunlight spreading like a beacon through the trees on that April day when the air smelled fresh with the aroma of newly turned soil and budding plants. It was the most beautiful day he'd ever seen with the sky colored like blue topaz.

He'd been wavering between courting Hildie or one of her younger and prettier sisters and he ruminated over which one to choose as they spread the food on the tablecloth and ate, complimenting Hildie on the delicious meal of fried chicken, rolls, slaw, and pie. Afterward, he watched as Hildie braided a basket out of vines while her sisters ran around playing tag and collecting wildflowers. He liked the fact that Hildie, who was the plainest and sternest of the bunch, was constructive with her time, intertwining the vines and lapping them into an intricate basket. "These wisteria vines are beautiful, and they smell good, but you've got to tear them off a tree because they will keep growing into braided twists that strangle it," Hildie had said.

Clark had seen vines wrapping round trees like coiled snakes and he agreed with her. He thought, "Now she's got common sense and would make a good wife." Even though she'd gone to college, she was a country girl who wouldn't mind getting dirty and putting her muscles to work if he needed help on the farm. A stout girl who could cook and didn't mind hard work was a definite asset. Besides, he thought, she's the only one who wouldn't think I was a "step down" the ladder. Truth be told, he like her straightforward manner and creativity. He remembered his mother admonishing him about finding a virtuous woman: "Looks don't matter all that much; it's a woman's character that counts."

Clark was twenty-four that spring day when he'd leaned against a tree and smoked a pipe carved out of oak. It was good to be able to make things and he appreciated the fact that Hildie was handy with weaving. He watched as she finished her basket. Then he stared at a woodpecker boring holes into a tree and thought for a long time about his future. Would Hildie consider marrying him? She was a few years younger than he was and a lot more sensible than her sisters who ran around, laughing and chasing each other. Mary, the youngest at sixteen, began switching the back end of his hounds, sending the dogs into a fit of howling. H wished the dogs would run away so she'd stop and was irritated that they loped around in playful circles, enjoying the attention.

Suddenly, Hildie jumped up and chased Mary, wrenching the stick away with such force that their hands were scraped and bleeding. "Leave the dogs alone and go walking with your sisters," Hildie demanded. Casting a hateful look back at Hildie, Mary reluctantly left to join her sisters who were collecting wildflowers.

The dogs began eating food out of Hildie's hands, and she didn't wince when they licked her face with their tongues. It was at that minute that Clark fell in love with Hildie. He saw their future together as clearly as the circle of sunlight surrounding them. His heart felt light, and he had to keep from jumping in the air. Surely, everyone would notice the sudden change in him as if he'd suddenly grown wings.

"I feel like a butterfly coming out of its cocoon!" he surmised, a little astonished at his burst of poetic expression. He was glad his feelings weren't on display as the crew packed up the picnic and walked down the hill with the dogs tracking scents. They spent a happy afternoon wading in the creek where Stanton had claimed to see Jesus. Clark made everyone laugh by warning them to "be sure to say 'Howdy' if you see anyone walking on top of the water!"

The next day, after church, Clark drove to Hildie's house to ask her father if he could court Hildie. Herman Donnell was a grouchy man who acted like he had a burr in his britches. "No," Herman replied. "Hildie's a twenty-year-old woman who's gone to college and made a teacher of herself. Why would she want to saddle herself with an illiterate farmer? I hadn't got nothing against you, but you need to find someone else to court."

Despite this setback, Hildie and Clark eloped soon afterwards and fixed up a rundown house not too far from Hildie's school. Clark sharecropped until he earned enough money to buy land and build a house. It took many years of hard work, attending church, farming, and raising three daughters before gaining the reluctant approval of Hildie's Pa. Clark wasn't the type to hold grudges and was glad to prove to Hildie's family that he was worthy.

Walking deeper into the woods, Clark saw leaves angling to the ground when the wind loosened them from branches. It took decades for leafy mounds to pile deeply enough to compost into dirt. He wondered if he could uncover the past by tunneling deep in the ground to find evidence of the Indians who once lived in these woods. Had they walked in this same spot to hunt or fish in the creek on a fine autumn day? "Everyone who's ever lived has experienced my same feelings," he said aloud. They had experienced bouts of self-doubt, loneliness, laced like a braid through periods of contentment.

Hildie read about people digging up fossils to reconstruct the past. Maybe if he dug deeply enough, he could unearth a time when he was happiest—all those years with Hildie. If only for a day. . . he thought, if only he could bring back the time when they were together. And he wondered, "Where does time go? Where do people go when they're no longer around and why do they leave?" Could he dig deeply enough to find all those seasons when he and Hildie were together? If so, Clark would have dug to China to hold time like leaves in his hands, crumbling them to the ground as a landscape to recreate the life he once lived.

Clark stopped and picked up a stout limb so he wouldn't stumble while going down the cow path which flattened in stretches like a ziggurat before sloping gently to the valley. "Kind of makes it easier on my knees," laughed Clark. "I reckon cows are smart. They found a way to confound gravity and not have to work so hard getting back up to the barn for evening feeding. We could learn a lot from animals."

Clark smiled at Peppy leading the way, noticing the sunlight glinting off his fur. He could tell the by the position of the sun that it was about nine o'clock in the morning. He'd always been good at figuring the time and remembering events as he sealed birthdays, weddings, funerals, deaths, and other momentous occasions in his mind with the accuracy of a calendar. He even remembered mundane details like the rainy day when he helped Ma can peaches, the day when Pa taught him how to hitch and drive a wagon, and that day in April when he watched Hildie weave a basket of vines on that long-ago picnic. Strange that he could remember things from so long ago but couldn't recall a song he'd just heard on the radio.

Finally, they reached the valley. Cows and horses stood quietly chewing and staring contemplatively at him and the dog as they walked around the herd and further into the flat pasture before venturing into the woods, the leaves filtering to the ground in wavy spirals. Clark measured the distance by landmarks until he found the grove of ironwood and oak trees he'd initialed long ago with the names of Hildie and his daughters.

After they had married, Hildie had taught him to scrawl a few words so he'd be able to sign checks and write his name on voting day. He'd practiced his signature and the names of Hildie and his daughers over and over again on paper, his big hands awkwardly holding the pencil and concentrating hard as he looped the letters on paper. One day, he'd gone into the woods and carved their names and birthdays on a few trees in a grove. Gradually, he started carving pictures into trunks until the trees were a gallery of scenes. Hildie would have laughed at him for being so foolish: a grown man etching names and drawings on tree trunks.

Clark had respect for human achievements. It would be good to leave behind a memorial like the Indians had done when they piled up rocks or carved monuments as a testimonial to their lives. Being able to write something signified that a person had scope and insight. Maybe a hundred years in the future, someone would come across the names scratched on a trunk and wonder what he and his family looked like; where they lived; if they were friendly or not. It was similar to fossils of plants and animals. Hildie read that scientists found traces of footprints embedded in rocks. "Imagine a drop of rain or some animal walking on the ground—just a second in time—something so ordinary preserved forever." Carving names on trees was like being part of something alive. "I know one day my name will be on a tombstone, but a slab of rock ain't a living thing."

He continued walking until he came to a grove of trees covered with etching that he traced with his fingers. Odd that the trees grew taller, but the names and drawings remained at eye level. He thought about the deep roots of the trees keeping the soil intact as their branches provided shelter through so many seasons. Trees could live hundreds of years, and he was grateful that Foley, a grandson who lived close by, kept the paths clear of underbrush so people could visit his gallery of tree art.

Clark had also carved animals out of oak stumps next to the trees. Myron, one of his grandkids, had taken them home to preserve. For years, he'd been trying to get Clark to set up a show at the college gallery for the public to view, but Clark just scoffed: "These things ain't no count. Whoever wants the things can have them."

For many years, Clark and several of the grandkids had spent days clearing out thickets of thorns and privet. When the grandkids grew up and had other things to do, only he and Foley were left to clear the paths, piling up fallen limbs and brush into a large clearing in the pasture for a bonfire. It was always enjoyable to sit around the fire, talking or just being silent for hours watching the flames. They'd douse the remaining embers with spring water and dirt before Foley drove them home in his old truck. Clark still came to the pasture for clearing, but he sat on a foldable lawn chair and watched Foley and his sons cut and haul off the brush. They did such a good job clearing the way that a person could walk through the woods without tearing their skin on thorny bushes.

Clark walked further into the woods before he sat down on a big rock next to the creek and watched as Peppy jumped in for a long drink before climbing up the bank and lying down on the ground next to him. They spent a long interlude listening to the sounds of the trickling water as the day got warmer, watching blue skies and reflections in the shallow pools close to the bank. Minnows flipped silvery tails and flapped fins as they darted in the water. "I could stay all day," thought Clark, mesmerized by the water steadily flowing like passages of time.

He looked at the round rocks in the stream whose rough edges had been worn smooth by water, and mused aloud to Peppy, "Them rocks remind me of my family, digging in, so the water can't jounce them around. That one over there, separated from the rest, puts me in mind of Douglas, who was once my son-in-law. He never quite fit in with the rest of us. The first time I met him, I knowed he wouldn't be around too long. He had a restless soul like those whip-o-wills in spring. They holler until they find what they're looking for. Then they get quiet and only the memory of their song remains in your heart." There were evenings when he looked at the sunset to keep alive the colors of the dying day and thought about the young man—who had been a boy really—all those years earlier. Memories are like wading in a branch on a hot day. Your feet are freezing but you keep walking because when you climb out, you feel so good that even the pain is worth it. And when you're tired and hot, all you have to do is think about how cool you felt after dipping in the creek. That's the way memories are. They keep you going, and even the sad times are a reminder of your resilience.

Clark and Peppy sat for a long time watching the creek. Around 1 p.m, he ate a ham sandwich washed down with tea and gave Peppy the second sandwich. "Well, I reckon we'd better start back up the hill. Wilda Layne will be getting' home soon and she'll fret if I'm not there." Clark's daughters were always checking up on him. They were bossy women, but he enjoyed their company, even if they did sometimes irritate him with all their fussing. He picked up his knapsack. "I ain't too interested in hunting. Don't tell nobody, but I just wanted to come out in the woods," said Clark to the dog. They made their way to the pasture, careful to avoid stepping in cow manure.

They began walking up the old dirt road that ran uphill like a wedge separating both sides of his property. It was a shadowy road with overhanging limbs that gave it a haunted look; but Clark didn't mind because lonely places were good places to think.

When Clark lived in the house with Hildie on top of the hill, he never liked hearing the sound of a car passing in front of the house and down the steep hill late at night. It usually meant that revelers parked their car close to the pasture and walked on his property where they'd sit in lawn chairs to drink and sing. Too many times, after the party ended, intoxicated drivers rumbled back up the hill and got cars stuck on bedrock or trapped in a ditch. Then they'd walk unsteadily up the hill to knock on the door in the dark hours past midnight, asking for help.

Clark dreaded opening the door since he had a superstitious fear of phantasmagoria who did terrible things in the dark. Hildie was more practical. "Clark, there's no such things as spooks; and anyway, no haint is going to bother knocking on the door. It's people you got to worry about! Ain't no telling what those liquored up drunks will do to you one night if they get hold of a tire tool," Hildie warned Clark.

"I know," replied Clark, "even sinners need help, but I want nothing to do with haints."

One night a drunken couple caroused in the pasture before getting into their car and chugging up the steep hill. Midway up, the car got stuck on an outcropping of rock. The wobbly couple tried to nudge the car forward, but it rolled back on them, and they had just enough time to scoot out of the way and watch in drunken horror as it landed in a deep ravine. High atop the hill Clark woke up to loud knocking on the door. Rain was falling heavily when the bedraggled couple asked for help. Hildie, who had also woken up, told the couple to come in while she called the sheriff.

Around two in the morning, the sheriff and a deputy drove down the hill to retrieve the car, only to have their car slide into a muddy rut. Clark opened the door to an angry and exhausted sheriff and deputy. Since it was too wet and cold to wedge the car out of the ditch, the law officers and couple sat on towels trying to dry off in front of the fire, drinking coffee and waiting on an officer to drive them into town. Before they left, Hildie counseled the soaked woman about "living right." "You need to either find a good man to settle down with or get that sot to quit drinking and marry you."

The sullen young woman looked like she was about to say something she'd regret before wisely keeping silent. However, the drunken man began sobbing and wailing to everyone about his miseries, his huge shoulders shaking and rivulets of tears coursing down his face. The sheriff and deputy listened with bemused looks on their faces as if they were used to such demonstrations. But Clark and Hildie were dumbstruck in horror and relieved when the sodden crew left. It wasn't long afterwards that the county commissioner shut down the road. "Good," said Hildie. "Now you won't have to help all those derelicts in the middle of the night."

Two years after the incident, the couple came back to thank Hildie and Clark for their help and hospitality and to apologize for their behavior. They relayed how they straightened up after the incident. "I thought about what you said," said Layla, the woman. "At first I was mad and then I thought about how slutty I was being, so I got right with the Lord and quit drinking. I told

Arnot that h could either marry me or I'd find someone else. That's how we got married."

Arnot nodded and said, "Yep. I married her and then we moved to Detroit to work in an automotive plant. We are doing real well and come back to visit kinfolk every summer. They live in Elysium. You might know them. They're the Clarpfanters."

"Oh yeah, I know them," replied Clark with a smile. "I know your folks. I sat with Jeptha in the grocery store."

The two couples conversed before the visitors left. Afterwards, Clark thought, "Who would ever have guessed that getting stuck or stranded on bedrock could be so life-affirming? I guess we've all needed help being pulled out of a ditch at one time or another. And maybe it teaches us humility."

He climbed slowly to the summit of the hill where he unlocked the fence and walked to the field behind his house to examine the gray, weathered outhouse and chicken coop before entering the barn, inhaling the sweet earthy aroma of livestock, leather, and hay. Even though the barn was over a hundred years old, oaken beams and rafters kept it structurally intact. Its high rafters and sturdiness reminded Clark of a church and he paraphrased the scripture: "This is my church and the gates of hell will not prevail against it."

Foley stored rolled-up bales of hay in the back entrance of the barn. When mother cows were birthing calves, they stayed inside the stalls. Occasionally, Foley brought the horses inside the barn to rest and eat oats before saddling them up for a ride. Clark inhaled the leathery smell of the saddles and harnesses that Foley kept on a sawhorse. Inside the barrels, Foley stored feed to keep out the vermin. Clark said a prayer of thankfulness for Foley's efforts to take good care of the barn and maintain the farm. A barn needed someone to take care of it and Foley did a good job.

Clark climbed the ladder to the loft. He hadn't been up there since Hildie had gotten sick several years earlier. During her last spring, Hildie spent most of her time in bed, only getting up to go to church or to receive company. Clark, who thrived on routine, cooked meals and cleaned as well as he could, although Hildie chuckled at his haphazard efforts. Every evening, Clark went to feed the cows and to sit in the loft and ponder in silent prayer.

One April day, while moving hay, he lost his pocket watch. He figured he must have broken the chain with the pitchfork and searched everywhere for it, even bringing Lodell and Foley, his son-in-law and grandson, to help him look. They scoured every inch of the barn and never did locate it. How could something just disappear? Maybe a crow had carried it to its nest since they like hoarding shiny objects, or a cow had stepped on it and splintered it into a thousand pieces.

Clark was upset about the loss since it held such sentimental value. Hildie had given him the pocket watch on their fifth anniversary back in November of 1928. Shortly after hosting a Thanksgiving meal, Hildie scoured dishes, swept up and put everything away, and then summoned Clark into the kitchen. Looking up at Clark, she gave him a box. He opened it and was overcome to see a heavy chain and watch made of gold. On the back of the inscription read: "To Clark with eternal love. Hildie."

She had spent years saving up enough money to buy the watch. Clark treasured it, keeping it securely tucked inside his overall bib pocket fastening it to a button so it wouldn't slip out. At church, he put it insider the coat pocket of his suit. At night, he placed it on the bedstand, enjoying the quiet ticking as the minute hand circled the hours. It was a ritual they both enjoyed when Hildie asked Clark for the time just so he would take out his pocket watch and announce the hour and minute.'

When Clark lost the watch, he was grief-stricken. It represented all the hours that he and Hildie had together. He was bereft without the cherished timepiece so he kept quiet about losing it. Oddly, in the last weeks of her life, Hildie never asked about the time—as though she knew her life on earth was ticking away by the minute.

She died on his seventy-fourth birthday, May 8th. May had always been Hildie's favorite month, when her favorite flowers blossomed, and graduations occurred. She always turned wistful towards the end of May, sad to say "goodbye" to another class of students. On her last Sunday when she'd been taken by ambulance to the hospital, she looked at the flowers and breathed in the sweet spring air one last time, knowing she'd never return.

At the hospital, she spent her final days in a haze of morphine-induced dreams, often addressing the family as if they were students. Then abruptly, she'd be back in reality again. During her last moments, after being reassured by her daughters that they would take good care of Clark, she took one lingering gaze and died.

After the funeral, Clark felt smothered by a white-hot cocoon of sorrow, too paralyzed by grief to do anything. For a few months, he stayed alone in the old house, trying to keep occupied, but the silence rattled him. Also the isolation of the house bothered him. A reclusive old shut-in made an easy target for thieves and ne'er-do-wells. Even though his shotgun and rifle were kept on a rack ready to use, he was uncertain if he could fire them at a trespasser. In the back of his mind, he worried about falling or hurting himself and being unable to use the phone to call for help. At night, family members took turns staying with him, but the house seemed strangely uncomfortable without Hildie. He alerted to each squeak and groan of the house, haunted as if something sinister was about to attack him.

He felt a mixture of sadness and relief when he moved into the small clapboard house adjacent to his daughters that his son-in-law had built for him. He missed the old house and felt guilty for abandoning it but felt much safer since he was in closer proximity to his family. Although he was grateful for his daughters' visits and nightly meals, he sensed they were distracted with chores and in a hurry to get back to their responsibilities. The grandchildren visited rarely since they were busy with their own jobs and families. They weren't interested in hearing stories about a world that no longer existed. After they left, he'd sigh and think: "I guess being young means you've got your whole life ahead of you. Being old means you've already lived most of your life." On holidays, his house was crowded with family. Every few years, newly-born great-grandchildren expanded the family. He was proud of his progeny, and looked forward to these occasions, but felt a painful twinge in his heart for Hildie in all the bustle.

Clark mounted the steps into the barn loft and walked around. Out of habit, he looked for the watch but didn't find it. Then he sat on a pile of hay for a long time listening to Peppy investigating the unfamiliar sounds and smells of the barn. He walked over to the loft opening spayed with shafts of sunshine to look at his old house in the distance. He remembered Jenny, a beautiful black mule that he'd loved. She had a vicious sense of humor, often nibbling the back of his britches when his back was turned, drawing back her lips in a toothy smile when he turned around. He always forgave her because she made him laugh. She was a good companion and hard-working despite her perverse sense of humor. After unhitching her, Clark gave her lumps of sugar and carrots, enjoying her soft fleshy lips on his hands. He'd raised her from a foal to a mule of thirty-six and cried like a baby when he found her slumped on the ground early one morning when he went out to feed the livestock. He could see her grave in the barnyard, marked with a wooden cross with her name and day of birth and death etched on it. On spring days, when he watched his son-in-law plow with tractors, he'd think of Jenny and miss the days when they turned the rich soil in deep furrows.

He walked back to sit on a hay bale and think about the day. A dim light glowed close to him before transmogrifying into a phosphorescent being as bright as a lightening bug. Clark squinted and was shocked to see the outline of a corpulent man dressed in finery sitting beside him. He jumped up to flee, but the spirit motioned for Clark to sit back down.

"Clark, sit down. I'm not here to hurt you," the man said in a mildly annoyed but kindly voice. Something familiar about the man tugged at Clark's memory.

"Wait a minute! You're that same man I seen in the woods when I was just a boy!" Clark shouted.

"How astute that you remembered," chuckled the apparition. "I've come to relay some news to you and guide you on your journey."

"But who are you? Are you from the good or bad side?" asked Clark.

"Well, from neither. I'm in an in-between place. Some people refer to it as Purgatory and others call it 'Limbo'. However, they both refer to a state of being hovering somewhere in the netherworld between heaven and hell—a transitional place for people who weren't quite good enough to march stalwartly into heaven, but not so immoral that they deserve everlasting damnation. Let me explain. You see, during my life I pursued—how shall we say—the 'comforts of the flesh'. I was engaged in fulfilling my senses with wine, women, and song."

"You mean you ran with a fast crowd?" asked Clark incredulously. He had heard of thrill-seeking people whose lives ended in dissolution.

"Well, yes, in way, although, I like to think I was more of an Epicurean: discreet and polite in all my pursuits. You see, I was a wealthy man of renowned status when I was alive. I'd inherited a fortune from my family and, therefore, had the time and energy to pursue my every whim. I searched high and low in pursuit of learning while enjoying the luxuries of travel, fine wine, and beautiful women before my life culminated in the arms of my mistress after a passionate interlude. It was a most provocative way to exit. I was whispered about for years after my demise. Upon reaching judgment, I apologized to God for all my transgressions. He would have sent me hell but said that my saving grace was compassion. All my life, I had given generously to the needy, building houses and donating huge sums of money secretly to help the destitute. My Lord and Savior granted me a reprieve whereupon I had to wander the earth helping people in difficult situations. You're my last case and I must say I am tired. If I can get you to appreciate the gift of life, then I can sail on to my heavenly reward."

"Well, that is fine and dandy, but since you have talked to God, I need to know something. Is Hildie in heaven? Is she happy up there?" asked Clark.

"Yes, very happy. Take the most blissful moments of life and multiply them a thousand-fold, and that is what one second of heaven is like. It glows with love. People visit with the Trinity for wisdom that surpasses all understanding. Of course, I only see it from a distance, but I hope to walk inside the pearly gates today if you will cooperate. Hildie sings, weaves, cleans, and loves the Lord; but she is annoyed that you are mired in her memory and can't enjoy life. She wants you to be happy. You'll be reunited with her one day. But for now, she wants you to break the bonds that are holding you captive to misery. In other words, she wants you to 'get on with your life and quit moping'—as she puts it."

"Tell me, how do I do that?"

"By creating your art. Myron wants to display your work at the University Art Gallery. You have over one hundred pieces that need to be exhibited to the public, not for pride or publicity, but to demonstrate that even an illiterate old man can make profound statements in art. It is through creativity that we give credit to God by using our gifts to interpret the world around us."

"But that night in the bedroom when you told me to look at the woods—what were you telling me?"

"I was telling you that your salvation belongs with God, but that you have to honor Him through your work, which is comprised of love and insight. Also, you were a very sick little boy. Your lungs were filled with fluid, and you were about to die. The angel of death was hovering over your bed and I had to get you up and moving around so she couldn't target you. When you jumped up, you caused the owls of death to fly away with your sudden movement and loud keening wails. Don't you remember that your mother came in shortly afterwards to quieten you down and lay a poultice on your chest? In a few days, you were cured."

"Well, I recon you're right. I remember now. Ma went in the woods every day for week gathering herbs. Seems like nothing worked until she made that poultice. I gained my health back after that."

"Yes, I know. We have ways of guiding people to do things they need to do. Now, that my mission is accomplished, I need to go. If you promise to show your carvings, I'll leave behind a present from Hildie."

"Why sure. I'll even carve some more figures. I've had ideas in my head for a long time. And I'll show all my wooden statues at that gallery."

"Good. You have made God and Hildie very happy and have helped me to attain my wings. Goodbye and I hope to see you one day. Now, if you'll excuse me, I'll be in paradise."

With those final words, the spirit began fading until he disappeared.

Clark awoke in a daze. It was just a vivid dream that he sometimes got when he napped in the middle of the day. He was disoriented for a while until he got his bearings. Just as he was about to leave, he saw the pocket watch and chain right beside him. It had been polished and amazingly, was in perfect working order after all these years. Clark wondered how he'd overlooked it and carefully pocketed it in his overall pocket with shaking hands. He felt the watch ticking like a living being; a birth that fill him with the kind of joy he had felt when he cradled his new-born offspring for the first time.

He climbed down the ladder and summoned Peppy. "Come on. We've got to get back home. I've got to call up Myron and collect all them carvings," he said, suddenly feeling more hopeful than he had in years. He thought about the dream he'd had. Was it just a dream? If so, how did he happen to find the watch in pristine condition right next to him? It was a quandary he never solved. Just to make sure it wasn't an illusion, he took out the watch and looked at the inscription and read the words: "To Clark with eternal love, Hildie." Out of everything on Earth, love is the only thing of permanence.

The afternoon sun illuminated the sky in golden hues. It reminded him of that long ago April day in the woods when his soul had been shocked into a profound love for Hildie. It would always be there—this love that God created to awaken souls. Hildie had often quoted scripture to him: "Seek and you shall find. Knock and the door will be opened to you."

Clark had gone on a hunt to find what he needed, and he had been found. He needed to drive home one final time before he put his keys away. He would miss driving, but he felt a revival in his spirit as his old self was baptized with new life. A butterfly alighted on his hand wings folded up like hands in prayer. Then it spread its wings and flew south for a warmer destination. "Come back in the spring!" Clark said. And he smiled as he watched it fly away, knowing that it would be resurrected in a beautiful promise of hope.

THE GREENHOUSE EFFECT

by Harold Raley

"Mr. Chastain, there's an applicant in my office who insists on speaking personally to you," Gail Freeman said apologetically, aware as were her fifteen co-workers that Director Chastain did not like to be interrupted during his methodical morning assessment of the departmental agenda.

"Gail, you know the protocol as well as I do," he replied with the dreaded note of annoyance in his voice. "Have you compiled the preliminary data?"

"No sir, but—"

"And why not, may I ask?" he broke in curtly with a rising tone of irritation.

"Sir, there are . . . complications in this case. If I could step into your office for a moment to explain . . ."

"Very well. Bring the case folder with you, but not the applicant" he said impatiently. "And come prepared to be brief and to the point. I have meetings this morning."

"Yessir. Right away."

For Albert Chastain, 32, the day—a May Tuesday—was settling into the unpromising continuation that began the night before. He had slept poorly, kept awake partly by the infernal barking of his neighbor's dog, but mostly because of uncertainty about his life in general. As if to remind him, he saw two more gray whiskers in his close-cropped black beard in the bathroom mirror the next morning. Later he discovered his belt was too tight in its normal notch. Since Christmas he had put on five pounds, instead of the ten he had resolved to lose this year. "Damn!" he muttered.

He was successful by external markers. His salary was good, and his stocks were soaring in the prolonged bull market. After rising quickly through the bureaucratic structure, he was appointed Director of the Office of Public Assistance at the relatively tender age of thirty. With skill, determination, and knowledge as Vice-Chair—and real brains—of the Commission on Welfare Reform, he took the lead role in streamlining the bloated, corrupt system and saving the city millions of dollars annually. His efforts won him praise and notice by the state's highest elected officials of both parties. Several major cities adopted versions of his humane reforms, and key features were incorporated into the updated state system. He was ready, so insiders told him, to run for a major elective office. But all that was three years ago, and nothing had come of it since. None of it mattered very much anyway; in his opinion, it was his physical shortcomings, not his public profile, that had stopped his quick rise and now kept him awake at night.

By his own reckoning, his personal limitations had overtaken his abilities. He was a realist about himself. Still, he would run for office if the chance and support ever came his way, but by his own assessment he did not look the part of a polished politician. He was under no illusions; he knew that in politics first impressions were usually the only ones that count with a majority of voters. He judged himself by what he saw in the mirror: a man too short, too ample in the midriff, and with facial features unfavorably defined by an oversized, off-centered curved nose and close-set, intense dark eyes. To describe his appearance with an ugly word, he was ugly, or so he told himself. If his all-business attitude inspired respect and productivity in his coworkers who knew him, he had no doubts that his physical traits would repel average voters who did not. His early successes were the payoff for thorough preparation, tenacity, and depth of knowledge. He was trusted by those who knew him.

Yet something was missing. With his thirty-second birthday now behind him, the irritating emptiness of his personal life outweighed satisfaction with his professional accomplishments. Not that he was likely to do anything drastic to alter things, even if it were possible. His life was set, and it was not his style to make dramatic changes. He was a realist, not a dreamer. He tried to be as truthful with himself as he was with other people. He knew he deserved his reputation as an efficient director unsullied by scandal and unethical behavior. He had done it right, walking a straight and narrow road in his career. The problem was he sensed that the road was about to end, and he could not foresee what the next phase of his life would be.

"Here's the application, Mr. Chastain," Gail said apprehensively.

"Folder 10. What about the first nine? Are they ready for adjudication?"

"All but the written resumés, but I could use some help on this one."

"Is the applicant still in your office?"

"Yessir. He was waiting at the door when we opened this morning."

"Give me your preliminary assessment of his case."

"That's why I'm here, sir. I don't know what to make of the man and the validity of his request. In fact, it's hard to understand him and what I do understand doesn't make a lot of sense."

"If he's a foreigner, get someone on the case who speaks his language. That's why we pay those people."

"It's not that, sir. He does speak English after a fashion."

"Well so do you, Gail, and it's your job to make a preliminary judgment based on the merits of the case. I remind you that's also why we pay you."

Redhead Gail, 37, blushed in silent but obvious resentment at his cutting remark. "Sir, that's what I'm trying to do, but I could use your advice on a couple of matters."

"Go ahead, Gail, and use my own dig against me: 'that's why we pay you'. Isn't that what you were thinking?"

"I trust your judgment," she responded, avoiding a direct answer.

"What two things are we talking about?"

"Mr. Landry, Gilbert Landry—that's his name—keeps saying something about being 'the railroad Gilbert'. I don't have the foggiest what he means by it. And keeping him on topic is like the proverbial job of herding ducks."

"What's the other matter you mentioned?"

"He keeps saying 'It's for 'my little Mary, not for me, for my little Mary.'"

"What's so strange about that?"

"There's no such name in the application, and I can't get him to tell me who this 'Mary' person is. He just keeps asking to see the Director."

"Gilbert, Gilbert Landry," Director Chastain muttered the name under his breath. Then suddenly he pressed the intercom button to his secretary.

"Sir—" Gail started to say.

He held up his hand to stop her and spoke to his secretary: "Frances," call the Commissioner's office and make my apologies about our lunch meeting. Something has come up. Reschedule at her convenience; and tell her I'm buying for the inconvenience."

"Is something wrong with the file?" Gail asked.

"It's okay, Gail, but I'd like to handle this case personally. You can write up your reports on the others."

"I didn't mean to dump the case on you, Mr. Chastain. I can handle it. As you said, that's what you pay me to do."

"Gail, don't take it as a slight. But the name rings a bell. I don't have time to explain. Just get him in here and you get busy with the other reports. And if you finish with yours, you can help Reeves with his. Okay?"

Gail nodded and left without another word, but by the look on her face she was skeptical that Chastain was being straight with her. Their relationship had always been correct but at times tense in the four years they had worked together. Though neither mentioned it, both knew she had never fully adjusted to being passed over by a younger person for the directorship.

A moment later, a tall elderly man with an unruly shock of snowy hair limped in, leaning heavily on a black cane. Albert got up, shook hands with him, offered to help him to a chair, but the man waved him off.

"Thank you, sir. My ole wobbly leg makes me about as slow a three-legged dog, but I can still get around."

If Albert had any doubts about Mr. Landry, the Deep South accent convinced him of what his eyes could hardly believe. He recognized the old man as the same Gilbert Landry, the train engineer, who had figuratively, if not literally, saved his life many years earlier back in old Picayune, a world gone so long from his experience that it was almost an ancestral memory. Albert had not heard or spoken the local accent since his boyhood in Deep South Mississippi, and it aroused long dormant emotions. With an effort, though, he stifled his feelings under his professional persona and spoke in brisk upper Midwest English.

"Mr. Landry, I have your application, but it's got some blanks in it. We'll need more information before we can proceed. I take it that you have a family emergency of some sort and need assistance. So I'll need to ask you some questions to complete the file."

"Ask away, sir. I tried to explain everything to the lady in the other office, but she was in such a hurry and spoke so fast that I got bumfuzzled. Anyway, it aint for me that I'm asking. It's for my Mary. That's who the money's for, my little Mary."

"And who is Mary?"

"She's my granddaughter, my only grandchild, sir. Didn't I say that? I guess not. Well anyway, she's all the family my wife Lottie and me have left up here in the north. All her family and the other Landrys—my brother and sister and some nephews and cousins—live down yonder in Picayune. That's south Mississippi, if you don't know that part of the world."

"I do know where it is. Tell me the circumstances, if you will."

"Well, first off, our daughter Virginia got sick with cancer year before last and had to quit working. So we brought her and our granddaughter Mary up here from Chicago to live with us, me and my wife Lottie. Her husband died in the Vietnam war. The cancer was too advanced for the doctors to do much for Ginnie—that's what we called our daughter—and we lost her this past January. Now here's the thing, sir. I spent all the money I could scape up to move them up here, to pay for doctoring, hospitals, and Ginnie's funeral, and then get Mary back in college so's she could finish her degree. My railroad pension ain't much to start with, so I had to borrow, and then borrow some more, till my credit run plumb out. So here I am, broke as a dog, and up to my eyeballs in debt."

"But you still have your pension, don't you?"

"I do, but it don't cover expenses, the main one being Mary's college costs. They have to be paid by the end of this month or she'll lose the semester and have to drop out and get a job. She already lost some time because of Ginnie's illness. A family she knows back yonder in Chicago owns a store and will hire her to work in the pharmacy. She's willing to go back, but I ain't. I don't want her to be down there all by herself. Chicago's a rough place. Besides, Mary's got her heart set on being a doctor, always has had. She's bright enough to make it, too, and I aim to do everything I humanly can to keep her in school. But I just don't know what else to do. So that's why I'm here."

"So she's enrolled in a premed curriculum?"

"Yessir, I believe that's what they call it. Course I don't know much about such things. Never got to college myself. I spent all my working years as a railroad engineer, driving trains between here and New Orleans."

"I know. I rode one of your trains."

"No, sir. That wouldn't have been me. I worked on freight trains, not passenger trains."

"It was a freight train. You let me ride with you to Chicago."

Mr. Landry leaned forward, his face a study in astonishment. "What is your name, sir? I plumb forgot my manners and didn't ask you."

"Chastain, Mr. Landry, Albert Chastain. But you probably

don't remember me. I was just a kid then, barely sixteen, and I was hanging on to a boxcar ladder and about to lose my grip when you spotted me. You stopped that long train right out in the middle of nowhere and let me ride up there with you. It had three engines coupled together, and the ground shook when they fired up. I remember it like it was yesterday."

"I can't believe it! I do remember! You were as thin as a rail and two thirds starved. I don't mean to be disrespectful, but I recollect that you done away with most of my lunch! Well glory be! They say it's a small world, and I guess it is! But just look at you now! Head of a big city department and a man respected and looked up to. I'm just real proud of what you've done with your life and glad I had a little part in helping you on the way."

"Sir, I remember too. The twenty dollars you gave me in Chicago got me on up north to Wisconsin and into Minnesota. One thing led to another, and here I am today. Now the application is one thing that will have to be decided in the normal way. But the twenty dollars is personal, and I'd like to repay it here and now."

Albert removed a twenty from his wallet, but Mr. Landry put up both hands to reject it. "No sir, I wouldn't want to undo a favor that helped you a bit on your way. I'm just glad I was able to help, and I prefer the memory to the money."

Landry left a few minutes later with only Albert's assurance of a quick decision on the application. It was not in the old engineer's character to remind Albert of reciprocity, but it was firmly fixed in the Director's mind.

Albert already knew what the official decision had to be: the fact that Landry had a pension automatically disqualified him for public assistance regardless of other circumstances. Albert himself had insisted on the stipulation in order to prevent freeloaders from misusing public funds. It was a main reason why the welfare reforms were necessary to start with. He slept less than ever under the moral dilemma he faced. Despite all the rationalizations he could think of to justify the denial, it still reeked personally of ingratitude. But one thing was certain: he could not compromise the very rules he had fought for on the Commission, not even for Mr. Landry.

All this was much on his mind as he walked to his mailbox the next afternoon. Among the throwaways and bills was a dividend statement from one of his investments. The market was red hot, and the amount was higher than his most optimistic hopes.

Then the solution to the dilemma hit him. Of course. What dilemma? He texted Frances to reset a meeting until the afternoon, then went to his brokerage and made a formal request for a cashier's check to be ready for him to pick up the next day. Despite the barking dog, he slept soundly that night. The next day he picked up the check, set the GPS for Landry's address, and drove to one of the city's more modest suburbs.

"Mrs. Landry, I take it," he said to the elderly lady who opened the door, I'm Albert Chastain, I'm sorry to show up without first calling, but I need to speak to Mr. Landry, if he's home."

"Why, Mr. Chastain, you come right on in. I'm Lottie Landry, Gilbert's my husband. He was so excited about meeting you the other day. He told us all about it. Do have a seat and I'll go find him. He's out there in his greenhouse with our granddaughter Mary, probably planting some more Mississippi herbs and flowers. He loves his greenhouse and Mary helps him all she can."

Mr. Landry came in as quickly as his bad leg permitted, followed by a tall slender girl of twenty-two or so.

"Well, hello again, Mr. Chastain, and welcome to our home, such as it is. But you didn't have to drive all the way out here. I know you have more important things to do."

"Thank you, sir, I do have things to do, but none I enjoy more than seeing you again. I hope I'm not intruding."

"Not at all, sir, not the least bit. You are more than welcome any time. This here is our granddaughter Mary, Mary Turner. Mary, this is Mr. Chastain, Director of the office I told you and Lottie about."

"I'm pleased to meet you, Mr. Chastain. Grandpa said good things about you."

"Call me Albert, Miss Turner—you all. I'm Mr. Chastain only during business hours. We call it being 'in harness'."

"Well, I'm Mary, just Mary, Mr.—Albert."

"Have a seat, Albert. Lottie, do we have any tea left?"

"We do. With sugar or without, Albert?"

"With, please, Mrs. Landry. If I remember, civilized people always drank it sweet in Mississippi."

Mr. Landry laughed. "You do remember some things about life in the South."

"Some, but a lot I've forgotten. I was only sixteen when I left, as you know."

"You don't sound like a Southerner," Mary observed. "If I had to guess, I would say you are a Wisconsin native."

"And you don't sound Southern either, Mary. Your grandfather told me that you lived in Chicago. Did you grow up there?"

"Practically. We moved there when I was ten. I probably remember much less than you do about life in Picayune."

Mrs. Landry returned with tea and cookies. There was a lull

in the conversation. Good Southerners that they were, they waited politely for Albert to state the purpose of his visit. After a couple of sips of tea and a cookie with compliments on each, he set his glass aside and took an envelope from his blazer.

"Mr. Landry, I told you a quick decision would be forthcoming on your application. I regret to say it was negative. The reasons are explained in this letter."

Landry's hand shook slightly as he accepted it. "Well, Albert, I guess that was the decision I expected. We didn't have high hopes to start with. But I appreciate your time and especially the trouble you took to bring it all the way out here in person. That was good of you."

"But I do have another letter for you," Albert said as he removed it from another pocket. "It has better news for you."

"$3,000! But, Albert, this is more than I requested. How . . . where did it come from?"

"From an anonymous donor account. Your case was selected to receive funds from it. I can't tell you the exact source, but the money is yours, free, clear, and completely legal. I think that tells the whole story. I knew the need was pressing, so I decided to bring it to you in person. You helped me many years ago; delivering this check was a small payback for your generosity."

Mr. Landry got to his feet and embraced Albert. Mrs. Landry hugged him, and although Mary was less effusive, she squeezed his hand and her eyes teared over with joy. With a lump in his throat, he thanked the Landry's for their hospitality, shook hands with Mary Turner, and went home to his apartment. Even the dog's yapping did not bother him that night. What better use could he make of the money? He thought as he drifted into deep sleep. It was his and he could do with it as he chose, and he believed he had chosen well. He had to some degree made a payment on a debt to Gilbert Landry he could never repay completely. And the look in Mary's lovely brown eyes was a reward of an entirely different kind that he had not known before and would not forget.

A week later Albert received a formal invitation through office mail to attend Mary Turner's graduation and reception. He accepted and bought a new suit and tie for the happy occasion. He racked his brain for a proper gift for her. It must not be too personal, but neither too impersonal. He had no experience in matters like this and no one to advise him. At his wit's end, he finally settled with uncertainty on an expensive gold pen. He reasoned that since everyone knew he was well paid it was not out of line to give her an upscale gift. He hoped he was right, but apprehensive that he might be wrong. He sat with the Landry's and cheered lustily with them as Mary walked across the stage. She was gorgeous and radiant with happiness, but Albert did not express his personal impressions of her to her proud grandparents who were again effusive in their thanks to him for his part in making it all possible.

He visited the Landry's several times in the following weeks. Talking with them, eating Southern cooking, visiting the greenhouse, listening to music, and hearing tales and anecdotes about the old days in Picayune, he began to recover forgotten expressions from his boyhood and some of the vowels in certain words lengthened into softer melodious Southern diphthongs. It raised a few eyebrows in the office personnel who were unaware of his boyhood connections. He was feeling better about himself. Mary liked his gift and complimented him on his taste. He was flattered and relieved.

Mr. Landry suggested on Albert's Fourth of July visit that Mary show him the greenhouse which he and Mary had stocked with several more species native to southern Mississippi.

"I'd go back there with you," he said apologetically, "but my gouty legs are acting up more than usual. I think I had too much of Lottie's sausage the other day."

"I'll be glad to show him around, Grandpa, if you'll promise me you didn't slip a snake or two in there, or maybe even a baby alligator. You know I wouldn't put it past you. Albert, over these last few days we've planted half of Mississippi in that greenhouse, and some of those critters might've slipped in too."

"Don't you doctors have to deal with critters?"

"Just the two-legged kind and the tiny ones you can't see. The others I leave to the vets."

"Well, lady, you just stick close to me for protection," Albert said with rare humor as they started down the pathway.

"Tell me why I don't feel much safer," she laughed.

Albert had wondered aloud a time or two why the Landry's stayed there. The natural thing, so it seemed to him, would be for them to go back to their roots. He mentioned it again when Mary opened the greenhouse door and he saw all the Southern flowers and herbs.

"I'll tell you why, Albert. They're still here because of me. I worry about the cold winters and the fact that for days on end they can't get out and go places. But when I bring it up, they let me know that the only way they will move back south is if I go with them."

"What about you, Mary? Do you have other family up here, your father's people maybe?"

"I do have an uncle and his family down in Illinois, but I

barely know them. I was just a baby when Dad died, and we pretty much lost contact with the Turners."

They looked at the plants and smelled the flowers, but neither knew very much about the imported fauna. Albert saw species he recognized but could not recall their names. Eventually, they turned to topics closer to their hearts.

"Albert," she said after a long silence. "I want you to tell you again how grateful I am to you for helping make all this possible. I couldn't have graduated without the money you got for Grandpa."

"All I did was deliver the check to your grandfather. I was glad to do it, but it was no big deal."

She smiled and took his hand in hers. "Albert, something tells me that you are a pious fraud."

Stunned by her words, he removed his hand and stepped back. "Leave out the pious part, Mary, and you'll be right."

"Oh, damn, I've hurt your feelings, and I didn't mean to. All I meant was that you didn't exactly tell us the truth about the money, did you? You acted with the best of motives, but the money came from your own pocket, didn't it?"

"What makes you think so?"

"Aha! So, I'm right. When people answer a question with a question, it means they're being evasive and hedging the truth."

"Well, for the sake of argument, let's say I did what you said. How in the world would you, or could you, know that?"

"Because I know you, Albert Chastain."

"You only met me a few weeks ago., how could you know much about me?"

"I just know and that's that. It's a conviction that admits no denial and accepts no rebuttal."

"You sound like a lawyer."

"No, just somebody who appreciates you and admires you for what you did. And I'm not the only one. My grandparents think you hung the moon."

"Well, I feel the same way about them. Even if I did come up with a little money—and I'm not saying I did—you can't put a price on what Mr. Landry did for me back in the day. If not for him, I might not even be alive today. I was close to the edge when he came along. It's a debt I can never repay."

"Who you are and what you've made of your life is payment enough for Grandpa. You know he never had a son; now in a way he does."

"That, Mary, is the kindest thing anyone has ever said to me. And I thank you for it. But look, your grandparents are probably wondering if one of those snakes or gators bit us. And I need to be on my way. You'll be going out of state soon to that medical school, and I may not see you again, at least not for a long time. But when you graduate, I hope I get to come to the ceremony. I know you'll be a great doctor. It's a conviction that admits no denial and accepts no rebuttal, as someone said just recently."

"Just a minute, Mr. Chastain. I haven't given you permission to just walk out of my life. I think we have more things to say to each other, and the first one is that I'm not going anywhere. I got accepted to the medical school right here in the city, the one I really wanted to attend all along."

"Congratulations, Mary, that's really great news. Your grandparents must be really happy."

"I haven't told them yet. I got the phone call yesterday, but the official letter hasn't come yet. I'll be in a holding pattern until it does. But yes, I am so happy, and not just about the school. This way I can be close to my grandparents and look after them and some other things in my life."

"I'm really happy for you, but I don't feel right wasting your time. Look, let me be frank with you. You are a beautiful girl, tall, smart, prettier than any model I ever saw, perfect in every respect. And here I am, short, fat, with a nose and face that would scare away snakes and vermin if there any around here. I'm not all that bright, just pit bull stubborn, and to top it off, a lot older than you. I wish I were different, but I am what I am. You deserve better."

He turned to open the greenhouse door, but she caught him by the arm.

"Albert Chastain, you hush that kind of foolish talk—as the Southerners say—and be the man you really are. You've tried to describe *what* you are, but, Mr. Chastain, I know *who* you are, and there's a world of difference between them. The point is if you believe all those things you say about me are true, then it's time for you to do something about it, not run away with your tail between your legs like a beaten dog."

"That's serious talk, Mary,"

"That's because I'm a serious girl, Albert."

"Are you saying, serious about me?"

"That's right. I'm saying I'm serious about you."

"But you're taller than I am, and I'm older than you. What kind of a couple would we make?"

"Well, I think a happy one. But it'll be whatever we make it, not what people say about us. Anyway, my folks have taught me that it's not how high a person's head or heart is from the ground but what's in them that counts."

"Your grandparents are going to think the critters really have done away with us down here."

"I think they know what we're up to down here. I've talked to them about it. At least they know what I'm up to."

"And what's that?"

"Better show than tell. You should make the first move, but to get things started, I'll do it. Kiss me."

"Kiss you? But your grandparents might come to check on us and catch us."

"I hope they do, Albert. It's okay; if we lived back in the age of arranged marriages, you would be the arrangement. Now kiss me, or do I have to get rough with you?"

He did and that's when things got serious. A long time later, the Landry's opened the Greenhouse door.

"Mary, what's wrong with Albert? Mr. Landry asked with a twinkle in his eye. "He looks like some of his cars derailed. Or did one of my snakes bite him?"

"No, Grandpa," Mary laughed, "something even more serious happened to him. It's called the 'greenhouse effect'. In medicine they describe the main symptoms as an accelerated heartbeat, elevated temperature, rapid respiration, and temporary pulmonary insufficiency."

"Man o man! That does sound serious. Is there any cure for it?"

"Well, yes, Grandpa, with proper care. But the treatment is drastic, and in the worst cases the effects can last a whole lifetime."

The Landry's were delighted. And arranged or not—Albert was never completely sure—their marriage brought happiness to all concerned.

But all that and what happened to them is another story for another time.

CROWN OF RIGHTEOUSNESS

by Landy Raley

The old woman made huffing sounds at random intervals. The ICU staff paid her little attention. She was old and in their considerable experience, she was not far from death. They were not unkind to her, but she required little attention and would most likely soon be moved to a regular room to live out the remainder of her life.

The sounds the old woman made were laughter. Occasionally, she would remember something, a joke or an event which would cause her to laugh. Once, she remembered a bawdy joke Lathel had told her. She had not thought of it in years and her huffing/laugh had caused her to have a coughing fit, which did get the staff's attention.

Her mind wandered along random, mostly pleasant paths. She supposed she was on medication to keep her calm and pain-free. When she had first entered the hospital seven days ago, she had expected to get better and go home as on three previous occasions in the past three months. She soon realized that this hospitalization was different from the previous ones and that she was not going home this time.

The realization did not distress her. She had passed her "three score ten" fifteen years ago. She had seen many people die. Most of the people she had known through life were now dead. She knew that she was not going to avoid death and she had done what she could to be ready.

The youngish doctor who had been treating her since Dr. Warnke retired came by to check on her. He called her name, but she did not want to be bothered, so she kept her eyes shut. He made some medical observations to the underling with him. They had to do with the success of body's attempts to keep living. His observations were interspersed with technical and medical jargon, but it seemed that her body was losing the battle. Dr. Warnke would have simply said "She's dying." It came out to the same thing.

She wondered how Dr. Warnke was doing. He had been her physician for over a quarter of a century. He was of German stock who had settled the county. His manner tended toward brusqueness, but not unpleasantness. She remembered her last office visit when he told her that he was retiring and the doctor who just examined her would be taking over his practice. It had made her sad and she felt the need to thank him for his care over the years. She did not always follow his advice, but he did not always do what was best for his health either, so he did not hold that against her. When she finished her short, awkward thanks, she put her hand out to shake his. Except for the necessary requirements of medical examination, she did not remember him ever touching her. He put his left hand on top of her hand as they shook and held it there briefly. She would not have been more surprised if he had kissed her on the mouth. Then he said, "Take care of your feet, Vera." Her eyes had filled with tears. She had a problem with her feet that he was well aware of. But it was as he had said, "Take care of yourself, old friend. I wish you well." She had not seen him since, although she had heard that he retired to Smith Lake. She hoped he was well and happy.

Sometime later, she realized she was awake. It seemed darker so she assumed she had slept. How long she had no way of telling.

She had not seen any of the children for a while. She supposed she may have slept through the short visiting period allowed in ICU. She wondered why she had not seen Lathel. He didn't like hospitals, but he would have come to see her. "Oh my! Lathel's dead," she thought. "He's been dead for more than 25 years. My mind must be slipping." She and Lathel had walked through life together. But it had not been an easy hike. They were not suited for each other and over the years she had been sharp-tongued to him on many occasions. He was an amiable man—well-liked by almost everyone. He was happiest when he was in the woods or talking to a neighbor. But they had children to feed, to clothe, to shelter. To her, it seemed that he forgot everything when he went to the woods. He would not respond to her tongue-lashings— either verbally or by correcting his actions to please her. She was not an angry person by temperament and did not enjoy fussing. She tried to fulfill her biblical responsibility to be a "help meet" for him. However, he did not seem to want or appreciate her help. She became even more frustrated with him for making her treat him so unkindly. She hoped in heaven they could become friends again like they were in their early ears when everything was still possible. Would she even know Lathel in Heaven? The Bible says, "We will know as we are known." But what does that mean? She wished some things had been made plainer. If one of her children had given her an answer like that, she would have accused them of "double talk". She supposed that if the greatest minds humankind had to offer had not completely figured it out, she should not be surprised if she, an old woman in a drug-induced delirium on her deathbed, failed to unravel the meaning.

She laughed her croaky laugh at the thought. "I'll know the meaning pretty soon now anyway."

She was sure the children had been to see her. They would be okay without her. It had taken some of them time to find their way, but they each seemed to have done so without too many missteps. She had encouraged them to get as much education as they could. Her success in that area had been mixed, but they seemed happy in their lives, and they all had a roof over their heads and plenty to eat. They came to see her, and they knew she loved them, and she knew they loved her. She saw that not everyone had that solid a relationship with their offspring. Yes, they would be okay.

She woke again.

She dreamed of her father. Thinking of him, she remembered a talk they had when she had committed some infraction. She did not remember what she had done, but she knew it was not trivial. Mother handled the trivial discipline. Father was called in for more serious (on ongoing) problems. She remembered what he said to her. "Daughter, just do the best you can with the sense you have. That is all that God requires of you. But he does require that." This last sentence he uttered with raised eyebrows, a tilted head, and the beginnings of a wry grin. She and her female siblings knew that any sentence that began with the word "Daughter" was instructional and must be heeded. Their mother was the religious teacher for her brood. Their father did not speak often of God. When he did his children paid attention. He probably had no memory of their conversation, but throughout her life Vera would think of his words at times of stress or uncertainty. They did not provide any answer, but they calmed and comforted her. After all, what else could you do?

She dreamed of Ebenezer School.

Her second-grade teacher was Miss Avelle White. She was sweet, pretty, and patient with the children. She was Vera's all-time favorite teacher, and it caused her great sadness when Miss White told them just prior to Christmas break that she was going to marry and would not return as their teacher. She was replaced by Miss Berta Black. Of course, the children noted the difference in the last names with humor. Luckily, Miss Black did not have the opposite temperament from Miss White, and she too became one of Vera's favorite teachers.

One original thing that Miss White did was to select a Princess or Prince for the week. This was based on the honored student's comportment and diligence during the previous week. The winner was announced on Friday afternoon and was given a crown to wear during school hours. (When a boy was selected, he was given a medal to wear because the boys considered a crown to be foppish.) Miss White had gone to some trouble in making the crown. It was "home-made" but was made of stiff cardboard paper and had been colored and sprinkled with glitter. The children in the Ebenezer School were not accustomed to glitter in their homes and considered it both elegant and exotic. The week Vera wore the crown was one of the proudest times of her life. When her reign was over, and she returned the diadem, she listened as Miss White told her that the Bible tells us that we will have crowns in Heaven. After learning this, Vera asked her mother to show her verses about crowns. It turned out that there were more than one such verse. Her favorite was: "Henceforth there is laid up for me a crown of righteousness, which the Lord, the righteous judge, shall give me at that day, and not to me only, but unto all them also who love his appearing." She committed it to memory that day and still remembered it three-quarters of a century later. In the years to come whenever a preacher or teacher mentioned a crown in a sermon or lesson, her ears "perked up" and she invariably thought of Miss White, Ebenezer School, and her crown.

She wondered if there would be real crowns in Heaven. Preachers usually said that things like that were probably figurative. She rebelled against this, thinking "if we have spiritual bodies, then we can have spiritual crowns. I guess I'll see soon enough."

She thought of the song "Blessed Assurance." It was one of her favorites. She began to sing it. She had known the words by heart for as long as she could remember. The medical staff heard her making a continuous verbalization. Two of them checked on her, thinking she might be attempting to summon them. After determining that there was no medical problem, they stood in her doorway for a moment and one of them, Rita, who was a fifth cousin to Vera, although this was unknown to both of them, said to her co-worker, "You know, I think she's trying to sing. I can't make out the words, but she's trying to carry a tune." The other worker returned to the nurse's station. Rita listened for a little while longer, trying to make out the melody. Finally, she shook her head and returned to the nurse's station as well. At 2:33 a.m. that morning, Rita sat up in her bed and said aloud, "It was that song with 'This is my story, this is my song. Praising my Savior all the day long' in it." The title did not come to her.

Vera drifted off again, remembering her life, her children, her grandchildren, places she had lived, memories of her childhood, and crowns . . .

AFTERWORD

We shall be glad if you have enjoyed these stories and even happier if they have spoken to your heart and suggested similarities to your own experience. We have obeyed as best we could a compulsion to express in words the ineffable workings of the spirit. In this sense these tales are true, even though they are more than factual and less than final. For we share a conviction that God is the first and final chapters of our life. Our task is to make the best of the interval.